CHOSEN

"With each book in the series, not only have Stein's characters become stronger but so has her writing . . . Hard-hitting urban fantasy with a hard-hitting female lead."   —*Fresh Fiction*

"From the opening chapter of this terrific series, Stein has sent her gutsy heroine on an uncharted journey filled with danger and bitter betrayal . . . In this pivotal but emotionally brutal book, skillful Stein reveals some critical answers and delivers some devastating blows. Like a fine wine, this series is improving with age. Brava!"   —*RT Book Reviews* (4½ stars)

RETRIBUTION

"The fifth book in the exceptional first-person Anna Strong series is a powerful entry in an amazing saga."   —*RT Book Reviews*

"Ms. Stein has a true gift in storytelling and continues to add exciting new elements to this well-built world. *Retribution* is an engrossing read with an action-packed story line and secondary characters that are every bit as intriguing as the heroine. This is a must-read for fans of the series!"   —*Darque Reviews*

LEGACY

"Urban fantasy with true depth and flair!"
          —*RT Book Reviews* (4½ stars)

"As riveting as the rest . . . One of my favorite urban fantasy series."   —*Darque Reviews*

THE WATCHER

"Action fills every page, making this a novel that flies by . . . Dynamic relationships blend [with] complex mysteries in this thriller."   —*Huntress Book Reviews*

"An exciting, fast-paced novel . . . First-rate plotting."
          —*LoveVampires*

BLOOD DRIVE

THE BECOMING

Ace Books by Jeanne C. Stein

THE BECOMING
BLOOD DRIVE
THE WATCHER
LEGACY
RETRIBUTION
CHOSEN
CROSSROADS
HAUNTED
BLOOD BOND

BLOOD BOND

JEANNE C. STEIN

ACE BOOKS, NEW YORK

THE BERKLEY PUBLISHING GROUP
Published by the Penguin Group
Penguin Group (USA) Inc.
375 Hudson Street, New York, New York 10014, USA

USA I Canada I UK I Ireland I Australia I New Zealand I India I South Africa I China

Penguin Books Ltd., Registered Offices: 80 Strand, London WC2R 0RL, England
For more information about the Penguin Group, visit penguin.com.

BLOOD BOND

An Ace Book / published by arrangement with the author

Ace Books are published by The Berkley Publishing Group.
ACE and the "A" design are trademarks of Penguin Group (USA) Inc.

For information, address: The Berkley Publishing Group,
a division of Penguin Group (USA) Inc.,
375 Hudson Street, New York, New York 10014.

ISBN: 978-0-425-25887-3

PUBLISHING HISTORY
Ace mass-market edition / September 2013

PRINTED IN THE UNITED STATES OF AMERICA

10 9 8 7 6 5 4 3 2 1

Cover art by Cliff Nielsen.
Cover design by Judith Lagerman.
Interior text design by Kristin del Rosario.

*To the readers who have taken Anna Strong into their hearts.
I am so appreciative of your support. I hope you approve of this
new chapter in her story.*

ACKNOWLEDGMENTS

Anna and I have come a long way—but there are people who have been with me from the very beginning, and I would like to acknowledge their contributions now.

First, my husband, Phil, and daughter, Jeanette—because you can never have too much love, support and encouragement.

My critique group (members past and present): Mario Acevedo, Margie and Tom Lawson, Warren Hammond, Angie Hodapp, Aaron Ritchey, Terry Wright, Tamra Monahan, Jeff Shelby, Sandy Meckstroth, Heidi Kuhn and Jim Cole—because no matter how hard you try to get it right the first time, you seldom do.

My editor, Jessica Wade at Ace Books, and my agent, Scott Miller from Trident Media—because you need people on your side who know what they're doing.

All the good people at Ace, from Jesse Feldman to Rosanne Romanello, senior publicist—because you guys really make it happen.

The heart of the Hand Hotel Writers: Susan Smith, Vicki Law, Carol Berg, Cindi Myers, Marnie Kirstatter, Lynde Iozzo, our host Michael Stone and unofficial hostess Stella McDowell—because the creative energy that sparks off this group and the others who join us from time to time is unbelievable (to say nothing of the great food and the way we've come to think of the Hand as home).

ACKNOWLEDGMENTS

Sisters in Crime and Rocky Mountain Fiction Writers—because that's how it all started for me.

I'm not even going to try to list all the wonderful friends and family who come to my signings, buy my books and just generally offer encouragement, because that would take a dozen more pages. Just know I love you all.

This is the end . . . and the beginning.

PROLOGUE

WHAT CAME BEFORE

S UDDENLY, MAX IS STANDING AT THE FOOT OF my bed.

I sit up, rubbing my eyes. Did I fall asleep?

He smiles. "Hey."

He's wearing jeans and a T-shirt. He looks good. "Hey, yourself. When did they let you out of the hospital?"

"An hour ago. I was afraid you weren't going to wake up in time."

My head is fuzzy with sleep. I give it a shake and focus on Max. "You really look good. I just left Texas a few hours ago. You made a miraculous recovery."

"In a way." He takes a seat on the end of my bed. "I have something to tell you. And I don't think I have much time."

I smile. "Why not?"

"Oh, you know, places to go, people to see."

"You realize Pablo is in custody."

"Yes. But that's not why I'm here."

I prop myself up straighter against the headboard and try to concentrate. My brain isn't cooperating. It seems to be trying to cut into my thoughts, to tell me something. I tell it to shut up, that I only want to listen to Max. I lean toward him. "Go on."

He sighs. "First, I owe you an apology. I didn't treat you very well when I found out you are a vampire. I was afraid of what it meant—to me. Stupid because it meant nothing. Not really. Above all, you are a good woman, Anna, and my biggest regret is that I realized it too late."

I shrug. "You can make it up to me."

He shakes his head. "No. Believe me, it's too late. But there is someone else. Learn from me. You have a real chance at happiness now. Take it."

My turn to shake my head. "If you mean Stephen—"

"No. Not Stephen. There is another. You know who it is." He stops, tilts his head as if listening. He nods. "I only have a few more minutes. Don't regret what happened in that hangar. I know you've been wondering whether you will always be stronger than vampire. You only need to want it. All the strength you need is within yourself. You are right about Culebra. He has found new meaning for his life with Adelita. He has found a way to make up for past mistakes. He has finally found peace. Make sure he understands he is not to blame for what happened to me. He needs to concentrate now on the future. Let the past die."

I tilt my head. "But how did you know what I was thinking at the hospital? You were unconscious the entire time."

"All the same, I heard your thoughts. Loud and clear. In

fact, it was those thoughts that kept pulling me back when I was ready to let go." He laughs. "Your will is too strong. I was relieved when they sent you home."

"I don't understand," I say while my gut is saying, of course you do. You know.

"It was my time, Anna."

Anger wells up, and with it, fear. Fear of losing a friend. Fear of losing Max. "No. I don't want you to go."

"It's too late. It's a tribute to your power that I was allowed to hang around this long. To say a proper good-bye. I'll miss you, Anna."

"No." I lunge forward on the bed, reaching for his hand.

It slips through mine as though made of fog.

He smiles a slow, sweet smile and raises his hand in farewell.

And then before I can reach out again, he is gone.

FUNNY HOW SOME DREAMS ARE FLEETING AS SPRING snow while others stay with you long past waking. It's been that way with the "dream" I had the night Max died. Only it wasn't a dream, was it?

It's all I think about on my way to Monument Valley. Max's message to me is like a beacon drawing me to Daniel Frey. And when I get there . . .

CHAPTER 1

JANUARY

I WISH I HAD A CAMERA. THE EXPRESSION ON DANIEL Frey's handsome face when he opens the door and sees me standing on his porch in the middle of the day in the middle of Monument Valley is priceless. It's a combination of surprise, delight, unease, trepidation and just plain confusion. It hikes his eyebrows, furrows his brow and turns a half frown, half grin into something that resembles a gargoyle's grimace.

"Anna. What are you doing—?"

"Is John-John here?"

"No. He's still at school." A glance at his watch. "He won't be home for another three hours."

I push him into the living room, slam and lock the door and shove him down on the couch.

He grins up at me. "I take it you have a reason for sur-prising me like this?"

"Can you guess what it is?" My hands are busy unbuckling his belt, pulling at the top button of his jeans.

"You missed me?" It comes out in a hoarse whisper, his fingers tugging my blouse free, slipping it off my shoulders.

In another moment, he's got my jeans unzipped and we're both squirming—frantic to have nothing between us except heat and skin.

And then he's inside me and neither of us speaks again for a long time.

FREY IS STROKING MY HAIR. I HAVE MY HEAD ON HIS chest, listening to the strong, steady beat of his heart.

I nestle closer. "This is right, isn't it?"

His hand stills. He tilts my chin up so that our eyes meet. "For me, it's been right for a long time. Maybe since the first day I saw you walk into that school auditorium with your mother. I'm just sorry it took so long for me to get the courage to tell you how I felt." He pauses. "And when I finally did, you didn't believe me."

I think back to that conversation—could it really have been only a few weeks ago? I shake my head and smile sadly. "John-John had just lost his mother. Staying with him, being a real father for the first time, starting a new life. That's a lot of emotional upheaval in a very short time. I believed you missed me. I believed you wanted me. But I didn't believe you were ready to love me."

"And," he reminds me, "there was Stephen."

I nod. "Yes. There was Stephen." A human I thought I could build a future with because he knew and accepted my true nature. But he was human, after all, and love was no competition for the lure of a public career that I could never, as vampire, be a part of.

I poke his chest with a finger. "And you were right. A match between a human and a vampire is doomed from the start."

"Oh. So, I'm the consolation prize."

I reach up and kiss him, urgently, passionately. When I pull back, we're both breathless. "Does that feel like a consolation prize?"

He puts his arms around me and pulls me closer. "So, tell me, Anna, what really brought you here today?"

I slide my hand down his abdomen. "You mean besides this?"

He laughs. "Besides that."

"Max."

"Max?" He pulls back so he can see my face. "What does Max have to do with us?"

"He told me you were the one."

His voice softens. "Before he died?"

"No. After."

Frey doesn't laugh or express incredulity. In fact, his expression grows thoughtful. He and I have been through so much together—faced witches and skinwalkers and rogue creatures of every denomination. The idea that I may have been visited by a man who was once a lover, who was killed in front of me while saving the life of a young girl, who proved to be as strong and bravehearted as any human I ever knew, all this he accepts with a nod and a tightening of his arms around my shoulders.

"Then I owe Max a debt of gratitude," he says.

"We both do."

CHAPTER 2

MARCH

I PULL THE JAG INTO THE PARKING LOT AND RE-luctantly shut off the engine. My business partners, David and Tracey, are already in the office. I know because I'm parked right next to David. He and Tracey have taken to driving together and I can tell where they spent the night by whose car is in the lot. This morning, it's David's big, yellow Humvee.

I should have been inside by now, too, knee-deep in tax reports. The not-so-fun side of a successful bounty-hunting business. To make it worse, the sun is bouncing off the bay with the intensity only a cloudless San Diego spring day can generate. I want to be outside basking in it—not trapped inside, working.

But duty calls.

Halfheartedly, I drag myself up the path to the door.

Tracey looks up and smiles a greeting, but David frowns.

"You were supposed to be here an hour ago. We have to get this stuff to the tax attorney by noon."

I slump in my chair. "Yeah, yeah. What do you want me to do?"

He hands me a fistful of receipts. "Sort these by date."

I take the pile and spread the receipts on the desk. Mechanically, I sort.

Boring.

"We've had a good year," Tracey remarks, her eyes zeroing in on the bottom line of an income statement.

"Too good," David grumbles. "And if we don't get this tax stuff to the attorney *by noon*, what hard work giveth, the tax man will taketh away."

"I hear you, David. Look. I'm sorting, I'm sorting."

David drops his eyes back to the pile of paper on his side of our partners' desk. Tracey has pulled a chair up so that they are seated side by side and it strikes me what a good-looking couple they are. David, ex–football player, six feet six inches tall, still the same weight and shape he was when he played for the Raiders. Tracey, ex-cop, bundle of energy, her auburn hair pulled back in a ponytail. I can't remember why I was skeptical of her when David first brought her on board. I had no reason to be. We even have the same fashion sense—each of us perennially dressed in jeans and T-shirts. That in itself should have been enough to bond us.

David looks up, catches me watching him. But instead of making some comment about how I'm not working, his expression shifts from irritation to sly mischief.

Uh-oh. What now? I brace myself.

"So, Anna," he says. "You went out of town last weekend."

"Did you do anything special?" Tracey pipes in, batting her lashes.

What the— I shift my gaze from Tracey to David, narrow my eyes. "Why don't you tell me? And since when have my weekends been a topic of conversation?"

David leans back in his chair and laces his fingers behind his head. "Since you started spending a lot of time with that friend of yours in Monument Valley. Is there something you want to share with us?"

"Like what?"

"Like is it getting serious between you two?"

I frown, sifting several variations of "none of your fucking business" through my head until I come to the realization with a start. It is their fucking business. They are my partners and my friends. I turn that old frown upside down. "Yes."

David almost slips backward off his chair. Scrambling to regain his balance, he grunts, "Wow. That's a first. He's not just a fuck buddy? You actually admit you have a serious relationship?"

Tracey leans forward, all big eyes and girlish enthusiasm. "Ooooh. Tell me about him. When will I meet him? What's he like?"

I have to mull that over in my mind. There are more things I *can't* say about him to my human business partners than I can—like the fact that he's a shape-shifter, that his other form is panther, that his son is already manifesting his powers as a shape-shifter years ahead of the curve, that he's saved my vampire ass more than once over the past year and a half I've known him.

I draw in a breath and meet Tracey's gaze. "He's generous, handsome, strong. Has tremendous endurance." A wink to her here. "Has a five-year-old son that I'm crazy about. And he loves me almost as much as I love him."

I hear a gasp from David. "Holy fucking shit. You sound like a girl."

"She is a girl, stupid," Tracey snaps. "Jesus." She turns to me. "He sounds wonderful. And I'm getting so jealous. When do I get to meet Mr. Wonderful?"

"In two weeks. His son has a school break the middle of March and they're spending it here."

"What's his name?"

"Daniel Frey."

"Frey lives in Monument Valley now? And he has a son?" David asks, startled. "Since when?"

I forgot that David met Frey several months ago. They spent some time together at a local bar while I slipped out to attend to some vampire business. "He moved a while ago. I didn't find out about his son myself until just recently."

A white lie. Frey told me about his son the same time he distracted David so I could sneak away. I did just meet John-John, though, right after Christmas.

"Wow, that's so romantic," Tracey says.

David sticks a finger in his open mouth and makes a gagging sound. "Jesus. Is this what I'm going to have to listen to in the office now? You two hard-asses cooing like characters in a romance novel?"

I get out of my chair and cross to his side of the desk,

leaning down so we're eye level. "I have just three words for you," I growl. "Gloria. Fucking. Estrella."

"Who's that?" Tracey asks.

Color floods up David's neck.

I grin. "Ask him to tell you about her sometime," I reply. "Now *that's* a story out of a romance novel."

David grows suddenly quiet, busying himself with a stack of papers he's probably been through a dozen times.

"Who's Gloria Estrella?" Tracey repeats. Then she stops. "Wait a minute. *The* Gloria Estrella?"

You can see the gleam of recognition spark in her eyes. "You told me you had dated a Gloria, but Gloria Estrella? She was your ex?"

"That was before you moved to San Diego and joined SDPD," David blurts. "It's been over for a long time!"

"You mean you missed the glamorous couple on the cover of *People* every other week?" I can't believe I'm spouting off like this, but once started, the sarcasm pours forth. "The actress and the football player. They were news, baby!"

David shoots me a look that's pure poison. "That's enough, Anna. Unless you want me to enumerate your less-than-stellar relationships."

But his tone is more hurt than angry and I'm suddenly flooded with guilt. It was unfair to bring Gloria into the conversation. Gloria Estrella was the big, stupid, "you are the love of my life" mistake every one of us makes at least once. David loved her to the depths of his soul, refusing to see what lay beneath the gleaming façade.

Yes, she was beautiful, a successful model and actress, but she was also vain, self-centered and utterly without conscience. David is handsome, trusting, an ex–football player of some local renown. Perfect for Gloria to use as a camera-friendly public consort and since I was his partner and friend, perfect to use me to save her ass with the police when she screwed up. Which she did on more than one occasion. Big-time. But it came to an end when I saw what she was doing to David. I made a bargain with her. I'd help get her out of yet another scrape (a very big one) if she promised to let David go. I did and remarkably, she's kept her word.

It took David a long time to get over her.

And now, I've raised the specter again. Just when he and Tracey were beginning a relationship of their own. Tracey is an ex-cop, almost as tough as I am, and just as street-smart. She and David do make a good couple, and she's more than a match for any of David's exes, except maybe Gloria.

Tracey is about to start asking questions again, I can see it in the confused way she looks from David to me.

I made this mess; I'd better clean it up.

I wave a hand and laugh. "Foget it, Tracey. Gloria is old news—a joke between David and me. It was over a long time ago."

I see David's shoulders relax ever so slightly.

But so does Tracey. Her eyes tighten at the corners. "Are you sure?"

And then, as if stage directed to enter at precisely the right moment, someone opens the door to our office.

The three of us swivel toward it. I might be imagining it, but a wave of relief at the interruption is so palpable, our visitor seems to feel it, too. He pauses, hand on the door, his expression curious but detached.

"Am I interrupting?" Detective Harris says.

Shit. "When aren't you interrupting?" I groan under my breath.

He comes in and closes the door behind him. He is smiling, but he's a cop. A middle-aged, built-like-a-boxer, craggy-faced bulldog of a cop. His smiles can't be trusted. He was involved in the Gloria Estrella fiasco, which brings David's shoulders up again. But we both know he isn't here about that long-closed case.

Harris strides over to the visitor's chair and pulls it up to the desk. He turns it around and straddles it backward, grinning. "Hope you all had a good holiday."

Small talk? And now he's grinning. Christ. This can't be good. When no one follows up with the usual banalities about how good their holidays were, I pipe in. "What can we do for you?"

Harris ignores my question and directs one to Tracey. "How's the bounty-hunting business treating you, Officer Banker?"

"Ex-officer," Tracey spits back with the malevolence of a striking rattlesnake, her ferocity startling us all.

Jaw clenched, she adds, "As you well know since it was at your recommendation that I was *granted* disability retirement."

I snap to attention at this unexpected bit of information—and at the heat in Tracey's response. I'd assumed Tracey had agreed to retirement after an off-duty scuffle with an armed bank robber resulted in a hero's commendation and a back injury. Should have known after seeing Tracey in action with us that it hadn't been her choice to retire from the force.

She's on her feet now, gathering the tax papers we'd assembled and the sheaf of receipts I was working on and stuffing them into a large envelope with jabs that would do a boxer proud. "I'll take these downtown," she says, jaw tight. "Finish it there. See you later."

And she's gone . . . fairly flying out the door. David and I look at each other and then at Harris.

"Well. I don't think she likes you very much," David says.

Harris shifts in his chair. The fact that he didn't jump to defend his actions with Tracey makes me think he might realize he acted precipitously in forcing her to retire. "I'm sorry she's still so angry," he says.

David shakes his head. "It's not Anna and me you should be apologizing to. It's Tracey." He pushes back his chair and gets to his feet. "I'm going with her." He's looking at Harris, daring the detective to try to stop him.

Harris lifts his shoulders. "Tell her I didn't mean to upset her," he says quietly.

David mumbles something that sounds a lot like "right, you fucking jerk" and brushes past Harris.

Then it's just the two of us alone in the office.

Yippee.

"I see your social skills haven't improved."

Then, since I think I'm going to need fortification, I get up and head for the coffeemaker in the corner. "Want coffee?"

If Harris hears the reluctance in my offer, he ignores it. He joins me at the credenza and takes a mug off the counter. He pours creamer and what looks like a quarter cup of sugar into it before swirling the mug until I think the contents are going to spill over the sides and onto the floor. They don't.

I watch the performance with raised eyebrows. "Ever heard of a spoon?" I ask dryly.

He's already tipped the mug to his lips, but he allows a smile. "Haven't spilled a drop yet."

We take our coffee back to the desk. This time he plops himself down in David's chair. We drink for a couple of minutes until I can stand the staring contest no longer.

"Christ, Harris, are you ever going to tell me why you're here?"

He tilts his head back, draining his mug. "You can't guess?"

Sure, I can guess. He's been badgering me ever since the former chief of police, Warren Williams, was found murdered, burned to ashes, outside of Palm Springs several months ago. Of course, he doesn't know that Williams was a vampire. But the details of his death and the unconventional forensic evidence found at the scene, two-hundred-year-old DNA to be precise, and the fact that Williams and I were known to have had a contentious relationship have elevated me to the top position in his list of "persons of interest." No matter that there is not a shred of evidence to link me to the crime.

But I want him to bring it up so I stay quiet.

Finally, he does.

"It's about Judith Williams."

Not what I was expecting, though as bad luck would have it, I have knowledge of *that* Williams' death, too. Warren Williams' wife, also a vampire, met her own grisly end at the point of an arrow.

I feign innocence. "Chief Williams' wife? Didn't I read that she'd gone missing several months back?"

"You did. Is that all you know, what you read in the newspapers?"

Now I've been around long enough to know the cops don't generally ask questions they haven't already answered—at least to themselves—so I frame my reply around a question. "I thought the FBI had taken over the case?"

"They had, yes. But I was informed yesterday that they're no longer pursuing it. Which means to us real cops that they hit a dead end. Decided to clear it off their books and throw it back to the locals."

He pauses, watching me, as if waiting for some kind of response. You'd think he knew me well enough by now to know the odds he'll get one are as infinitesimal as the odds we'll ever share a bed. When I stare back at him, mouth clamped tightly shut, he finally gives up.

"So," he says, picking up the conversation as if he'd never hesitated, "I've got all these reports from the FBI investigation. And I'm exercising due diligence by going over each and every one, and imagine my surprise when a familiar name pops up." He gets up and walks back to the coffeemaker, casual as an old sweater, taking time to pour himself a second mug and going through the "sugar, cream, swirl and slosh" routine. Then he takes a breath and turns to face me with the smug expression of a movie detective about to expose the villain in a room full of suspects.

Only there's no room full of suspects. Only me. I know what he's going to say. Before he gets the chance, I figure I'll pop his balloon. "It's no biggie, Harris. Yes. I was in Monument Valley same time as Judith Williams. But I only saw her once. Ran into her at the lodge. She was with a man I'd never seen before. I was there with Daniel Frey, visiting his son. We said hello to her, went our separate ways. End of story."

I touch the tip of my nose. Nope. It's not growing.

Harris puts his mug down on the credenza. "That's what the report said. Funny thing, it's just about word for word the same thing that you said about being in Palm Springs when Warren Williams was killed. And Daniel Frey was with you then, too."

I eye him over the rim of my mug and snort. "My, that is a coincidence."

I shouldn't have pushed it with that last sarcastic remark. Harris' patience explodes with the impact of a rock through a window. "There are a hell of a lot of coincidences with you, lady. I don't believe in coincidences. The FBI may have dropped the case, but I won't. Not ever. Get used to this face because I'll be looking over your shoulder every minute until I figure out how you managed to be in the vicinity of not one, but two murders." He pushes out of the chair. "There's something not right about you. You're a puzzle. I don't like puzzles. But I'm damned good at solving them."

He turns on his heel and storms out of the office. His threat, because that's just what it was, trails behind him like a bitter wake.

I put my head against the back of the chair. Harris and I have a relationship that teeter-totters up and down. Not too long ago, I thought we might be on our way to becoming if not exactly pals, at least tolerant of each other. Obviously I overestimated.

His words echo in my head. *Something's not quite right with me?*

I get up and take our mugs back to the credenza.

A little overly dramatic but what a master of understatement. I'm vampire, for shit's sake.

I'm surprised he didn't ask me again about the mysterious two-hundred-year-old DNA found where Warren Williams' was killed.

At least that's one sleeping dog he didn't kick.

CHAPTER 3

I TAKE MY COFFEE OUT TO THE DECK THAT SPANS THE back of our office. I sink into a chair and let the sun soothe my frazzled nerves. Harris is not going to let his suspicions about me go, no matter how circumstantial they appear to be.

Only I know his instincts are dead-on. Just my luck to get a really good detective on the case.

I'm still on the deck when Tracey and David come back to the office less than an hour after Harris' abrupt departure.

David looks in to make sure Harris is gone.

I get up and come inside. "It's safe. Harris left to find somebody else to harass."

He motions Tracey inside. She goes right to the coat-rack, grabs her jacket and waves a hand at me before standing on tiptoe to give David's cheek a peck.

"See you at the condo?"

Her good humor has obviously been restored.

David gives her shoulder a squeeze. "I'll stop at Sammi's for takeout and see you in twenty."

She smiles at me. "See? You're not the only one who found a good guy. Want to join us for lunch?"

"Good guy?" I feign shock and look around. "Where?"

Tracey laughs and I continue. "Rain check for lunch. I have some stuff to do."

"When your guy gets to town, we'll double-date for sure." She reaches up and pinches David's cheek. "Won't that be fun?"

David groans and closes his eyes. "I can't think of anything funner."

Tracey heads out. When the door has closed behind her, David drops the comedy routine and turns anxious eyes to me. I expect him to tear me a new one over the Gloria Estrella thing this morning. Instead, he surprises me.

"What did Harris want?" he asks.

Relieved, I fill him in. Ever since David started having fractured memories of an evening not too many months ago when he and Judith Williams spent the night together, he's had more than a casual interest in her, too. I could help him fill in those gaps but doing so might trigger another memory I'd rather leave buried . . . the memory of Judith telling him that she was a vampire.

And that I was one, too.

The fact that she disappeared (and I know is dead) granted me reprieve but left David with questions he'll never get answered. I made up a story of a drunken rave where he was drugged and had sex with not only Judith, but others as well. A story part true—he was drugged and he actually did have several sexual partners that weekend—part fiction—there was no drunken rave. Judith Williams kidnapped him to ensure my presence at a little soiree she had planned. But casual sex is so far out of character for David, he was determined to question Judith Williams himself.

Something that now is never going to happen.

David listens to me as I reprise Harris' frustration that he can't pin either Williams' disappearance on me.

"Why would he do that?" David asks, his own frustration adding an edge to his voice. "Just because you were a friend of her husband's? He's making you a scapegoat for his own incompetence. If he comes sniffing around again, I think you should file a harassment suit."

He grabs his jacket from the back of the chair. "Got to run. Finding a place to park around Sammi's at this time of day is going to be a bitch."

"David?"

He stops at the door and turns around.

"I want to fix up the guest room in the cottage for John-John. I don't have any experience decorating for a boy. I thought maybe you could help me pick out some stuff?"

His eyes widen. "Wow. You aren't kidding about this relationship being serious, are you?"

I shrug. "And who knows? Maybe this will be good practice for you and Tracey?"

He holds up a hand. "Whoa. Not even remotely ready for anything like that." Then he grins. "But I'd love to help you. When do you want to go?"

I look over the desktop calendar. "We don't have anything going on tomorrow. After lunch?"

"Sounds good. I know just the place to go, too."

Before I can ask where, he's out the door. Is it my imagination or was that smile on his face one of genuine delight at the prospect? Who would have thunk it?

THE CLOSER IT GETS TO FREY AND JOHN-JOHN'S VISIT, the first time they'll be staying at the cottage, the more excited I get. I had all the furniture in my guest room moved into a storage area I share with my parents and set about deciding on a color for the walls. They're vanilla-bean bland right now. Perfectly suited for the (very) few adult visitors I've ever had and for the cherry bed and dresser formerly occupying the space. Not suited for an active five-year-old. I spend the afternoon looking through home-decorating magazines and the next morning at Lowe's picking up swatches and paint samples.

It's one when I get to the office.

The voice mail indicator is blinking. Since Tracey and David are MIA, maybe at lunch, I dial in and take the message. It's one of the bondsmen we work for out of L.A. and he has a tip. A skip he's been looking for was spotted eating lunch at Jake's in Del Mar. I call him back, tell him we're on it. I pull the guy's file. Wanted for two counts of aggravated assault. Skipped his first hearing. If he's not in custody by five p.m. this afternoon, his bond is forfeit. Fifty thousand dollars. Not a big payday for us but it'd take care of the tax bill, so after scribbling a hasty note to David and Tracey, I take off.

Since becoming vampire, much of my life has been consumed with adjusting to a dual nature. Most of that has been concealing that dual nature from the people I care for most. Every once in a while I enjoy giving the vamp free rein and setting out on my own to bring in a skip (especially one wanted for violent crimes) without Tracey and David along. I don't have to pretend I'm not as strong as I am or as fast or as invulnerable.

The guy is right where the bondsman said he'd be. He's seated in the patio area in the back of the restaurant so I watch as he finishes his meal, pays the check (with cash), takes one last pull of a cup of coffee and starts for the door.

He isn't a big guy, five-nine I'd guess, and slight of build. He's wearing a suit and tie and good shoes. He looks like any other businessman grabbing a quick lunch before heading back to the office. He doesn't look like the type who beat the crap out of his ex-wife twice before she got the nerve to press charges. What he's doing here in Del Mar I have no idea. And I couldn't care less.

The suit is well tailored and I see no telltale bulges that would indicate a gun. 'Course, he could be wearing an ankle holster. Or carrying a knife. The vampire hopes he goes for it.

I've already set the trap. The hood on my Jag is up and I'm leaning over the engine with a puzzled look of feminine bewilderment.

He has to stroll right by and right on cue, he stops, whether from my predicament or the outline of my ass against a pair of tight jeans, I can only guess.

"Having trouble?" he asks.

I straighten and sigh. "It's the third time this week. Can't get it to start."

He joins me so that our hips are touching. "Don't know too much about foreign cars, but let me have a look."

He bends over and begins touching this cable and that piston, checking gaskets and pulleys. "Well," he says at last, "I can't see anything. Do you have AAA?"

I nod. "Just called them. It'll be about thirty minutes."

My left hand is resting on the edge of the engine well and he places his right hand over mine. "You're cold. Let's go inside. I'd be happy to buy you a drink while we wait for them."

I slip my hand out from under his, grasp his wrist and he's handcuffed before he can say, "What the fuck?"

He struggles, but not too much. My grip is tight. He looks at me and snipes, "You're strong for a woman. What are you? A fucking dyke?"

Nice. I pat him down, none too gently. No gun. No knife.

I manhandle him into the backseat of the Jag. He's cursing and yelling and demanding to know what I'm doing. But he doesn't try to fight back or make a break for it.

Damn it.

I ignore his howls of protest, snapping the cuffs through a metal bar I've had installed on the door of the Jag for just this purpose. Once I get him to SDPD, he'll catch on. Now I'm just disappointed I didn't get to have any fun after all.

DAVID AND TRACEY ARE WAITING FOR ME WHEN I GET back. The whole episode didn't take more than two hours. I throw the paperwork on the desk and David looks it over.

"Didn't give you any trouble?"

Not really a question. Little veins are bulging at his temple. He's pissed.

I pretend not to notice, knowing what's coming. "Nope. Cakewalk."

He purses his lips. "I thought we decided we wouldn't do any lone-ranger pickups. This guy is wanted for aggravated assault. He could have given you trouble."

I can't say what I'm thinking—that a little trouble was what I went looking for—so I just smile like I don't understand his irritation. "Worked out fine. Came along gentle as a little lamb."

"Damn it, Anna, don't play innocent." He slaps the file down on the desktop. "You should have waited for backup."

I look at Tracey, but she's shaking her head. "He's right, Anna. One of us should have gone with you."

Two against one. I raise my hands in surrender. "Okay. You're right. Next time I'll wait."

Tracey smiles, but David isn't ready to let go of his frustration. I understand. I know he's remembering a time when a skip got away from us and I was raped and beaten while David lay unconscious a few feet away. What he doesn't know, what he can't know, is that attack resulted in my becoming vampire. The reason he's so protective is the reason he no longer needs to be.

He shoves the file into the cabinet and slams the drawer shut.

I clear my throat. "Does this mean you don't want to go shopping with me this afternoon?"

"Of course he'll go shopping with you," Tracey answers before he can, her tone as barbed as a fishhook. "I'll stay here and tend the office."

"You speaking for me now?" David snaps.

But Tracey takes no umbrage from his tone or annoyed glance. "It's all you've been talking about," she says in a voice so honey sweet you could smear it on toast. "You've been as excited as a little kid at the prospect of picking out furniture and toys. Don't try to deny it."

"Really?" I layer my own sugary sweetness atop Tracey's. "I do need your help, David. I don't know what little boys like these days."

Then, because it's the kind of guy David is, he gives in. "Yeah, yeah. Cut the bull. Jesus, you two going to gang up on me all the time now?"

"Probably," Tracey says. "Now go. I'll hold down the fort."

DAVID IS DRIVING. HE HASN'T SAID A WORD TO ME, and in spite of Tracey's insistence that he wanted to help me pick out things for John-John, his attitude now is one of resentful indifference.

"So," I say, deciding to break the silence when he obviously is not about to, "you and Tracey? Things seem to be going well."

Silence.

"She's a good match for you. Tough. Won't let you get away with anything."

Irritated sideways glance.

"I like her. It's a big improvement from—"

"Don't."

"Don't what?"

"Don't say her name."

"Look, David. I'm sorry about yesterday. I shouldn't have brought Gl—"

"I. Said. Don't. Say. Her. Name."

Jesus. I shrink back into the seat. Either he and Tracey had a big fucking fight over Gloria last night or . . .

"Tell me you aren't still in touch with her."

David isn't a good liar. Worse, he knows he's not a good liar so he doesn't try to be. He's brutally honest. The fact that he's not answering me is his way of not having to lie so that I won't have to accuse him of lying.

"God, David. What about you and Tracey?"

"What about us?"

"She's crazy about you. Does she know you're seeing—" I catch myself before uttering the G-word. "She who cannot be named?"

"It's complicated."

"No. It's not. It's very simple. Shit. Now I know why you reacted the way you did yesterday. You're cheating on Tracey."

"I'm not cheating on anyone," David snaps back. "I'm not exactly seeing—" A sideways glance to me. "You know. But she's called me a few times. And we talk."

"What's a few times?"

A very pregnant pause while I drum my fingers impatiently on the dashboard and David pretends to be busy driving.

"David? How often do you speak with her?"

"Oh. Maybe three or four times."

"Three or four times since you broke up?"

Color is flooding David's face. "A week."

"Oh. My. Fucking. God." The words explode out in a howl of outrage so loud, David jumps. "Are you kidding me? After all she put you through with that murder investigation? She slept with the guy she was accused of killing, remember? She manipulated you and me and a goddamned fourteen-year-old kid to save her own skin. And you're still in touch with her?"

David's jaw is tight. His eyes are fixed straight ahead. His shoulders are bunched so tight that I think if I poked him in the arm, they'd shatter.

We're pulling into the parking lot of an IKEA. David finds a space to park and it's not until he's shut off the engine that he says another word. Then he doesn't turn to look at me, but simply says, "Look, Anna. We're never going to agree about this. But you know me. I won't break Tracey's heart. She has nothing to worry about. You have nothing to worry about. Can we just let it go at that?"

Then he opens the door to the Hummer and jumps to the ground.

CHAPTER 4

I T'S NOT UNTIL WE'VE WOUND OUR WAY THROUGH a maze of living room, dining room, office and kitchen furniture to arrive at the "kids stuff" that David again acknowledges my presence. He's standing in front of a bed shaped like a race car.

"I would have killed for a bed like this when I was a kid." He's running a hand over the frame. "It's not too big for John-John, is it?"

His voice has lost the anger and bitterness of our conversation in the parking lot. I jump at the chance to smooth things over. "I think it's perfect! And John-John makes Lego cars all the time."

David has moved from the bed to an area with rugs and toys. He points to a rug laid out like a racetrack. "Get this, too, and those wooden cars. And that lamp and desk."

He's picking out things faster than I can write the item numbers on an order sheet. IKEA is a big warehouse with the displays in one area and the pickup in another. I start to laugh. "Hold on there, cowboy. I can't keep up."

But David has already moved onto sheets and towels and shower curtains. "That bedroom has its own bathroom, doesn't it?" he asks. When I nod, he starts loading our shopping cart with sheets and towels and a brightly color-splashed shower curtain.

In less than an hour, we have everything. I've never seen David move so fast. I follow along, caught in the undertow of his enthusiasm. It's a side of David new to me. A side I would not have expected.

When we've had everything loaded into the back of the Hummer, and are on our way to my place, I risk igniting the firestorm again.

"What do you and Gloria talk about?" I ask softly.

I wait, shoulders bunched, for the explosion. Instead, David says, "Mostly how her career's going. Where she's going on location next. Who she's dating . . ."

Sounds like Gloria. There's Gloria and then there's the world. "Does she ever ask about what *you're* doing? Who *you're* dating?"

"Of course she does," he replies with more than a hint of impatience. "Why do you always assume the worst about her?"

I grunt. Let me count the ways. But instead, I say, "I worry about you where Gloria is concerned. She seems to have some mystical hold on you I've never been able to figure out."

He glances sideways at me. "You mean besides the fact

that she's beautiful, famous, rich, an international star and sex with her was—"

"Okay," I interrupt. "TMI." At least he didn't say sex with her *is*. I regroup. "Which brings me back to the question I asked you before. Where does all this leave Tracey?"

He raises his shoulders in a half shrug. "I told you. I won't hurt Tracey. Gloria is fantasy. Tracey is real. Someone I can rely on to be honest. Someone I can count on."

I shake my head. Does he even know how demeaning that sounds? "Do you think you're being fair to Tracey?"

His jaw sets. "I've always been honest with Tracey. I've never promised her more than I can deliver."

"Maybe not in words, but I see the way she looks at you."

He shrugs again. But we're pulling into the back of the cottage and I have to jump out to open the gate before he can answer. Then we're busy with boxes and packages and I get caught up in the excitement of tackling John-John's room.

David is unloading one of the cartons containing the bed from the Hummer when he asks, "Want some help putting this stuff together?"

His tone is full of eager anticipation. He sounds as enthusiastic as I feel. Who am I to deny him such pleasure? Besides, I looked at one of the instruction sheets. It's written in three dozen languages not one of which was fumble-fingered female. "I'd love it!"

It takes us twenty minutes to unload everything and haul it up the stairs to the second story. I dump the white goods on my bedroom floor and David and I tear yards of bubble wrap and cardboard from the furniture pieces. Then we hunker down and piece the bed together. I read (or interpret) the instructions. Most are stick-figure drawings with one or two words to clarify what you're looking at. Not that David needs much direction. He's got that bed put together and we're standing back admiring it in less time than it took us to buy it.

"How about a beer?" I ask.

"Sounds good." David has wandered over to the open closet. Inside, I'd stashed the cans of paint bought to transform the stuffy adult room to something more to a kid's liking. He's looking at the color swatches. "This is great. Why don't we get started?"

"What? You want to help me paint?"

"Right after that beer."

I REALIZE, STANDING SIDE BY SIDE WITH DAVID, SWIPING paint rollers of pale yellow over the walls of what's to become John-John's bedroom, how much I've missed doing simple, human things with him. How much I've missed our friendship.

I actually have to swallow down a lump in my throat before I can say, "You know what this reminds me of?"

"Painting our office two years ago," he replies without missing a beat.

I hear the smile in his voice. "You spilled a whole pan full of paint," I say.

"Because you bumped the ladder," he says.

"I did not. You saw a spider in the corner and jumped off the ladder so fast, everything went flying."

A chuckle. "Well, it was a big spider."

I snicker. "We've had some good times."

He's quiet. When I glance over, his shoulders are slumped, that little muscle at the corner of his jaw is jumping.

"What's wrong, David?"

He continues to paint, eyes tracing the swaths of color onto the wall as they appear from the end of his roller.

"If something's wrong, I wish you'd tell me."

His hand pauses in mid-stroke. "Nothing's wrong."

David keeps painting, pushing the roller back and forth. I've stopped painting now and turn to face him. "That's bullshit, David. What is it?"

The silence stretches on. I don't take my eyes off him, fixing him with what I hope is a laser stare until finally he gives in with a growl.

"You've never forgiven me."

My stomach does a small roll. I know exactly where this is coming from. What I did this morning, going after that skip alone, has awakened the dragon. Angry at myself, I blurt, "That's because there's nothing to forgive."

He lays the paint roller down in the pan and wipes his hands slowly and deliberately with a rag. "You know that's not true. Because of me, you were raped and beaten and left to die."

His words are sharp, enunciated carefully with bitter recrimination as he continues.

"Because of me, your life changed. You've had one boyfriend after another. Your family lives halfway around the world. I don't ever see you with friends. I don't ever see you out of the office. You're not the same. And it's because of me."

I can't look at him. My heart aches and my mind is full of things I *want* to say. Things I should say.

Things I can't say.

I release a long breath, put my paintbrush down along-side his. My hands are trembling when I turn to face him.

"You're right. My life changed that night. But not be-cause of anything you did."

"Because I did nothing," he retorts bitterly. "I was knocked out. Like a fucking amateur. And Donaldson beat you and raped you and would have killed you if someone from that bar hadn't come out to stop him. I don't know how you can stand to look at me. I walk into the office ev-ery morning expecting to find your letter of resignation. You should hate me, Anna. It's what I deserve."

He's still looking down at his hands, rubbing them with that rag as if they were the last year and a half and if he scrubbed hard enough, he could wipe them out of existence.

I put my hands over his to stop it. "David." He won't look at me. I take his chin in my hand and lift his face. "None of what happened with Donaldson was your fault. He was on PCP, remember? He surprised both of us. I got over it. I wish you would. It almost sounds as if it would be better for you if I left. Is that really what this is about? You have Tracey now. She's a good partner. Do you want me to go?"

He closes his eyes. "God, no, Anna. The business wouldn't be the same without you. It's just—"

"Then stop. If you want me to say the words, I will. I forgive you. I fucking forgive you. But you know I don't mean it because in my heart, there's nothing to forgive."

That gets a tiny smile from David. The tension breaks. "You make me feel so much better."

I grin, so relieved my knees feel shaky. "It's what I live

for. Listen, I know we don't do all the things we used to. It's not because I don't want to, it's because we lead complicated lives. You know all that's happened. First there was Trish and her bitch mother. Then there was all the drama with Gloria. My folks inheriting a winery. You getting kidnapped. I admit my love life hasn't been the most stable. But neither has yours. I think we both have a real chance now at getting it right with Tracey and Frey. Let's put the past away once and for all." I reach up and tweak his cheek. "Think we can do that, big boy?"

That actually elicits a laugh. "God. Now you sound like Tracey."

"Better get used to it."

David sighs and picks up his brush. "Let's get this done. I'm ready for another beer."

"You've got it. And David?"

He looks over, eyebrows quirked.

"You're going to make a great dad."

He grins. "And you're going to make a great stepmom."

We finish in companionable silence. I don't know what David is thinking, but I'm thinking, I should be a novelist. The story I just spun is worthy of a Pulitzer. But David deserves to have that burden of guilt lifted over what happened to me. Only I can ever be aware of the irony. An attack by a "skip" who left me for dead turned out instead to be an attack by a vampire that made me immortal.

CHAPTER 5

I CAN BARELY SIT STILL.

I'm in front of the first terminal at San Diego International Airport, one eye on the cop coming up five or six cars behind me, one eye on the doors. If Frey and John-John aren't out in the next thirty seconds, that cop will wave me on and I'll have to make another lap around the parking lot.

Down to ten . . . the cop is eyeing me.

"Anna! Anna!"

The voice of an angel. I'm out of the car in time to see the cop turn on his heel and start back down the row. In another nanosecond, I've scooped John-John up and we're spinning around the sidewalk. Over the top of his head, I see Frey approach, pulling a roller, a car seat balanced on top, and clutching a couple of duffels.

"A little help here?" he says. But he's smiling.

I set John-John on the sidewalk and pop the remote to the trunk. Frey settles the bags inside. Then we're face-to-face.

He touches my cheek. It's not enough. I put my arms around him and squeeze. John-John hides his eyes behind his hands.

"Mushy stuff."

Frey leans his lips close to my ear. "Later."

The one word is breathed with so much promise, my heart starts to race.

Frey steps around and hefts John-John's car seat into the back. I've put the top down on the Jag so it takes only a few moments to secure it and get John-John settled in.

Frey takes his place beside me in the front. "Your place or mine?" he asks.

I glance back at John-John. "Mine. I have a surprise."

"For me?"

"You betcha."

"What is it?"

I put the car in gear and pull out. "If I told you, what would be the fun in that?"

"Then go fast, Anna."

And we do.

I'M NOT SURE WHO IS MORE EXCITED BY THE TIME WE get to the cottage.

"Leave the bags," I tell Frey, grabbing John-John's hand. "We'll get them later."

And then the three of us are through the back gate, across the yard, I've fumbled the lock open and John-John and I are racing up the stairs.

I throw open the bedroom door. "Ta-da!"

At first I get the sinking feeling John-John doesn't like his room. He's stopped at the doorway. In profile, I can see only one wide eye and an open mouth. Frey has come up behind us. His hands rest on my shoulder. I hear his breath catch.

Then John-John whoops and runs to the bed. "Is all this for me?"

And he's everywhere at once, touching the cars and the Legos and books and climbing up on the race-car bed and down again to examine the rug.

"Do you like your new room?" I ask with a hopeful tone.

John-John whirls to look at me. "I love it. You got everything right."

"Did I?"

Then it's Frey who pulls me around. His eyes are shining and I've never seen such warmth in a smile.

"You did," he says. "You got everything right."

JOHN-JOHN IS ASLEEP. FREY AND I ARE UPSTAIRS ON the deck outside my bedroom, watching a full moon rise over the ocean. There's a circle of light around the moon, a golden nimbus reflected in the still water offshore. The only sounds we hear are the waves gently breaking off the seawall. Even the air is still, heavy with the fragrance of night-blooming jasmine.

Frey and I are seated in deck chairs, glasses of wine sitting untouched on a small table beside us. I feel the heat from his body, hear his soft breathing. His presence is a balm to my soul. This afternoon with John-John was all I'd hoped it would be. It felt like a beginning and an ending. The beginning of our becoming a family and the end of my being alone.

Frey's fingers brush mine.

"The room is wonderful. I can't thank you enough."

"I didn't overdo it? I wanted everything to be perfect for him. I love John-John. I'm so happy he likes me."

Frey pushes himself off his chair and perches on the end of mine. "He more than *likes* you. Do you know he talks about you all the time when we're in Monument Valley? He sees you the way I do, Anna. He wants you to be a permanent part of our life."

Frey reaches into the pocket of his shirt and pulls out a small box.

"Another gift from Sani?" I ask, holding up my left hand where the moonlight reflects off the silver band of turquoise the Navajo shaman made for me.

Frey doesn't answer with words. He takes my hand, slips the silver ring from my finger and replaces it with another.

A white-gold band with a single, sparkling stone big as the tip of my little finger.

For the first time in my life, I'm speechless.

As if from far away, I hear Frey laughing. "You should see the look on your face. I hope what I'm seeing is 'oh my god yes' and not 'no are you out of your mind'?"

I can't seem to form words. My throat is suddenly too dry, my tongue is stuck to the roof of my mouth. My heart hammers against my ribs until I think it will burst.

Frey pulls me to my feet. "Talk to me, Anna," he says. "I've never heard of a vampire having a heart attack, but you look as if you're about to have one."

I rest my head against his chest. Where do I start? My thoughts and feelings are churning like a maelstrom, my mouth still so dry, I don't think I can speak.

"Anna?" Frey tilts my chin up, his eyes clouded with worry. "Did I overstep? Did I misinterpret your feelings?"

Come on, Anna. Get it together. I swallow hard and reach up to touch his cheek. "You hear about girls who have fantasies about how this moment will be. When the man they love proposes."

Frey strokes my hair. "Was I not romantic enough?"

I look into his face. "I never had a fantasy like that. Ever. I always thought I'd be alone. Even during the love affairs I've had, I knew deep down I wasn't destined for a happily ever after.

"Then I became vampire and the idea that I might someday marry, have a family, seemed even more unattainable."

"And now?" Frey's tone is still unsure, hesitant.

"Now, I'm not so sure."

Frey's arms tighten around me. "That's the nicest declaration of love I've ever heard," he says. Then we're kissing and I'm so happy, my heart soars.

IT'S MORNING AND ALTHOUGH FREY AND I INTENDED that we'd get up before John-John and make ourselves presentable, a timid knock on the door brings us both straight up in bed.

"Does John-John know that you were going to propose last night?" I whisper, frantically scrambling to throw on a pair of sweatpants and a T-shirt.

Frey is doing some scrambling of his own. His suitcase

is still downstairs so he has no choice but to slip back into the same clothes he arrived in. "Yes. I thought we'd wait a little while, though, to let him see us—" He gestures at the rumpled bed. "Together in bed. I don't know if he knew of the affair between his mother and Kayani."

But Frey forgot the powerful abilities of his shape-shifter son. A small matter-of-fact voice sounds in our heads.

Mother explained that two people who love each other often sleep in the same bed.

I throw open the door and scoop him into a hug. "Your mother was right. Your father and I love each other. Very much. And I love you, too, and I hope you'll let me become a real part of your family."

John-John throws his head back and holds out his arms to his father so that in the next instant we're tangled in each other's arms.

I can't remember ever being so happy.

IT TAKES HARRIS TO BRING US BACK TO EARTH.

After breakfast the three of us trek to the office so I can officially introduce Frey and John-John to David and Tracey. A fishing boat is coming back to port and we're all on the deck, watching seagulls dip and swoop for chum, when the front door to the office opens.

David glances in, then gives a low groan. "Shit. It's Harris again. Remember what I said, Anna, tell him you're about ready to sue for harassment."

I leave everyone on the deck and go inside. "What is it now?" I ask.

He's looking through the slider to the group outside.

"Good. I see Daniel Frey is here. I have some questions for him."

"How did you know he'd be here?"

But even as I ask the question, I can guess the answer and the idea of a harassment suit becomes more appealing.

"You're having me watched?"

He holds up his hands. "All legal and aboveboard. After all, we're investigating two open cases and you admit you and Frey were around for both."

John-John bounds in and runs up to me. "Anna, Anna— come back out, the birds are catching fish right out of the air."

Harris bends down. "And who is this?"

I have to fight the impulse to physically place my body between Harris and John-John. Instead, I do the next best thing. I pick him up. "John-John, this is Lieutenant Harris. He's a policeman. Lieutenant Harris, this is Daniel Frey's son."

Harris looks surprised. I guess the fact that Frey has a son slipped his mind. I set John-John down and turn him back toward the deck. "Go get your daddy, will you, John-John, and ask David to come here a minute?"

When he's scampered off, I direct my fury to Harris. "I'm going to ask David and Tracey to take John-John for ice cream. Don't you ask a single question until they're gone, do you understand?"

Harris returns my glare but does as I ask. I tell David what's going on and he and Tracey leave to take a giggling John-John to the ice cream shop at Seaport Village. Then Frey and I face Harris.

"Does he know why I'm here?" Harris asks, jerking a thumb at Frey.

"He does," Frey answers, and I'm suddenly glad I took the time last night to fill him in. "So if you have questions for me, ask them."

Harris plops himself down on David's desk chair. I take my own. Frey pulls the visitor's chair to my side of the desk.

"Judith Williams," Harris begins. "What do you know about her?"

"Nothing." Frey leans back in his chair. "Anna and I ran into her in Monument Valley. Anna introduced us. It was the first time I'd ever seen her."

"So you didn't know her personally?"

"No. Should I have?"

"What were you doing in Monument Valley?"

I wonder how Frey will answer but he doesn't even hesitate before telling his story. "Anna and I went to visit my son. He lived on the Navajo reservation with his mother. While we were there, John-John's mother was killed in an accident. I stayed on to care for him. Anna came home."

Harris' eyebrows jump. "Another accident?" He makes a show of taking a notebook from his pocket and scribbling a few words.

I shake my head. Our friend, Kayani, will be getting another call, I'm sure. Harris' next words confirm my suspicions.

"While you were both there something else happened, too. Judith Williams went missing. I understand you were questioned about her disappearance by an Officer Kayani of the Navajo police."

Frey nods. "I was. Briefly. But since I couldn't help with the investigation, Officer Kayani didn't question me again."

Harris shifts in his chair. "What about Warren Williams?"

"What about him?"

"You knew him."

"Not well. Met him once or twice through Anna."

"His body was found outside of Palm Springs. You and Anna had been at the Palm Springs home of Anna's boyfriend, Lance Turner, at the very same time. In fact, according to our reports, Williams was killed coming back to San Diego just hours after you two left to come home."

Frey's expression remains neutral, betraying neither interest nor surprise at the revelation.

His detachment seems to trip Harris' temper. "So you and Anna are in the vicinity of two murders at two different locations and times, know the victims and are alibi witnesses for each other. Is that about it?"

At that, Frey registers shock. "Do we need alibis, Detective?" he asks.

Harris lumbers to his feet. "You two have it all figured out, don't you?" He shakes his head at us, then his eyes widen as they settle on the diamond ring on my left hand. He looks from the ring to Frey and shakes his head again.

"Better be careful with this one," he says. "Her track record with men is lousy."

CHAPTER 6

WE WAIT FOR HARRIS TO CLOSE THE DOOR behind him before I explode. "I don't think he's ever going to let go of this."

Frey's expression remains cool and undisturbed. "What can he do? He has no evidence to link us to either crime. He thinks by pushing he's going to get us to crack. He doesn't know who he's dealing with."

"Or what he's dealing with," I growl. "But I want you to know that if it comes down to it, and somehow he finds out it was you who shot Judith Williams, I'm going to take the blame. I'll confess. I won't have you punished for something that was my fault."

Frey smiles one of those cat-and-canary smiles that really means, *I'd never let you do that.* But on this, I would insist. Frey shot Judith Williams because I told him to. It was a complicated situation and she was a rogue vampire, but he shot her at my insistence nonetheless.

Frey catches up my hand. "Let's go get John-John, shall we? Enjoy this beautiful day?"

I call David and tell him to wait at the ice cream shop, that we're on our way. I lock the office door and we stroll hand in hand down the boardwalk to Seaport Village. Soon, I feel my irritation dissolve like snow in sunshine.

Frey has my right hand, the one where Sani's ring now sits after being displaced by the brilliant diamond that I can't keep my eyes off.

Frey catches me glancing down for the tenth time and laughs, squeezing my hand. "So you like it? It's not too old-fashioned?"

"God, no, it's gorgeous." The words pop out before I can censor the reply. After all, I am Anna Strong. Vampire. Bad ass. Getting sentimental over an engagement ring is out of character. But it's so beautiful. My eyes seek Frey's. "You've made me happier than I thought possible. I almost feel human again."

He drops my hand and puts an arm around my shoulders. "You are human, Anna. More human than ninety percent of the mortals I know. You just happen to have another aspect to your nature. It's a big one. But it's only one part." He holds up my left hand and lets the sun play on the ring, sending sparks of rainbow light dancing. "You're like this diamond. It takes all the facets of this ring to make it brilliant. It takes all the facets of your nature to make you who you are."

I've never been a sappy romance-novel type of gal, but I swear, Frey may turn me into one. We've known each other from the very beginning of my existence as a vampire. Has he always felt this way about me?

Frey tugs on a strand of my hair. "Too much? What are you thinking?"

I pull him over to guardrail, out of the way of other boardwalk strollers. I pull his head down and wrap my arms around his neck. "I'm thinking I've wasted too much fucking time." And then I kiss him, putting all I am, all I hope to be for him and all I promise our life together will be into that kiss.

I must have done a good job because the way he kisses me back makes my face flush, my blood heat and my toes curl.

DAVID, TRACEY AND JOHN-JOHN ARE SITTING ON A bench watching a mime, big double-dip cones melting in the bright spring sunshine. John-John spies us and thrusts his cone out toward Frey.

"Want some, *Azhé'é*?" he asks.

Frey leans his head down and takes a lick. "Good stuff."

David looks over his head at Frey and me. "How'd it go?"

Tracey rises from the bench, digs a hand into her pocket and pulls out a dollar. "Why don't you put that in the mime's tip jar?" she tells John-John.

He happily complies. While he's gone, Tracey says, "I'll take him to see that clown over there. Give you three a chance to talk."

David gives her cheek a kiss. "Thanks, Trace."

John-John bounces back and he and Tracey leave to visit

the clown making balloon animals farther down the boardwalk.

David moves over so Frey and I can take a seat. "What did Harris harangue you about this time?"

"The same," I reply. "Warren Williams' death. Judith Williams' disappearance. Things Frey and I know nothing about."

I wonder how Frey feels about the easy lies that spew from my mouth. At the same time, lying to mortals is what our lives as supernaturals are all about. I know he understands that.

Frey has his arm around my shoulders again and he squeezes. "Harris has two major open cases that he can't close. It's no wonder he's grasping at straws."

David is like me—not so generous in his appreciation of Harris' predicament. "I told you, Anna, you should file a harassment suit against him. He has no right to keep bothering you."

"Well," Frey says. "Maybe this is the end of it."

David takes my left hand and holds the ring so he can examine it. "This is one beautiful ring. You've set the bar high for the rest of us bachelors."

"Are you thinking of asking Tracey—?" I stop in midsentence, remembering what David said yesterday, remembering that Gloria may still be in the picture.

"No." He lets my hand drop, fixes me with a steely gaze. "Just saying, if I was thinking of asking anyone to marry me, I'd have to go some to top this ring. How many carats is it—two, three?"

"Two and a half," Frey answers.

I look at my ring again. I knew it was a good-sized stone but two and a half carats?

"The stone was my great-grandmother's," he continues. "I had it reset for Anna. The original setting was pretty ornate."

I can't believe I didn't think to ask about the ring. Frey is a schoolteacher and it never occurred to me to think how much a ring like this would cost. "Your great-grandmother's stone? Frey, I'm honored. I'll treasure it always. And when John-John finds someone to marry, we'll pass it to him."

David chuckles. "What about when you and Frey have children? There may be a daughter you'll want to have it. Or another son."

Of course, David would assume there might be children in our future. It's obvious Frey can procreate and we're certainly young enough. It's the other biological imperative, that I'm vampire, that makes it impossible. Something unknown to David.

Frey picks up the thread smoothly. "Maybe. We'll have to let nature take its course."

David stretches his arms over his head. "Well, judging by what a good kid John-John is, I'd say you're a great father."

I see a subtle shift in Frey's expression, sadness clouds his eyes. "I can't take much credit for that," he says. "John-John was raised by his mother."

David's expression changes, too, sobering. "I'm sorry. I know Anna told me that John-John lost his mother recently."

Frey shrugs. "Yes. An accident. But Anna and I hope to

make a good life for John-John. No one can take the place of his mother, but he'll always know he's loved."

There's a brief pause, a kind of silent acknowledgment of John-John's loss, and then David says, "On a different note. When's the date?"

Frey and I look at each other. We hadn't discussed it yet.

David smiles. "Just remember—if Tracey and I aren't invited, there'll be hell to pay."

Frey holds out a hand to David. "Might even have to tag you for best man duties."

David returns the handshake. "It would be my pleasure."

A squeal of laughter from down the boardwalk captures our attention. John-John is running back toward us, a balloon animal clutched in his hands.

"Look," he says. "It's a horse. Just like mine at home."

And Frey and I exchange another look. Another question we've yet to answer. Home. Just where will that be?

Frey kneels down to examine the "horse" made from brown and yellow balloons while I sit back to watch them. It occurs to me that I can't wait to let my folks know about Frey and John-John. That we'll have to call them when we get back home this afternoon.

That it scares me how much I love Frey. And how perfect my life seems at this very minute.

That I wish I believed it could be like this forever.

My cell phone chirps. I dig it out of the pocket of my jacket and glance at the caller ID.

"You must be psychic, Mom," I say. "I was just about to—"

"It's your dad, Anna." His voice is sober, serious.

My back stiffens.

"Dad? Is everything all right?"

There's a hesitation, dead air on the line as ominous as any threat of peril. My heart races. "Dad?"

His breath catches. "It's your mother, Anna. I think you need to come to France. Now."

"What's wrong?"

Frey looks up at me. He must see the fear and uncertainty in my face because his pales. He stands up and steps close.

I listen to my father's next words. Tell him we'll leave right away and disconnect.

"What is it, Anna?" Frey asks, touching my arm.

I don't recognize my own voice. "My mother. She's dying."

CHAPTER 7

THE NEXT HOURS ARE A BLUR OF ACTIVITY THAT for a time, at least, dulls the pain. I call my pilot, arrange for him to file a flight plan. John-John and Frey have passports but they're in Monument Valley so we plan a layover in Farmington, New Mexico—the closest airport large enough to handle my jet. A call to Frey's friend Officer Kayani and he agrees to pick up the passports and meet us at the airport, a good two and a half hours from their home.

At first I thought it might not be good for John-John to be exposed to a situation so close to what he's recently been through—the loss of his own mother. But when Frey and I sat him down and explained that I had to go to France because my mother had been taken very ill, his only question was when were *we* leaving? Whether he had picked up on my fear and sadness or whether it was just a child's intuition, he seemed to know his presence and that of his father was something I desperately wanted. I never loved him more.

At two, David and Tracey arrive to take us to the airport. Frey and John-John never had a chance to unpack so it was simply a process of loading their suitcases into David's Hummer. I finished my own packing just as David and Tracey got to the cottage and my single duffle was the last item to get put in.

Jimsair, the private terminal at Lindbergh Field in San Diego, is set apart from the main airport structure. When we pull up, I go inside to let my pilot know I've arrived and he sends a baggage handler out to the Hummer to transport our luggage to the plane. On a pleasure trip, it never fails to impress me how much nicer it is to travel by private than commercial jet. Today, though, all I can think about is how it will get me to my mom that much faster.

My mom. Dying of cancer.

We board after saying good-bye to David and Tracey. John-John gets treated to a tour of the cockpit by my pilot as Frey and I settle ourselves in. The cabin of the plane seats six and we swivel seats around so that we can all three fly facing each other. When the jet engines roar to life, the copilot brings John-John back to us.

He's sporting a pair of wings on the collar of his jacket.

I smile a thanks to the copilot and lift John-John into his seat. He points to the pin. "Look. Just like the pilot."

I buckle him in and give his cheek a kiss. "Just like the pilot."

Frey and I buckle in, too. "Watch out the window, John-John," Frey says. "You'll see we fly right over the ocean."

Excitement shines in John-John's eyes and he turns his face to press it against the glass.

Frey takes my hand. "I don't know what's going to happen in France, Anna," he says. "But you're not alone. We'll face it together."

Tears sting my eyes. A few hours ago I was so happy. I felt positive about the future. Couldn't wait to tell Mom about Frey and John-John. Well, I'm going to get the chance now. But not in the way I envisioned.

It's a relatively short flight to New Mexico. Frey asks the pilot to call ahead. We are told Kayani will be waiting for us when we arrive at the terminal.

Security allows him to come on board. He's in his Navajo Nation Police uniform, looking as crisp and tailored as the last time I saw him. He sweeps a round-brimmed hat off his head. His eyes are serious. Frey told him the reason for our trip on the phone and he expresses his sympathy to me.

For John-John, he has a smile and a hug.

He hands a manila envelope to Frey. "Travel safely, *sida*," he says. "I will take care of the house and horses while you are gone."

Frey reaches out his hand. "Thank you for making such a long trip. Anna and I appreciate it."

Kayani smiles. "Not nearly as long as the journey you are about to make." He drops Frey's hand and turns to me. "Be well, Anna. I wish the best for your mother. I will remember her in my prayers."

He stoops and speaks to John-John in Navajo. John-John nods solemnly and holds out his arms. Kayani embraces him, and in that simple act, it comes rushing back to me how close Kayani, John-John and his mother, Sarah, used to be. I have no doubt he once looked forward to the three of them being a family the way I look forward to Frey, John-John and I forming that bond. My heart knows it can't be easy for him to see the three of us together.

Impulsively, I follow him to the doorway of the plane. I take his hand. "Thank you, Kayani."

He looks toward John-John. "Take care of the little one. I want only for him to be happy."

"I will. And you will always be a part of his life. Frey and I will see to it."

He releases a breath. "*Hágoónee'*, Anna."

"*Hágoónee'*, my friend."

WE PUT JOHN-JOHN TO SLEEP IN THE BEDROOM AT THE tail of the plane and Frey and I sit close on the small couch opposite the bar. The jet was outfitted by an old-soul vampire who spared no expense—the bar and tables are teak, thick carpets run along the floor and up the sides of the fuselage, all the seating accommodations are of the softest leather. In the bedroom, there's a full bathroom, queen-sized bed and a dressing table. Where there might be mirrors, original oil paintings fill the spaces. Avery, the bastard, appreciated his luxury.

Now Frey and I are the beneficiaries of his decadence. For a long time, I refused any of the inheritance due me because of the right of blood vengeance. Avery, an old-soul vampire who pretended to want to mentor me when, in fact, he wanted nothing more than to control the Chosen One, betrayed me. I killed him in defense of my own life.

Slowly, over the last eighteen months, and because with Warren Williams' death, there was no one else to do it, I took over handling the estate myself. I kept the jet for my own use, agreed to my parents inheriting his winery in Provence and kept Avery's hilltop estate in La Jolla. But other things, his money, for instance, went to dozens of charities and foundations, donated anonymously. His art and a hidden treasure trove of ancient artifacts showed up mysteriously in the collections of museums around the country.

Now there's just the house, shut up, furniture shrouded with sheeting, a caretaker on premises to see the landscaping is tended to and the place secure. I haven't decided what to do with the property—it's in one of the most expensive areas in San Diego with a view that sweeps the Pacific—but in the back of my mind, I envision it being Trish's legacy. And now—my eyes drift toward the bedroom—John-John's, too. A brick-and-mortar security blanket available to them for college, setting up their own households, hell, anything they want.

I know I'll never live there.

Frey strokes my hair, bringing me back. "What are you thinking?"

I snuggle close, legs drawn up, head on his chest. "We've come so far to get here. When I introduced you to my family, I wanted it to be perfect. I've brought them so much unhappiness. Withdrawn almost completely from their lives. This—us—was to be a happy thing. Another grandchild. An extended family . . ."

My voice drops, strangled by a wave of emotion that chokes off the words.

Frey gathers me in his arms. "I think you may be misjudging the impact our being together will have on your family," he says. "For your mother, in particular. It's every parent's dream to see her child happy. When she sees you with me, with John-John, she will see what I see. A woman loving and loved. I think this is the best present you could give her."

"How do you always know what to say to make me feel better?" I ask, smiling into his chest.

There's a rustle of movement from the bedroom. I sit up. "It may frighten John-John to wake up in a strange place. Maybe we should join him, stretch out for a while." I glance at my watch. "We still have hours before we reach France."

Frey stands, takes my hands, pulls me to my feet. "One thing," he says.

He tips my head up, draws me closer, and kisses me. "I love you, Anna Strong," he breathes.

For a moment, I have to remember where we are, who we're with, why we're on this trip. His kiss ignites such passion in me, I can't keep from pressing my body against his, wanting more, wanting him inside me, wanting to taste him.

Frey senses the need. His arms tighten around me. "Patience," he whispers. "We have all the time in the world."

I suck in a breath, pull back, let my blood cool. "Keep reminding me."

He takes my hand and we walk back to the bedroom, cocoon John-John between us on the bed. I lay down, but I'm too keyed-up to sleep. Twenty-four hours ago I thought my life was perfect. I should have known better. That's when my dad called.

John-John cuddles closer.

I wrap the blanket tighter around him and snuggle him against my chest. He never seems to mind that my skin is cold. It's almost as if he's trying to share his body warmth with me. To make *me* warm.

I put my head to John-John's chest, listen to his heart-beat—steady, strong. I concentrate on it, and my mind starts drifting. In spite of all the uncertainty ahead, and with the soft rhythm of John-John's heartbeat in my ear, I've soon fallen asleep.

BETWEEN ONE FUEL STOP, THIRTEEN HOURS FLYING time and the crossing of nine time zones, we touch down at the Cannes Mandelieu Airport about nine a.m. There are airports closer to my family's estate, but they either don't have runways long enough to accommodate the jet or there are no facilities for parking the plane. I've given my crew the choice of either flying back home and waiting for my call or taking a paid vacation on the Côte d'Azur. Two confirmed bachelors. Guess which they chose?

I've been here three times before. I think it's one of the most picturesque airports I've ever seen, ringed by verdant hills on three sides and the sea on the fourth. We're guided to the hangar by a yellow-vested member of the ground crew who in turn is greeted by the pilots, first off. A customs agent comes on board, checks our passports and wishes us a pleasant stay.

I wish it were so.

Then the pilots supervise the unloading of the bags. John-John, Frey and I deplane to a beautiful, soft-breezed spring day, the cloudless sky the color of the Mediterranean.

John-John is all big eyes and breathless excitement. I let Frey take him ahead to the terminal while I give instructions for the bags to be taken inside, tip the baggage handler, make sure the pilots have my parents' telephone number and slip envelopes with some spending money to my crew.

One of the first things I learned upon deciding to accept responsibility for an airplane was that having a crew ready and eager to fly for you is essential. Paying them well is a budget stretcher, but it's worth it at times like this.

I leave them on the tarmac to see to the jet and follow John-John and Frey into the terminal. My father is picking us up at ten. We have thirty minutes to wait. I make a quick stop at a kiosk just inside the door to exchange dollars for euros then look around for John-John and Frey.

John-John and Frey are seated in the small restaurant area. Everything gleams in the sunlight. It pours through big plate-glass windows that muffle engine noise but reflect with quiet brilliance from the stainless-steel podiums and stair rails and walls. John-John has a cup of hot chocolate in front of him, Frey an espresso.

He pulls out a chair for me to sit. "Want anything?"

I shake my head. "Not now. Thanks. Dad will be here to pick us up at ten."

I say it like it's the reason for not wanting coffee, but now that there are no more decisions to be made—travel plans, the packing, the calls back and forth to let my dad know when we'd arrive—my stomach clenches like a fist. I've managed to push away thoughts of what I'm going to hear from Dad about Mom's condition by focusing on getting here. We're here. Dad will be arriving any moment. I can't keep those thoughts from intruding any longer.

John-John slurps up the rest of his chocolate. He is sober-faced when he leans toward me. "I'm glad you let us come with you," he says. "Daddy and I will help."

He has picked up the timbre of my thoughts. I feel tears sting. "You and your daddy have already helped," I say. "Just by being with me." I put my arms around his shoulders. "And I know you're going to love my parents' home. It's perfect for a young boy. Lots of room to run. Lots of trees to climb."

I release a breath. "And wait until you meet my dad and mom. And Trish. They're going to love you as much as I do."

I hear my name paged and my heart jumps. Time to go. The three of us walk through the stone-tiled passenger terminal to a concierge desk. I'm told my dad is outside at the waiting area. My luggage is in a cart beside the door.

I hold John-John's hand in my right, Frey's in my left and we step into the sunshine.

CHAPTER 8

M Y FATHER IS WAITING RIGHT OUTSIDE THE TER-
minal door in his classic 1971 Citroën. The white,
zeppelin-shaped car was included with everything else
when my parents *inherited* the vineyard and estate from a
long-lost relative.

Read "long-lost" as "imaginary." Avery, again. But it
gave my parents and niece a refuge, kept them safe from
any fallout that might be directed their way because of my
vampire existence. That it turned out so well is a constant
source of relief to me.

But now, seeing him standing by the car, face gaunt with
worry, I feel none of that relief. We've had to travel so far
to get here. If they were still in San Diego . . .

Dad approaches. He's trying to smile. I think for the
benefit of the little boy at my side.

John-John is looking at the car. "That's a funny-looking car," he says with the perspicuity of youth.

Dad kneels to eye level and holds out a hand. "It is. That's true. It's called a Citroën. Funny name, too, right? It means 'lemon.'"

John-John takes his hand. "It does look like a lemon! I'm John-John. Are you Anna's daddy?"

"I am. My name is James and I'm very pleased to meet you."

Dad straightens and turns to greet Frey. They exchange handshakes. Dad knows who Frey is—they met at faculty functions when Mom was principal at his school—and though we've made no announcement, he seems to understand that his presence here means something important.

Then we're loading luggage and ourselves into the car. Frey secures John–John into his car seat and climbs into the backseat beside him. I take the front with my dad. He steers the car out of the parking lot and we pull into palm tree–lined roads that lead away from the coastline and toward the highway that will take us to Lorgues.

We are all quiet for a time. I'm trying to find a way to phrase the question that I'm afraid to have answered. Finally, after we've traveled about ten minutes, my dad clears his throat.

"Your mother will be so happy to see you."

I turn in the seat. "How is she?"

"She's doing pretty well right now." A smile. "And that will get better when she sees you."

"Is she at home?"

"Yes. She wouldn't spend a moment longer in the hospital than she needed to."

"Pancreatic cancer," I whisper. "She's never been a smoker. She's not diabetic. How does this happen?"

He glances at me. "You've been doing your homework."

"Before we left yesterday. I didn't have time to do much research. But I did read that in most cases if the tumor can be removed . . ."

"It can't." Dad's voice is gentle. "It was found too late. There were no symptoms and by the time we realized something was wrong . . . Well, the cancer had metastasized."

"I just saw her in December." I hear the plaintive wail in my voice and snap my mouth shut.

"I know." Dad's voice is calm, quiet. "We found out not long after."

My shoulders hunch. I close my eyes. "How long?"

He's quiet and when I straighten to look at him, I see the muscle at the base of his jaw quiver. I touch his shoulder. "It doesn't matter. We'll stay as long as we need to."

He places his right hand over mine and squeezes it.

"How is Trish?" I ask then.

"She's such a wonderful girl," he replies, a small smile touching the corners of his mouth. "She wanted to leave school and stay home to care for your mother. But of course, that would never do! Anita insists she maintain a normal schedule. So she goes to class and keeps up with her homework, but she's curtailed all extracurricular activities. She spends her free time with her grandmother. She won't hear of anything else. She's strong-willed. A fighter. Like you."

I nod approvingly. "Good." It's not surprising. Trish needed to be strong to survive her upbringing.

We lapse into silence again. Our drive through Provence

meanders along beautiful country roads—now hugging the edges of steep hillsides, now dipping into picturesque valleys. Everything is spring green and alive. When I glance into the backseat, Frey meets my eyes and smiles. His smile warms my heart and I feel a little of my tension melt away.

I shift my gaze to John-John and discreetly probe his thoughts. This landscape, lush, green, rolling, is so different from his home in Monument Valley where the desert is stark and flat and stretches as far as the eye can see, broken only by monoliths of red rock. I wonder what he thinks of this? I pick up only youthful curiosity and wonder.

Then, *Anna, what is that?* His voice in my head.

Maybe I'm not probing as discreetly as I imagine. I smile and look out my window. A purple meadow rolls by on the right side. *Lavender fields,* I tell him. *Do you know what lavender is?*

John-John looks at his father, who must be explaining what the flower is. As usual, I can only pick up John-John's thoughts. An irritant until it dawns on me that maybe now that we're engaged, it might not be a bad thing that I can't read Frey's thoughts anymore. Nor he mine. It would take great effort to have to continually sanitize one's thoughts, especially if angry or disappointed. I swivel back around to face the front and leave father and son to their discussion.

I remember from past trips that it takes about an hour to reach the estate. I know we're close when we see the most famous building in Lorgues silhouetted against the cloudless blue sky. La Collégiale Saint-Martin church rises like a great fortress, towering above the countryside. It looks out over green fields broken in color only by the brilliant contrast of those fields of lavender, one of Provence's most famous crops.

Now that we're near, dread makes my heart beat faster. What will Mom look like? Will she be thin and pale? Will she be weak? Or in pain? How will I bear it?

I twist my hands in my lap. I have to be strong.

We pull off the main road and onto the winding drive that leads to the estate. As always, I marvel at how striking it is. The grounds set up like an old bastide, the house on a hilltop surrounded by the vineyards and gardens. The vines are just coming to life, delicate leaves on dark trunks. The gardens are alive with flowers—the pink of wild thyme, yellow of daffodils, vibrantly hued flowers on blooming cherry and almond trees. The house itself, now coming into view, is covered on the south wall by climbing wisteria and its fragile-looking flowers, purple tinged with blue, are in full bloom, pendulous clusters that perfume the air even from this distance.

But in spite of the beauty, there's something else I can't forget—that it was built by Avery centuries before. According to the records, the house was built in three distinct periods, the sixteenth, eighteenth and nineteenth centuries. It was updated and renovated many times in the course of history. Now, it's thoroughly modern inside, though the outside still retains much of its historic façade. Avery, again, and his penchant for good living.

My parents know nothing of its real provenance, of course. Only what was manufactured for them.

I push those thoughts aside. It doesn't matter who owned the property before. All that matters is that my family loves living here.

The house glows under the spring sunshine like a welcoming beacon. The front door opens as soon as we pull into the gravel turnaround. Trish runs out to meet the car. In her jeans and T-shirt, blonde hair pulled back from her face, she looks so young and fragile. But even as we embrace, I look beyond her, anxious to see Mom.

Trish follows my gaze. "She's upstairs. She's having a bad day." She hugs me again. "But when she sees you, she'll be so happy."

Dad shoos me toward the house and takes care of introducing Frey and John-John to Trish. Like my dad, Trish knows Frey. He taught at the school she attended when my family first became aware of her existence. They know him as human, not other-natured.

I faintly catch the exchange of greetings but my concentration is on getting to my mother.

I take the stairs two at a time. My parent's bedroom is at the end of the hall, a large, corner room with windows that overlook the vineyards and gardens. The door stands open and I force myself to slow down, tiptoe toward it, not wanting to risk waking her if she's asleep.

She isn't. She's standing beside the bed, slipping a dressing gown over a silk nightdress. When she sees me, she lets the gown drop to the floor and hurries into my arms.

Her hug is as fierce as ever. But beneath my hands, I feel the ridge of her backbone. In the months since I last saw her, she's lost weight. A lot of weight. And her hair is so thin, I see pink scalp between sparse strands of gold-gray. I have to bite back a sob.

I push myself gently away and lead her back to bed. "Come on. Get back under those covers."

Mom seems reluctant. "I want to go downstairs. See Daniel and meet his son."

"And they want to see you. But there will be plenty of time for that. Right now, it's just you and me. And I want to know how you're doing. How you're *really* doing. What do the doctors say? And if you want me to call in a specialist for a second opinion or—"

But Mom has my left hand in both of hers, her eyes suddenly as sparkling and bright as the ring she's examining. "Oh. Anna. Does this mean—? You and Daniel?"

I nod. "Did you ever think you'd see the day?"

And then we're both laughing and crying and clinging to each other and for one joyous moment in time, we are just mother and daughter. No intruding thoughts of vampire, no desolate thoughts of illness or death.

Frey was right. Being here, sharing good news, was the best present I could give her.

CHAPTER 9

MOM INSISTS ON COMING DOWN FOR LUNCH. She also insists she doesn't need help getting dressed and like Dad an hour or so before, shoos me out to check on how Frey and John-John are settling in.

The room next to Trish's has been set up for John-John, a small, comfortable nook of a room that shares a Jack-and-Jill bath with Trish's. When I peek in, Trish is helping him unpack and the two are chattering as if they've known each other forever. I catch bits of a conversation about horses and how Trish is learning to ride at the estate next door. John-John's thoughts are on accompanying her to her next lesson. They are obviously hitting it off.

I find Frey unpacking in the room that has always been designated as mine when I've come to visit. It's on the opposite end of the hall from my parent's, another corner room, this one overlooking side gardens of boxy shrubs and grass and an ancient oak, under which sprawls a large rect-angular wooden table. Dubbed the "outside dining room," it's where my family takes most of their meals in nice weather.

Frey looks up when I enter and waits until I've closed the door behind me to ask, "How is your mother?"

I join him next to the bed and help him ferry clothes back and forth to an open dresser drawer, composing my thoughts before answering.

"In some ways, she doesn't seem sick at all," I say fi-nally. "She's as bright and funny and excited about our be-ing here as ever." I flash my ring. "You should have seen the smile on her face when she saw this." I sigh. "But she's lost a lot of weight and most of her hair. She seems so fragile. And you remember how she was at school."

Frey nods. "Strong as steel. Unbreakable." He draws me to him. "It's good that we've come."

The sob I swallowed back at first seeing my mother rises to the surface again. This time, I don't hold it back. I press my face into Frey's chest and give in to it. His arms tighten around me and he rests his head on the top of mine, holding me while I cry.

He knows me. Knows this will be the only display of emotion I'll allow myself. Knows only with him will I give in to despair. It's up to me to be the unbreakable one now. For Dad. For Trish.

The sobs send tremors through my body, tremors he steadies with arms offering support and consolation. When I can't cry anymore, when I'm spent and quiet, he still holds on. I don't let go, either, wondering why it took me so long to recognize that it is Frey, has been Frey, since the very moment we met.

I pull back a little, to wipe my tear-and-snot-smeared face with the back of my hand. "I must look great." But it's not what I want to say.

Frey is smiling at me, his hands touch my cheek and I know what he's about to say. He has the kind of look in his eyes that means he's getting ready to say something sappy like *You will always be beautiful to me*. I stop him before he can, wrapping my arms around him.

"Why did I waste so much time?" I ask, voice breathless with anger and frustration. "There have been so many men. So many trivial relationships. Why didn't I see what was right in front of me? Why didn't I know it was you from the very beginning?"

Frey's shoulders lift slightly. "Maybe we had to travel different roads to end up here. Maybe we weren't ready before now."

"You mean *I* wasn't ready." I push out of his arms and cross to the dresser to yank a couple of tissues out of a box sitting on top. After I've sopped up my dripping eyes and nose, I turn back to him. "I hope you never regret asking me to marry you."

He gives me a teasing smile. "Would it do any good?"

"Fuck, no. You're committed now."

"Ah." Frey closes the distance between us and pulls me back against his chest. "There's the romantic little lady I've grown to know and love."

"You want romance?" I glance at my watch. "We have half an hour until we have to go down to lunch." I cross to the bedroom door and lock it. "John-John and Trish are getting to know each other." I take his hand and lead him to the bed. "Mom says she doesn't need my help to get ready." I give him a push with both hands and he falls back. "I'm feeling a little insecure about our relationship. I think a little romance is just what I need, too."

I've lowered myself on Frey so that the length of our bodies press together.

"Insecure, huh?" Frey says. In one smooth motion, he's reversed our positions, pinning me beneath him as he reaches down to run a hand from my thigh to my breast. "Let's see what I can do about that."

His fingers are in my hair and his mouth hot against mine. You'd think it would be difficult to undress each other, lying like that and unwilling to break off a kiss that has my blood raging. But we manage. I don't need to be coaxed or manipulated into being ready, either. When I feel Frey, his hardness, his heat, I take him right in. And when he nuzzles his neck against my lips, I know he's ready, too. I breathe him in, bare my teeth and find the spot.

His body tenses when I break through, just as mine tenses with the first mouthful of his blood. The rest is a tornado of desire and excitement, spiraling up and up, catching us in a whirlwind of passion that doesn't end until our bodies have nothing left to give.

WE'VE GATHERED AROUND THE DINING ROOM TABLE, a banquet of fresh breads and cheeses, fruit, olives, grilled salmon and Parmesan risotto laid out in a splendid array in front of us.

John-John's eyes widen. "Do you eat lunch like this every day?"

My father laughs. "Just about. What would you like to try first?"

He busies himself helping John-John fill a plate. I look toward the stairs where I expect to see my mother descend. For once, I won't have to *pretend* to eat. Nor will I have to feign not being hungry. Once the euphoria of lovemaking with Frey wore off, my stomach was once more in turmoil over Mom's condition. I couldn't eat a bite even if it were vampirically possible.

Frey and Trish are chatting about attending school here in France and how it differs from school in the States. I let my gaze drift around the table. It's remarkable how comfortable we all are, how ordinary this feels when the situation is anything but.

My folks, Trish, human. Frey, John-John and I, not.

Before we came down, Frey and I took a moment to let John-John know that my parents were unaware that I was a vampire and if I seemed to look like I was eating food that was why. He promised not to say anything, though I could feel his surprise and confusion that I wouldn't want to share something so important with my parents. We promised to talk to him about the situation later.

I hear a rustle from the hall and my mom is standing in the doorway, her eyes bright, her smile wide as she joins us. She has a scarf tied around her hair and is wearing a shift of multicolored silk over a pair of dark leggings. I jump up to hold out her chair.

She gives me the eye. "Don't fawn over me, Anna," she

scolds. But she grabs my hand and squeezes before looking across at John-John. "And who is this handsome young man?"

Frey brings John-John over to stand by her chair. "Mrs. Strong, this is my son, John-John."

John-John holds out a hand, but Mom leans over and hugs him instead. "I am so pleased to meet you," she says. "Would you like to call me Anita?"

"Yes, ma'am. Thank you for letting me visit."

Mom pulls back and winks at Frey. "Daniel, you have a very polite son. Is he always so well behaved?"

Frey and John-John exchange conspiratorial grins and father and son return to their places.

Lunch goes smoothly although I find I can't take my eyes off my mother. She's relaxed and the conversation flows smoothly, touching on every topic except the one that brought us together.

She managed to avoid it when I was alone with her, too, diverting the talk from her condition to my engagement.

When lunch is over, Dad takes Frey on a tour of the property while Trish and John-John leave to see the horses next door.

Mom and I start to clear the table. The housekeeper, Catherine, appears to finish the job, sending us to the living room. In her heavy Irish brogue, she promises to follow with coffee, so I hook my arm in Mom's and we settle into comfortable chairs around a big window overlooking the vineyard.

Mom's chin is set, her back straight. When she meets my eyes, I wonder if she's ready.

Ready to finally acknowledge the elephant in the room.

CHAPTER 10

"JOHN-JOHN IS A REMARKABLE YOUNG MAN."

Mom opens the conversation with a sigh of contentment.

And another diversion.

But I smile. "Yes, he is."

"And you and Daniel? How did you two become a couple? *When* did you become a couple? Last time we saw you, you were dating that reporter from CBS."

I laugh. "Yep. That wasn't meant to be."

Mom tilts her head to study me. "But I can see you're in love. And I can see Daniel loves you. It makes me very happy. It's what every parent wishes for their child. I'm so glad you found each other. Especially now . . ."

Catherine appears in the doorway, a tray in her hand. She's a large woman, stocky, wearing a plain shift of heavy cotton over which she's layered a starched white apron. She has a kind, moon-round face framed by a mane of gray hair pulled into a disheveled knot at the top of her head. She sets the tray on a table between Mom and me and pours us each a cup of coffee.

"Can I get you anything else?"

We both shake our heads. She starts for the door but pauses to turn and add, "Now don't overtire yourself, missus. Remember the doctor said you should get plenty of rest."

We stare at her retreating back as if knowing this is the signal we've been waiting for.

"What else do the doctors say?" I ask quietly.

Mom takes a sip of her coffee, places the cup carefully back on its saucer. She doesn't look at me but rather fixes her gaze on the vineyards outside the window. "Stage four, inoperable, caught too late for conventional cancer treatments." She rattles through the list briskly, matter-of-factly, unemotionally.

I can't be so dispassionate. "How can they be so sure? There are new breakthroughs every day. There are cancer treatment centers in the United States that are making tremendous progress. We could get you admitted to one of them now. Today. I have my jet here—"

Mom reaches over and stills my windmilling hands. "Anna, stop. Believe me, if I thought there was a chance, I would leave right now. But I don't want to spend my last days being kept alive by tubes in some sterile ward. Look at what I have here." She gestures to the window. "This beautiful place. Surrounded by the people I love most. I want the last things I see to be sunlight and vineyards and the faces of my family. You can understand that, can't you?"

I want to scream, *No! I want you to fight!*

But I do understand, so I whisper, "I don't want to lose you."

"You won't. Not ever. I'll always be with you and Trish and now John-John. Family is a bond that transcends life and death."

She doesn't say it, but with her last words I know she's thinking of my brother. The son she lost so many years ago. She believes they'll be reunited. It's a hallmark of her faith. It's what's giving her grace and courage now.

Is it what's keeping her from seeking treatment?

Immediately, I feel a pang of guilt. I know my mother well enough to know she wouldn't forsake Trish or me. She wouldn't choose the dead over the living. Still, I plan to question my father, make sure they've exhausted every possible remedy, procedure or technique that might improve her condition.

I catch Mom peering at me, eyes narrowed. "Don't go badgering your father about this," she says.

"What? You're psychic now?"

"Not psychic. I just know how you think. Believe me, your father has Googled, called about and written to anyone he thought might be of help. Trust me, Anna. Please. Let's enjoy the time we have left. I want to get to know John-John and catch up with Daniel. It's been a while since I heard anything about my school."

She gestures again toward the window. Frey and my father are just coming into sight, strolling across the vineyard, skirting the rows of grapes, heading for the house. Dad's face is animated as he makes a sweeping wave of his arm, no doubt explaining some vagary of wine making to Frey. Frey listens intently, hands in pockets, head bent. Seeing him un-expectedly like this makes my heart pound. When did I fall so in love?

I don't realize Mom is watching me until she chuckles and says, "This is a side of you I've never seen."

I take mental inventory. What's giving it away? Do I have a silly love-struck expression on my face? I frown, raise an eyebrow, feign ignorance. "What side?" But it's said with a lilt in my voice I can't disguise.

"See?" Mom laughs again. "It's even in your voice. When you look at Daniel, your face lights up. Ironic, isn't it? Considering how you two met?"

It is ironic. Frey and I met when I was searching for Trish. He was a teacher at her school and for a brief time, I thought he might be involved in a child pornography ring. Nothing could have been further from the truth. But Trish had run away and I was desperate to find her. In a fit of reckless abandon, I attacked and bit Frey, thinking I'd rav-age the truth out of him.

I got the truth out of him, all right. But in the process of learning his innocence, broke the psychic link between vampire and shape-shifter that allows us to communicate mind to mind. So now we can no longer read each other.

Again, I decide it's a good thing. This time, though, it's not because of any negative thoughts I might let slip. As I watch Frey approach, I'm flashing back to the sensation of our bodies intertwined on the bed upstairs and I'm filled with such a heady rush of desire that heat sears my blood.

"You're smiling again," Mom says, with a smile bright-ening her own voice.

Color floods my cheeks. I pull myself from the bedroom

back to the present, reach over and give her a hug. "It seems so strange. I'm happy—really happy—for the first time in such a long time. And I want to share it with you. I want you to be a part of our lives. But we need time—"

"I told you," she interrupts gently. "I'll always be with you. Don't feel guilty for being happy. Coming here, sharing your happiness, has been the best medicine I could have hoped for. In fact—"

Mom breaks off. She grasps my hands. There's a definite twinkle in her eyes that makes me go, *Uh-oh. What are you thinking?*

"I just had the most wonderful idea." She clasps her hands together. "It's the one thing you could do for me. You and Daniel."

"Go on . . ."

"Get married here. Right away. Let me do this for you. Your father and I could arrange the most beautiful wedding. Oh, Anna, it would be perfect."

The very last thing I would have expected her to say. I sit back, "But, Mom. It's too much. You can't tire yourself out. Planning a wedding is a lot of work. And Frey and I haven't even set a date yet. I don't know if he'd want to get married so soon."

"I've seen the way he looks at you. Of course he wants to get married right away. In any case, it wouldn't hurt to ask him, would it?"

"Ask who what?"

A voice from the doorway. Frey's. He and my father back from their walk. He comes over and stands between my mother's chair and mine. He smiles down at us. "Ask who what?" he says again.

I roll my eyes and look toward my mother. "Mom had an idea. Now, if you don't want to do it, I understand. It's kind of out of the blue and we haven't talked about it yet. So be honest. My feelings won't be hurt if you think it's too soon."

"Too soon for what?"

He's looking from one of us to the other. I take his hand. "Mom wants us to be married here. It's rushing things, I know and you can—"

"I think it's a wonderful idea."

Frey's answer stops me short.

"You do?"

"Of course. Why should we wait?" He looks at my mother. "My only question is how it will affect your health? Now between Anna and me and Trish and James, I'm pretty sure we can do most of the heavy lifting. But as mother of the bride, you have a big role to play. Are you really up for it?"

Mom's face radiates joy. "Nothing would make me happier."

Dad has come to join us. "What's this I hear? We're going to have a wedding?"

I look around at the three people gathered around me and find myself grinning. Not having given the ceremony any thought, I'd supposed Frey and I would elope—Vegas maybe—with David and Trish as witnesses.

But now . . .

A wedding.

We're going to have a wedding. I roll the thought around in my head, tasting it like some exotic food.

Anna Strong. Kick-ass vampire. The Chosen One.

I'm going to have a wedding.

Frey and Mom and Dad are already tossing ideas back and forth. The atmosphere is festive and full of excitement.

Hopeful. Happy.

I see the elation on my mother's face.

I'm sure it's mirrored on mine.

I'm going to have a real, honest-to-god wedding. I look at my mother. "Nothing fancy, though, okay? No long white dress and veil."

"No jeans, either," my mom quips back.

"Deal."

The four of us spend the next hour or so making lists and assigning chores. There isn't much for Frey and I to do except decide who we want to officiate and where we need to go to get the required certificates. With the help of the folks' trusty computer we soon determine in spite of all the paperwork required, a wedding in two weeks is doable.

My head is swimming. We put a call into the American Consulate in Nice and make an appointment to go the next day to set the wheels in motion. Mom says she has copies of my birth certificate. She'll dig one out to take with me to the consulate tomorrow. Frey is sure he can have a lawyer friend back in San Diego send his since most of his papers are still in the condo there. He gets right on the phone and makes arrangements.

I watch in shock and wonder. And a bit of trepidation. I can't help feeling I've pressured Frey into this. Mom plans a celebratory dinner and asks Frey and me to go into town to pick up a few things. I jump at the chance. It will give the two of us time to talk. I want Frey to understand that I love his enthusiasm but have to know it's not just for my mom's benefit. If we need to, we can get out of it.

Dad walks us outside and hands us the keys to the Citroën. "Do you remember the way into town?" he asks.

I nod. And stand on tiptoe to give his cheek a peck. "Thank you," I say.

"Are you kidding?" he shoots back. "This is the best thing that's happened to your mother in months. I can't wait to tell Trish and John-John." He stops and quirks an eyebrow at Frey. "Unless you'd rather I not say anything until you can tell him yourself, Daniel."

Frey grins. "You can tell him. He wanted us to be married as soon as Anna said yes to my proposal. He'll be thrilled!"

Once Frey and I are on the road, I ask, "Is that true? John-John wanted us to get married right away?"

Frey, in the passenger seat, glances over. "Are you afraid he would think it too soon after losing his mother?" he asks quietly.

I nod, keeping my eyes on the road.

He reaches over and squeezes my knee. "No. John-John loves you. He wants us to be a family. He'll always love his mother, but he sees in you what I do. Besides, neither of us wants to take the chance you'll change your mind."

The last is said with a hint of humor. I don't answer, my throat suddenly tight with emotion. How could I change my mind? I'm about to get everything I'd thought unobtainable to me since becoming vampire—a husband who is strong, brave and understanding and a child to love as if he was my very own.

CHAPTER 11

L ORGUES HAS THE FEEL OF A MEDIEVAL VILLAGE with the shopping amenities of a modern city. Frey and I spend an hour wandering the narrow streets hand in hand. Frey has never been here before and he's as taken with the vaulted passages, ancient stairs and elaborate stone carvings on the buildings and doorways as I was at first sight.

It's a beautiful spring day, and after checking off all the items on Mom's shopping list, we stop for coffee in an outdoor café on the Boulevard Georges Clemenceau. The sky is deep blue and cloudless, the air still.

Frey breathes it in. "I can see why your family loves it here."

I let my gaze wander up and down the street. Across from us, the open-air market we visited earlier teems with shoppers. The pile of our own packages, tucked under the table, holds bread, fresh vegetables, olives. It's still too early for the platan trees lining the streets and parks to have budded, and their white spindly trunks look like skeleton hands lifting bony fingers to the sky. Most of the buildings in Lorgues are painted soft pastels or brilliant primary colors with shutters of contrasting blue or green. It's an artist's concept of a French village . . . only real.

Once again I find myself grudgingly admiring Avery's choices. He couldn't have picked a more beautiful spot to set down eternal roots.

Frey picks up my hand and gently squeezes. "Are you thinking of Avery?"

I look at him in surprise. "How did you know?"

He points to the bridge of my nose. "You get a furrow, right there, whenever you think of him."

His comment makes me laugh. "Wow. Who needs mind reading when you have such keen powers of observation."

"It's true. I know you very well."

I place one of my hands over his. "Better than I know myself, I think."

Our coffee arrives and we settle back to enjoy it. One of the things I appreciate most about Frey is that we can be quiet around one another. As we are now, each alone with our own thoughts, but connected in a way that transcends words. It's a heady, comfortable feeling.

Until I *feel* him suddenly tense beside me. When I look at him, his face is drawn, tight with anger and taut with the primal instinct to defend. A low growl escapes his throat, the panther at the ready.

His reaction is so unexpected, it brings vampire to the

surface, too. I swing around, senses on alert, scanning the crowd until I find a face I recognize.

A face Frey recognizes.

A face we intuitively know is about to shatter the peace we've found as surely as the cup I've let slip from my fingers shatters on the sidewalk at my feet.

A waiter approaches and makes quick work of cleaning up my broken cup, tsking and mumbling in French but reappearing in an instant with a new cup.

Along with a third for the man now standing beside the table.

Chael.

CHAPTER 12

*C*HAEL. MY TONE IS GUARDED, CLIPPED. *WHAT ARE you doing here?*

In his perfectly tailored Armani, a white linen shirt open at the neck and polished brogues, he looks right at home in this French sidewalk café. Only his complexion and eyes, dark and exotic, emphasize his mideastern rather than French roots. He is, in fact, the head of the Middle Eastern Vampire Tribe and literally the last man, human or vampire, I would have expected to run into here.

With a snapping of fingers, and flawless French, he bids the waiter to fetch another chair.

Somehow his rudeness appeals to the waiter, who while only a moment ago was grousing at me for dropping a cup, now springs into action to not only grab a chair from another table but hold it out for Chael to slip into.

Irrationally, his imposing presence ratchets my dislike for Chael up another notch.

I asked what you are doing here. I did not invite you to join us.

Frey has my hand under the table. He will not be able to hear what I'm saying—since Chael speaks no English we must communicate telepathically—but he will understand Chael's side of the conversation. He squeezes my hand softly, as if assuring me that he has my back.

Chael, for his part, has taken a leisurely drink from his cup. His eyes flick to Frey. He knows him, from Monument Valley, knows he's a shape-shifter, knows he's my friend, but he neither acknowledges his presence nor bothers to demand he leave us while we talk.

He merely dismisses him entirely by ignoring him and shifting his gaze to peer at me intently over the rim. *You still see me as an enemy.*

Not an enemy. An annoyance. A rude annoyance. The words resonate in my head like a hiss. *Like a mosquito I'm about to swat.*

He laughs. *Colorful as ever, Anna. But there is a reason I am here. Just as I believe it was fate that you should arrive here, too, at just this moment. When I heard you were coming, I—*

A chill touches the back of my neck. We, Frey and I, had only found out about my mother's illness a day ago. No one else knew except David and Tracey. *How could you know I was coming to France?*

Chael lifts his well-dressed shoulders. *You are an important figure to the vampire community. I make it my business to know what you do as I'm sure most of the leaders of the Thirteen Tribes do as well.*

You have me followed?

Nothing so pedestrian, he replies, his tone registering disdain that I would think so little of him. *I have contacts in all major airports. When your pilot filed his flight plan, I was notified.*

Just like that? Anger sends the blood racing. Not for the first time, I want to slap that smug smile off his elegant face. Frey must feel my body tense, because he squeezes my hand again.

I exhale. *So why are you here? I won't ask again.*

This time, Chael lets the smile fall from his face. He leans toward me. *I told you in Monument Valley if you let me go, I would be indebted to you. I intend to honor that pledge. It's why I'm here. To warn you. But first, to help you.*

Help me?

Your mother. I know she is very ill. If you should decide to bring her over, to make her one of us, I offer my services to see . . .

My stomach clenches. *Don't speak of my mother.*

The anger, the challenge in my voice makes Chael blanche. He bobs his head, once.

Fine. Then there is just one thing we need to discuss. Something of utmost importance to the vampire world.

I release a sigh. Chael, melodramatic as ever. I keep my thoughts guarded. *Go on.*

Have you never wondered why there was no ambassador from Europe in attendance when you were acknowledged as the Chosen One?

Until this very moment, no. I'd never noticed. I was too busy fighting for my life. I meet Chael's eyes. *Explain.*

He leans back in his chair, cup in hand, legs crossed. *The European vampires refuse to join the Council. Have from the beginning. They are among the oldest, some say the first, vampires in existence. They are also the most powerful—at least in their own eyes.*

He takes a sip of coffee, wipes at his lips with a napkin. *They are well organized and disciplined. And answer to a vampire who calls himself King Steffan.*

That brings a snicker to my lips. How like an old-soul vampire to proclaim himself a king. But something in Chael's manner makes me swallow back the sarcasm. His thoughts are dark and his tone concerned. His usual cockiness and arrogance are not in evidence, either. Which, above all else, makes me uneasy. I incline my head in a go-ahead gesture.

There have been rumors circulating lately. Steffan is ready to begin the process that will end human domination over the vampire. He sees the collapse of the European Union and the decline of the United States as a world power as a signal that the time is ripe to put his plan into action.

I pass a hand over my face in frustration. As usual, Chael exercises his penchant for overstatement. Collapse of the EU? Decline of the U.S.? Another scheme to achieve vampire world domination?

I've heard this before. I glare pointedly at Chael. *It's a very familiar refrain. And just what is King Steffan's plan?*

Chael plunges ahead as if my voice exuded enthusiasm instead of dripping sarcasm. *I don't know the details. It's a closely guarded secret among Steffan's inner circle. But what I do know is that if he is to be stopped, it must be now, before he has a chance to rally his supporters. And I understand there are humans who are ready to fall in line with him, too. It's a serious threat.*

I throw up my hands. *Why would he listen to me if he does not acknowledge the Council? I would have to assume my title as the Chosen One would hold no sway over him.*

Chael smiles, but a smile that is cold and just a bit resentful. *True. But you have proven yourself a mighty arbiter. After all, you convinced the Thirteen Tribes to turn down my plan.*

Ah, for the first time a bit of the old Chael shines through. *Which makes me wonder again why you've come to me. Steffan sounds like someone you would want to join forces with.*

Chael and I have both been carefully guarding our thoughts, letting only what we wish the other to know to come through. Now he lets down the barrier completely, allowing me to *feel* as well as hear the sincerity of his words.

I am indebted to you. You could have taken my life in Monument Valley. You did not. For that, I owe you allegiance. I do not think Steffan is the kind of vampire to be allowed to risk our very existence in his attempt to overthrow our human brethren. You are the strongest vampire. If you cannot reason with him, you have only one alternative.

I raise my eyebrows, guessing what is to come next but wanting to hear Chael say it anyway.

You must kill him.

I sit back in my chair. *Chael, you sly dog. You are either the best actor in the world, or you've managed to find a way to cloak your real feelings. I don't buy for one moment that you'd prefer Steffan's death over mine.*

Chael shrugs, shakes his head. *I don't know what I can do to convince you of my sincerity. I can only report to you what I know. It's up to you to decide if the threat merits your attention.*

Shit. Along with everything going on in my life, my mother's illness, the upcoming nuptials, I now have one more thing to worry about? Chael knows I can't let this threat go. At least until I've met Steffan and can assess the situation myself. All this I keep hidden from Chael until I open my thoughts to say with a reluctant sigh, *Can you arrange a meeting?*

Yes. I will do so. How do I get in touch with you?

Is that relief I hear ring through, or satisfaction?

I give him my cell number. *I will be busy for the next couple of days. Try to set up the meeting for Thursday evening. Can you do that?*

Chael nods and pushes up from the table. *I will be in touch.*

And then he is gone, melting back into the throng on the sidewalk as subtly and artfully as he appeared.

Frey releases a long breath. "Do you believe him?"

But I have something else I want to say before I talk about Chael. I lean over. "Thank you. For being here. For putting up with this crap. You know it's not going to get any better. No matter where we go we might run into Chael or one of his counterparts."

"Comes with the territory," he replies matter-of-factly.

"I knew you were the Chosen One from the beginning. It's part of the package."

I take his hand and press it to my lips. "Some package." Then I sit back. "As far as I can tell, Chael was perfectly sincere in what he said. As for the rest of it, I won't know about Steffan until we're face-to-face."

"You won't be alone," Frey says. His jaw tightens. "I will be with you when you meet him."

I look away. That may not be possible, for Frey's own protection, but it's also not something I want to argue about now. In fact, I don't want to argue about anything. Nor do I want to think about Chael. I have two days before I hear from Chael about a meeting. I motion to the waiter for the check.

"Let's get back," I say, gathering the shopping bags. "I want to spend as much time as possible with my folks and the kids. I don't want to think about Chael or this King Steffan or anything remotely connected with vampires. I want only to think about you and our wedding. Happy things."

Frey's brow furrows. "Nice dodge. But I mean it, Anna. I want to be with you when you meet him. We're a team now. In everything."

Then Frey is distracted by the waiter arriving with our check. I watch as he presses some bills into the waiter's hand.

It would be nice to *think* we could be partners in everything. I *know* it's not possible. Just as Chael pointedly ignored Frey, didn't even acknowledge his presence, I have a feeling this *King* Steffan would be no less disrespectful. The attitude of most vampires is that we are the top of the supernatural hierarchy and every other creature not only falls far below, but is expendable. I would never risk Frey's life.

Frey is backing away from the waiter. Evidently my transgression in breaking a cup is forgotten because we're now being assaulted by an effusive stream of *mercis* that follow us all the way down the sidewalk.

Either that or somehow our association with the exquisitely dressed Chael has raised his estimation of this casually clad American couple up a notch.

CHAPTER 13

WHEN WE GET BACK TO THE ESTATE, MOM AND Catherine are marshaling the troops in the kitchen like a general and her aide. John-John runs up to me when Frey and I come in and hugs my legs. He doesn't have to say a word, his shining eyes say it all. Trish follows him over, encircling Frey and I and John-John in a group hug that threatens to topple us all over in its enthusiasm.

Laughing, I pull back. "What's all this about?" I ask innocently.

Then everyone, Mom, Dad, Trish and John-John are talking at once, each offering a suggestion about what they want to do to help with the wedding preparations. I can tell it's all they've talked about since Frey and I departed. Already, Mom has lined up a caterer, a party planner to handle renting tables and chairs and a local baker to make the cake.

"Wait a minute." I hold up a hand in protest. "This is supposed to be a *small* affair, remember?"

"It will be," Mom insists. "But there are some neighbors we'd like to invite and I'm sure you and Daniel will want to include friends from San Diego. David, for instance. Which reminds me, no time to mail out invitations. You'll have to call everyone. Better do that tonight. You said your jet was here? Maybe you could arrange to fly—"

She continues to babble happily on. I tilt my head, studying her. I'm happy to see her so animated. I find myself smiling, agreeing to every suggestion. No way will I ruin her glow.

At that moment a tiny germ of an idea takes root. Something Chael said this afternoon.

Maybe I won't have to.

THE TRIP TO THE CONSULATE GOES SMOOTHLY. UNTIL we're presented a list of the documentation necessary to marry in France. One item jumps off the page—medical certificate. Blood tests and a medical exam by a French doctor have to be completed before the marriage application can be approved.

The clerk helping us offers a list of doctors to consult, but for the same reason I have avoided my own doctor in San Diego, I know I can't go to just any doctor in France. I have no idea how vampire physiology differs from human, but I don't intend to find out now. I glance at Frey. Chances are, he would pass a normal exam and routine blood tests. He is more human than not.

Everything else, passports, birth certificates, certificates certifying that we are free to marry, proof of domicile—all are dispatched with alacrity. Frey has his lawyer friend in San Diego with whom he's already talked. I call David and he promises to get the bureaucratic wheels spinning for me. After, of course, an excited chorus of whoops from both he and Tracey when I tell him why I'm calling.

Then he says, "By the way, Harris stopped by the office yesterday. You are never going to guess what's happened? They've identified Warren Williams' killer! And the same guy confessed to killing Judith Williams, too. Can you believe it?"

My breath catches. Not possible. Warren Williams' killer is a vampire long dead. By my hand. Judith was killed in Monument Valley. Frey's hands were on that weapon, but I was at his side, urging him to take the shot. It takes me a second to compose myself enough to ask, "Who?"

"Some lowlife ex-con who had a grudge against the chief. Confessed to killing them both and burying Judith Williams' body in the desert. Left a beautiful letter addressed to the DA before blowing his brains out in front of SDPD headquarters."

Frey is watching me, reading my body language. We're back in the car, getting ready to head home. As soon as I end the call with David, he asks, "What's wrong?"

When I repeat what David told me, he's as shocked as I am. "Somebody engineered this," he says. "But who?"

"And why?" If I'm supposed to be relieved that Harris

will no longer be harassing Frey and me, the feeling is over-whelmed by a sense of dread. Whoever did me this "favor" will undoubtedly be around at some point to collect for it.

"Jesus, Frey. A man is dead. The case tied up with a pretty ribbon. What the fuck?"

Frey's eyes meet mine.

"I can't help feeling this has Chael's signature all over it."

Frey is shaking his head. "Well, we can't do anything about it now. When we get back home, we'll do some dig-ging." He spreads his hands. "Right now we have a wed-ding to plan, right? I saw how you reacted when you saw that medical requirement. Let's tackle that problem."

Frey is right. I close my eyes for a minute, push Wil-liams to the back of my head, focus on the present.

Where Chael is once again front and center. "Are you thinking what I'm thinking?"

"I know he wouldn't be your first choice as a go-to guy, but maybe Chael can help," he says, proving that we are indeed thinking the same thing. "He's obviously spent a lot of time in France. He speaks the language like a native."

I release a breath. "I hate going to Chael for anything. He's such a smug bastard. But you're right, he's been around for a long time. I'm sure there's a network he can tap into. I can't be the only vampire to ever get married in France." I glance at Frey. "What about you? Could you pass a routine physical?"

He smiles. "Of course. Have many times. Only my DNA contains the strand that would identify me as a shape-shifter and I doubt they're going to run DNA tests on us. Or recognize what it was if they did."

Frey is at the wheel and has guided the car onto the road

so I dig my cell phone out of my pocket. "Never thought I'd ever be calling Chael for a favor," I mumble, calling up his number from the contact list. He gave the number to me in Monument Valley and some inexplicable impulse made me program it into the phone even as I swore it'd be a cold day in hell before I used it.

Wonder what the temperature is in the Syrian Desert today?

The phone rings once before the call is answered with a brisk, officious male voice that rattles off an impressive greeting in Arabic.

I didn't think before calling that there's no mental connectivity through a phone line. Stupid. I hesitate before saying, "Anna Strong, calling for Chael."

There's not even an instant's hesitation on the part of the unidentified male on the other end. "Ms. Strong, how nice of you to call." The switch to English is done effortlessly. "I am Chael's assistant. Can I be of service?"

Okay, now what? May as well just tell him why I'm calling. Since he recognized my name, he must know my nature. "I am planning to marry in France. I need a doctor to handle the necessary medical paperwork. Does Chael know of someone who can help?"

Again, the answer comes instantaneously. "Of course. I will see to it right away. Is there anything else?"

I have the feeling if I'd asked for a full moon on the night of our wedding, he would have answered the same way.

And probably swung it.

"No, that's it," I reply. "Thank you."

"I will tell Chael that you called. He is a great admirer."

I hike my eyebrows at Frey as I ring off. "Maybe I need to get an assistant like that."

"Are we all set?"

"Oh yeah," I say, grinning. "We're good to go."

THE NEXT MORNING, BEFORE THE HOUSEHOLD HAS time to gather for breakfast, there is a ring at the front door.

Since Frey, John-John and I are already up, I rise from the breakfast table to answer it. A man in the familiar brown UPS uniform hands me an envelope and a clipboard.

I sign at the "x", the messenger bids me "bonjour" and is off down the driveway in his truck.

"Wow, that was fast," I comment to Frey, rejoining them in the dining room. "David must have worked all night to get this stuff together so fast."

But when I tear open the envelope, I see I am wrong about who it is from. Four official-looking French documents are inside. Along with a note, written in a precise hand:

Miss Strong, here are the documents you requested. Present them to the Mairie at the consulate. Chael suggested I take the liberty of including documents for your fiancé as well. I hope you don't think it presumptuous.

Chael also asked that I pass on to you the information that the meeting has been set as you requested. He suggests you meet him at Le Course café and he will take you to the castle. 6:30, Thursday.

Please do not hesitate to call on us if we can be of more assistance.

The note is signed with theatrical flourish: Pierre LeDoux.

I look up at Frey and hand him the documents. "I *definitely* need an assistant like this."

His brow furrows as he notes the set of certificates with his name on them. "How does he know my blood type?" he asks, scanning the pages. "And my exact height and weight. This is creepy."

I nod. "Yes, it is. But then *Chael* is creepy, so I guess we should be thankful he seems to be on our side now."

"What does the note say?" Frey asks, slipping the papers back into the envelope.

I read the first paragraph aloud, hesitating before going on to the second. For a split second, I consider not telling him that the meeting has been set. Wondering again if I should go alone.

But I don't want to lie to him. And I don't want to have to sneak away. I continue reading.

John-John catches the word "castle" and pipes up, "You're going to a castle? A real castle? Can I go, too?"

We both look at John-John, then at each other. "There are lots of castles around here," I answer, taking my place next to him at the table. "And if it doesn't work out this time, I promise we'll plan to go again, okay?"

He agrees with a bob of his head and digs a spoon into his cereal.

"So what's on the agenda for today?" I ask John-John, squeezing his shoulders.

"James said he'd take me on the tractor to show me how they water the vines," he replies with a grin. "Then when Trish gets home from school, we're going next door to see the horses."

"Sounds like a pretty good day," I say. "Much better than the one your daddy and I have planned. More running around to finish the paperwork for the wedding."

"We have to go shopping sometime, too," Frey adds. "A suit for me. A suit for the best man, here." He leans in and tickles John-John's ribs.

"And the bride needs a dress." Trish is suddenly in the doorway, grinning. "So tonight, we go shopping."

CHAPTER 14

SINCE I NEVER EXPECTED TO GET MARRIED, I'D never given much thought to all that goes into a wedding. Luckily, it seems my mother has. She prepares lists and makes calls and for the next couple of days, we—Frey, Trish, Dad and I—run around so she can check each item off with a satisfied stroke of the pen.

I watch her closely—watch for any sign that she's weakening or tiring herself out. All I see is a woman at peace, happy even, immersed in the details of a day that obviously means as much to her as it does to Frey and me.

Still, it's up to Trish, Frey and I to handle the in-town stuff—shopping for dresses and suits, visiting the caterer to plan menus, choosing a wedding cake. A cake I can't eat. So we leave the final choice to John-John and Trish. After polishing off the half dozen samples supplied by the bakery,

John-John decides he likes weddings. And the kids settle on a decadent chocolate mousse cake with a frothy whipped cream icing.

Thursday afternoon Frey and I make the trek back to the consulate, papers in hand. France requires a civil ceremony before any kind of religious service. Since a religious service is something I neither want nor plan to have, the consular employee who helps us suggests we look into a "humanist" wedding. An organization called Gracefully Personalized Ceremonies crafts individual services for couples who want a ceremony adapted to them and not the other way around.

Frey and I look at each other. If ever there was a couple who didn't identify with the traditional, it's us. So we take the pamphlet and contact information. We are assured such a ceremony fulfills the civil requirement that makes the marriage legal. And the service can be performed in any location. Sounds perfect for what we want.

We get back to Lorgues at six p.m. We purposefully planned the day so we would have an excuse to stay in town for the evening. In thirty minutes, Chael will pick us up for my meeting with the infamous King Steffan. So far, I've managed to push thoughts of it to the back of my mind, but I can't evade them any longer.

Frey and I sip glasses of wine while we wait in the café. We are both quiet.

At 6:15, Chael appears. One minute the extra chair is vacant, the next, he's sitting in it, joining us like the object of a magician's sleight of hand. He smiles and brushes an imaginary piece of lint off an impeccably tailored jacket.

"How does he do that?" I mumble to Frey. To Chael, I

ask, *Where is your car? I thought you were taking me to Steffan?*

Did you find the documents satisfactory? he replies, not addressing my question. *I was extremely pleased that you thought to come to me with your request.*

Yes. Thank you. The two words are slow to form, but he did help us out of a sticky situation. I keep thoughts of the part he may have played in the neat wrap-up to Williams' case back in San Diego tucked carefully away. Time to explore that mystery later. I gesture instead to Frey. *We are both appreciative. Now, about Steffan?*

Before Chael can reply, a Rolls-Royce pulls to the curb. It's a classic, a Phantom, the top down, and a gasp of appreciation goes up from the people sitting around us. The car is a deep royal blue and from what I can see of the inside, the upholstery is red leather. The paint is so highly buffed, I can see Frey's reflection in the door panels. Only Frey's. It looks like he's alone at the table.

I wonder if anyone else notices.

I'm so wrapped up in my own musings, it takes an instant to realize the driver is looking at me.

Ms. Strong?

A vampire. I nod acknowledgment.

Would you get in please?

Frey starts to push back from the table, but Chael puts a hand on his arm. *Only Anna. We will wait here.*

I see irritation tighten the lines around Frey's mouth as he shrugs out of Chael's grasp. This time it's my hand on his arm. "It's all right. You wait with Chael. I won't be long."

Frey shoots Chael a venomous look. "This isn't what we

agreed on." Then his eyes latch onto mine. "Anna, I don't think it's a good idea to see this Steffan by yourself. What if you get into trouble?"

"I've got you on speed dial." I lean in and brush his lips with mine. "And Chael is staying here. If anything happens . . ."

The panther, dark and dangerous, flashes in Frey's eyes. He nods and relaxes back in his chair. He understands. "We'll be right here."

By the time I get to the curb, the driver has slipped from behind the wheel and is holding the front passenger door, rather than the rear passenger door, open. It's not surprising. It makes perfect sense to have an unknown vampire sit where he can keep an eye on her. Casting no reflection means not being able to watch in a rearview mirror.

I climb in and he shuts the door, giving a two-finger salute to Frey and Chael. Frey frowns back. Chael merely smiles.

Once the driver has pulled the car into traffic, I turn in the seat to give him the once-over. He must have been in his thirties when he was turned. His face bears the look of one who spends a great deal of time outdoors—lines radiate from the corners of his eyes, his skin is smooth but deeply tanned. His dark hair is brushed back from his temples and touches the collar of his shirt and when his eyes find mine, they are green with gold flecks. He is broad shouldered, not dressed in the uniform of a chauffeur, the lines of his jacket cut in a classic style, his slacks tapered to the tops of polished loafers. His hands on the wheel look steady and strong, his fingers slender, his nails lightly buffed.

King Steffan obviously likes his employees to cut a stylish figure.

All the time I am studying him, he keeps his thoughts closed. Completely. He has been vampire for a long time to master such ability. Nothing comes through. Neither is he probing my thoughts. If I am of any interest to him, he gives nothing away.

King Steffan trains them well, too.

"Do you speak English?" I ask at last.

"Yes," he replies.

"Can you tell me where we are going?"

"We are almost there."

I look around. We have left the town limits and are traveling out into the countryside. But I see nothing that looks like a castle. In fact, I see nothing at all. This road, if I remember correctly, leads to a farming community and little else.

Strangely, I feel no concern. Where uneasiness should have vampire clawing her way to the surface, instead I find myself enjoying the ride: the purr of the stately old engine, the wind in my hair, the freedom of not having to guard every thought from intruding minds. The driver pays me no heed.

Fields surround us, the perfume of new grass and freshly tilled soil fills the night air. I look up at stars like pinpricks of fiery ice filling the darkening sky. They appear as if someone had thrown a switch at sunset to start the show.

A sliver of a moon dances on the horizon. Besides the stars, it sheds the only light, meager as it is, to illuminate the road. When the driver pulls off onto a side road, I stir and glance over.

"Where are we?"

He smiles but says nothing.

Okay. Enough is enough. "I thought I was going to meet King Steffan."

The driver slows the car at the edge of a bluff and stops. He turns in his seat and lets his eyes lock with mine.

Before he opens his thoughts to me, I know.

And feel foolish that I hadn't guessed.

This dashing driver, this old vampire with the impenetrable mind, *is* King Steffan. "Very cute," I say.

"Are you angry?" he asks.

I raise my shoulders. "Should I be angry?"

"Well, you were promised a castle."

I wave a hand. "I'd settle for a ride in this beautiful old car over a visit to a stuffy castle anytime." I brush a finger over the dashboard. "What year is it?"

"It's a 1929."

"And I suppose you're the original owner."

He laughs. It's musical and self-deprecating. "Yes. But you may change your mind when you see my castle. It's not stuffy, I assure you."

He is studying me the way I studied him when I first got into the car. After a moment, he says, "You are not what I imagined."

"Which is?"

He tilts his head. "After the stories I'd heard about you, I expected someone with a harder edge. Someone tougher. You look like the schoolteacher you once were. Not a bounty hunter. And certainly not like the vanquisher of half a dozen old-soul vampires."

"You've done your homework."

"Of course. Haven't you?"

"No."

He looks surprised. "And yet you agreed to meet me alone? You were not afraid?"

"Half a dozen old-soul vampires, remember?"

He laughs again at that. "You have confidence, Anna. And strength of conviction, I can see that. It pains me to think we may become adversaries."

"Then you know why I'm here. Why we are meeting."

He sighs. "Chael told me. I am sorry it is such a sad occasion that brings you to France. But as for the other, you must recognize that you are out of your depth in Europe. We do not accept your title or your Council. Now that I have met you, I see why others respect you. But you will find no allies amongst the vampires in Europe. They swear allegiance only to me."

"Then it's you I'll have to convince to give up your shortsighted plan."

He studies me another minute, this time letting his eyes travel from my face to my breasts and down my legs in a lazy, appraising path that is as obvious as it is insulting. "You are welcome to try. In fact, I think I insist on it."

Bristling, I draw myself up on the seat. "Not even in your wildest dreams." Does it sound as juvenile to him as it does to me?

"How provincial. You are engaged. To the shape-shifter, I know."

As if that is the only reason I could possibly reject such an opportunity. But his tone while condescending and scornful has an underlying hint of—disappointment. I try to probe for the meaning behind his reaction, but the mental brick wall is back in place.

He reaches down and starts the engine. "I'll bring you back to town—to your fiancé whom I imagine is getting restless waiting for you. But we will talk again. I think you and I have many things to discuss, Anna Strong."

I reach over and grasp his hand, forcing him to kill the engine. "So, let's talk. Why waste time? I know what you are planning. You must know if you attempt to upset the balance between mortals and vampires, you will have to face the opposition of the Thirteen Tribes. We will be a formidable opponent."

This time, Steffan eyes me with nothing but a disdainful glare. The kind of expression I'd expect from a *king*. A dismissal.

"I am not prepared to argue with you tonight. In fact, have you not more important matters to tend to? Your mother is dying. You are preparing for a wedding. When we speak again, I want your full attention."

The hair bristles on the back of my neck. "You may not like what happens when you have my full attention."

He looks hard at me, then moves my hand aside and cranks the engine over once again.

This time I let him. Mentioning my mother reminds me that whatever Steffan's plans are, I do have more important priorities. Europe seems to be in no imminent danger, even from one as arrogant as this vampire who calls himself a king.

He pulls the car onto the road, makes a U-turn and we're heading back for the city lights of Lorgues. We travel in stiff silence and it's not until we've come to a halt in front of the café and I'm preparing to open the door that Steffan stops me with a hand on my arm. He's looking at Frey who has risen to meet me. He leans close. His lips are warm on my ear when he whispers.

Think carefully about your future, Anna. You could do better.

I pull out of his grip, a cold anger rising. *You overstep, Steffan.*

Frey is approaching the car, and I climb out to meet him.

I don't turn to see what Steffan is doing, but as the car engine revs, Steffan calls to me once again. *Think about it, Anna, I could make you a queen.*

Then he is gone, leaving me with Frey on the sidewalk.

Frey casts an inquisitive look, not catching Steffan's last comment. Unfortunately from his place at the table, Chael does.

A queen? Well, you have made an impression, he says when we rejoin him.

Frey is frowning. He may have missed what Steffan said but not Chael's reaction. "What's this about a queen?"

I wave a dismissive hand, sink into a chair.

And fix Chael with a warning eye. *Nothing.* To Frey, "Some bullshit meant to impress. A bad joke."

Chael doesn't wait to hear any more but stands as if ready to take his leave.

Which makes me snap at him. *You knew it was Steffan in the car. Why didn't you tell me?*

It was Steffan's wish to keep the first meeting low-key. I trust it went well. He pauses. *I know you haven't resolved the issue tonight, and I will let you know when Steffan wishes another audience.*

My temper flares. What issue? All that we determined tonight is that Steffan is an overconfident prick. *When I meet with Steffan again, Chael, it will be on my terms. You can pass that on to his majesty and tell him I am the one who will be in touch.*

117

Chael's eyebrows rise. He gives a little half bow. *As you wish.*

And then he turns on his heel like a Prussian soldier and marches off.

Frey shakes his head at his departing back. "Quite a character. Now." He leans toward me, takes my hand. "It was Steffan in the car? What happened?"

I fill him in as we sip wine. "Not much." I describe the ride and where we ended up. Steffan's comments to me about having no influence here but agreeing to listen to my arguments anyway. "We danced around like a couple of circus horses," I finish with a sniff.

"So the grand scheme never came up."

"Not so you'd notice. The only one who did any talking was me. I think this was a scouting party. Steffan taking my measure." Immediately, I'm thinking of the ways his eyes traveled the length of my body, appraising, coming to a conclusion about—what? His last remark certainly caught me off guard. Was he baiting me? If he was trying to impress me, he failed.

I don't say any of this to Frey. I finish my wine. I want to forget Chael and Steffan and everything vampire. I want to go back to the estate, hug my mother and make love to Frey. I take his hand and press it to my cheek. "Let's go home."

Whether it's the heat radiating from my skin beneath his fingertips or the breathlessness of my voice, Frey raises no objection.

CHAPTER 15

NEXT MORNING, FREY AND I ARE THE LAST TO THE breakfast table.

I'm glad no one asks why. It would be embarrassing. Even an adult daughter doesn't want to acknowledge that she's late coming down because she and her fiancé were having sex. Lots of sex. Great sex. Sex so good I didn't want to stop. When I feel color start up the back of my neck, I decide what I'd better do is stop thinking about it.

I slink into a chair at the table and reach for the coffeepot. "Where are the kids?" I ask pouring myself a cup.

Dad avoids my eyes. Shit. Were we making too much noise?

Mom picks up the slack. "Gone next door. Trish and John-John arranged an early morning ride before Trish has to go to school." She casts an apologetic eye to Frey. "I hope that was all right."

Frey smiles. "Of course. Trish mentioned their plans last night. And John-John has been riding since before he could walk."

Mom grins then. "They left *hours* ago."

I lower my head. Yikes. I glance at Frey but he seems oblivious. He's buttering toast with the gusto of a man who's just experienced an earth-shattering orgasm.

I clear my throat. "So what's on the agenda today?"

Mom slips on her reading glasses and consults her ever-present list pad. "Well. After school you and Trish have to go into town to pick up the dresses. And you should call anyone in San Diego that you want to come for the wedding. And you need to decide who you want to officiate at the service."

"Which reminds me." Glad for a chance to banish the pesky image of sex from my head, and maybe Dad's, I jump up from the table and fetch the brochure we got yesterday from the consulate. "Have you ever heard of this group?"

For the next hour we do our homework, not only going through the brochure but pulling up the website for the organization calling itself Gracefully Personalized Ceremonies. Even Mom, who I know would have preferred a Catholic ceremony, had to admit she found the philosophy of a non-secular yet devout exchange of vows fitting.

"And the sooner those vows get said, the better," Dad mutters under his breath.

I wasn't wrong. What did he do, come up to get us for breakfast? Did he hear us on the other side of the door? Shit.

This time, Frey catches the subtext, too. His face reddens.

Mom slaps at Dad's hand. "Don't be such a stick in the mud. They're young. They're in love. Don't you remember how that was?"

The doorbell rings and I jump up so fast to answer it, I almost knock my chair over. Frey is right behind me.

"Did they hear us?" he whispers, following me to the door, his brow furrowed in dismay.

"Must have." I can't help but laugh at his expression. "We need to be quieter."

"Understatement. Maybe we should lay off sex until after the wedding."

A snicker escapes my throat as I open the front door.

Another delivery man. This one is holding a bouquet of sunflowers. A bouquet so big, he's hidden behind it.

"Mademoiselle Anna Strong?"

I accept the bouquet. It takes two hands to hold it. Frey digs in his pocket and pulls out some euros. The delivery-man accepts the gratuity, tips his hat and heads back to his truck.

"Did you do this?" I ask Frey, burying my face in the bouquet. "They are beautiful."

He shakes his head and plucks a card from the flowers. "Here."

I hand him the flowers while I tear open the envelope.

The note is brief. *Until next time. Steffan.*

I turn it around so Frey can read it. He grunts. "Chael didn't exaggerate," he says through a tight jaw. "You made quite an impression." He takes the note, crumbles it into a ball, stuffs it into the pocket of his jeans. "Next time you meet with Steffan, I'm going."

I smile. "Let's just tell my folks these are from you. For my mom, shall we?"

He grins. "Good plan. Maybe it will win me a few points with your father."

I reach up and kiss his cheek. "And then maybe we won't have to give up sex until after the wedding?"

He laughs. "To keep from having to give up sex, I'd buy your mother a field of sunflowers."

I turn his shoulders and push him back toward the kitchen. "I believe you would."

The rest of the morning runs smoothly. I don't know whether it's the flowers or if Mom talked to Dad while we were out of the room about the way he raised an eyebrow in disapproval whenever he looked at Frey, but the storm seems to have blown over.

John-John calls from next door. The neighbors have invited him to stay on and help groom the horses after Trish leaves for school. Noting the excitement in his voice, we happily grant him permission.

Next, we contact the wedding people. They assure us that a wedding three days from now is tricky but certainly not impossible. They will email us a questionnaire about what kind of ceremony we envision. Once we've filled it out and mailed it back, we only need to meet with them for a short time before the ceremony to decide on vows.

We call David and Tracey and tell them we've set the date. No shocked protestations about the short notice. They are as excited as we are. We go on speakerphone mode and Mom invites them to come out a day ahead and stay as long as they'd like after. There are certainly enough bedrooms in the villa. They happily accept. I let them know I'll telephone my pilot next and arrange for them to be picked up in San Diego. I'll have the pilot contact them with the details.

Which I do.

By this time, Catherine is in the doorway announcing lunch. I'm seated right beside Mom on the couch in the living room. I rise and turn to offer my mother my hand when she suddenly pales and sinks back onto the couch. Her pad and pen fall to the floor. My heart stutters in my chest.

"Mom?" I lean over and feel her forehead. Stupid. My hands are so cold, any human flesh feels feverish. I look up at Frey and he takes my place beside her.

"Anita?" His voice is soft. He takes one of her hands in both of his own.

In the next instant, Dad is standing over us, too.

Even Catherine has crossed the room to cluck at us, wringing a towel in her hands. "It's too much," she scolds. "She shouldn't be out of bed. She should rest. Conserve her strength."

I look up at Catherine, at the concern on her face. It takes the housekeeper to make me recognize with a rush of anger that I never asked to speak with Mom's doctor. I'd assumed she'd let us know if she wasn't strong enough to deal with the task she'd taken on. I should have remembered how stubborn she can be . . . how unlikely to admit she might be tired or in pain.

"Let's take her upstairs," Dad says.

Frey sweeps Mom into his arms. She starts to protest that she can walk, but he doesn't falter.

She looks like a doll, small and fragile, huddled against his chest. I become conscious again of how much weight she's lost. I follow them upstairs, listening as Dad stays behind to ask Catherine to prepare a lunch tray. I turn the bedclothes back and Frey lays Mom down. She settles back against the pillows while I slip her shoes off and pull a blanket up around her waist.

She reaches out a hand and brushes a fingertip across my cheek. It surprises me to see that her finger comes away wet.

I didn't realize I'd been crying.

"Oh, Anna," she whispers. "I'm so sorry."

Her words cut into my heart. Why should she be sorry? Bitterness stiffens my shoulders. I'm ready to lash out that I'm the sorry one, that I've manipulated her life in ways in which she's not even aware, that I've been lying to her about what I am, about who Trish is, about every fucking thing that matters. I suck in a ragged breath.

Frey's soft hand on my shoulder stays my tongue. Once again, he *reads* me. Knows without words what I'm feeling, understands the guilt threatening to overwhelm my good sense. With a touch, he has grounded me.

I sit beside my mother on the bed, wiping away the tears with the back of my hand. "You have nothing to be sorry for, silly. Look at the wedding you've made for Frey and me. Everything is perfect. Trish and I will go into town this afternoon and finish the shopping. Frey and John-John have final fittings tomorrow morning." I tick off more items on my fingers. "We've chosen the menu and the cake, the party planners and florist will be here to decorate the morning of the wedding, our guests have been invited. It's done. No wonder you're exhausted!"

Mom smiles. "I think we are done, aren't we?"

Catherine appears with a lunch tray. "Do you want me to stay with you?" I ask Mom.

She waves me off. "No. You and Daniel go have lunch with your father. I'll have lunch up here and take a nap. You wait, by dinnertime I'll be right as rain."

I lean over and kiss her cheek. "Then we'll see you at dinnertime."

Frey follows me out of the bedroom and I close the door softly behind us, beckoning him past the stairway and into our own room. Behind the closed door, I collapse against him.

He holds me against his chest, stroking my hair.

It's a long moment before I can speak. "Thank you."

He doesn't ask for what or mumble some meaningless conciliatory remark. He just holds me.

It's absolutely the right thing to do. He gives me strength but, once again, I find myself wondering if there isn't something more for my mother that I can do.

CHAPTER 16

THE NEIGHBORS BRING JOHN-JOHN BACK IN TIME to join us for lunch. His presence brightens the mood at the table considerably. He's full of lively talk about the neighbors (real nice) and their horses (a breed called Arabian) and the ride he and Trish took out into the countryside (through fields of lavender.)

He provides the perfect distraction, drawing Dad and Frey in with his enthusiastic chatter and leaving me alone with my thoughts . . . and my concern for Mom.

After lunch, Dad takes John-John out to show him the winepress. Frey and I take glasses of wine to sit at the big table under the shade of a huge oak.

"You were quiet at lunch," Frey says, kneading the back of my neck with the palm of his hand.

I sigh and relax against him. "I wasn't prepared for how hard this would be."

"No one ever is."

I sip my wine, looking out over the vineyards, unsure how to broach the subject. After a while, I say, "I keep thinking about Max."

Frey looks surprised. "Are you thinking of him because he died recently?"

"No." I draw in a breath. "Because I could have saved him."

The glass in Frey's hand stops midway to his lips. "Saved him? You mean 'turned him,' don't you?"

"You don't see it as the same thing?"

The corners of his mouth turn down in a sharp frown. "You do?" His eyes narrow. "What are you thinking, Anna?"

He doesn't wait for me to respond. "You can't think your mother would want—"

"Want what?" I interject hotly, angry words rising like lava. "To be like me? A monster? A freak?"

He puts his glass down on the table with a sharp crack and gathers me into his arms. "That's not what I mean and you know it."

Irrationally I'm angry, so angry I struggle violently to break free. Frey tightens his grip until I can scarcely move. When I stop fighting, he still doesn't loosen his grip. He bends his face close and whispers in my ear, "When you got back from Mexico, you told me that you didn't turn Max because you couldn't be sure that it was what he wanted. That you wouldn't do to someone else what had been done to you. Is that what you're thinking now? That you'll ask your mother if she wants to be turned? Do you realize what that means? Her life—your Dad's life, Trish's life—nothing will ever be the same."

He pushes back now, tilts my chin up so that I'm looking into his eyes. "Think about it, Anna. You have so little time left to spend with her. Once you tell her that you're vampire, regardless of her decision, your relationship with your mother will be changed."

A wave of fatigue overtakes me. Everything Frey says is true. But another truth interjects itself as well. I don't want my mother to die. Trish needs her. My dad needs her. I need her.

I close my eyes and lean my head wearily against Frey's chest. Maybe I'm being selfish, but if I didn't at least offer her the alternative to what she's facing, I will never forgive myself.

Frey glances at his watch. "Listen, Trish won't be home for another hour. Why don't you go upstairs and take a nap. You look exhausted. I'll come and get you when Trish is ready to go to town."

Numbly, I nod and get to my feet. "Are you coming with me?" I ask.

He smiles, slow and sweet. "If I come, how much sleep do you think you'll get? No, I'll go find your dad and John-John. I'd like to see that winepress myself."

He steers me toward the house, then takes off down the path to the outbuildings where the wine is processed. I watch him go, glad that I didn't tell him my decision. First chance I get to be alone with my mother, I'm going to tell her.

About what I am.

About what it could mean to her.

I have to.

I GO UPSTAIRS, PAUSING OUTSIDE MOM'S DOOR. IT'S quiet inside her room, only the sound of her soft breathing. She seems to be resting quietly, no labored gasps, no moans of pain.

I could wake her now.

My heart flutters in my chest.

No. Better she rest.

No rest for me, though. Instead of stretching out on the bed, I sit at the window looking over the countryside and go over the ways I can explain to my mother what I am.

And imagining her responses.

There are only two, really.

She will be horrified and order me out of her house.

She will be horrified and have me committed.

Frey is right. Do I dare risk our last few days together?

On the other hand, does it have to be our last few days?

What if Mom understands what I'm offering and is willing to accept it to stay with her family?

For how long?

Immortality is something I'm wrestling with all the time. Frey and I haven't discussed it, but he knows the reality of our situation. He will age, naturally, gracefully, while I will stay forever the same. I will watch him die, John-John and Trish, too. And I will stay forever the same.

Can Mom cope with that? Watching Dad die—watching Trish and maybe her grandchildren from a self-imposed distance because they can never know the truth?

But she and I can be together, then, right?

Is that selfish?

Yes.

Still . . .

A car is coming down the drive—Trish's ride from school. I go into the bathroom and splash cold water on my face. I will talk to Trish this afternoon. See how she's holding up. She's had a rough life and now this. It's so damned unfair. Maybe she will help me decide what to do. Maybe her devastation at Mom's loss will tilt the scales in favor of presenting my case.

Maybe I'm grasping at something, anything, to take the decision out of my hands.

CHAPTER 17

TRISH AND I ARE STANDING IN THE DRESSING AREA of one of Lorgues' nicest boutiques. The attendant has just brought in the dresses we chose on our shopping trip a couple of days before. They are in three white garment bags, which she hangs on a wooden rack. She leaves with smiles, a flutter of hands and effusive assurances that she is right outside if we need any help.

Trish goes to the rack and reads the tags. "Here's yours, Aunt Anna. Try it on! I can't wait to see you in it!"

I take the bag from her outstretched hand and step behind the changing screen. I'd chosen a champagne-colored peau de soie sheath, simple, knee-length, tailored, adorned only with seed pearls at the portrait neckline. The silk is light as air against my skin. I can't see myself in the mirrors surrounding the dressing area, so I'll have to judge by

Trish's reaction when she sees me whether or not I made a good choice.

Her eyes sparkle and her smile beams. "It's perfect," she breathes. "Oh, Aunt Anna, you look beautiful. Wait until Daniel sees you!"

I twirl around, laughing, before taking her dress down from the rack. "Your turn!"

She disappears behind the screen only to reappear a few moments later looking so breathtakingly grown-up, a gasp catches in my throat.

She'd chosen a simple silk dress, too, pale rose, fitted at the top, pencil skirt. She holds her hands in front of her mimicking holding a bouquet and walks slowly toward me.

I have to brush away a tear.

Trish holds up a hand in dismay. "No crying! Tears are murder on silk!"

Which makes us both burst into tears and scramble to find tissues before we spot our dresses, which in turn makes us burst into gales of laughter. We collapse on a bench and compose ourselves.

Then, our eyes turn to the third garment bag. I unzip it.

Mom's suit is inside. The same pale rose as Trish's dress, this is wool bouclé, an elegant jacket and skirt, cap-sleeved silk camisole. I skim my fingers over the fabric. "She'll look beautiful in this."

Trish's expression softens, saddens. "She looks beautiful in everything."

I sit down beside her. "How are you doing? Really?"

She looks away, her breathing shallow and quick as if swallowing back a sob.

I put my arms around her shoulders. "I'm so worried

about you. I know how hard this has to be. Finally, you have a real home, grandparents who love you, and now—"

She leans her head on my shoulder. "I'm doing okay. It's Grandfather I worry about. He and Grandmother are so close. How will he cope when she's gone? When there's just me?"

Her voice catches and I sense an undertone of hesitation, of concern. As if she's afraid once Mom is gone, Dad won't want her around anymore. I know how utterly baseless that fear is, how much my father loves her, but I also realize my saying that won't change the way she feels.

I put an arm over Trish's shoulders. "Go change, honey. Let's get some dinner."

She disappears into the changing area and I remain on the bench, gazing at Mom's suit. I wanted help in making my decision.

I just got it.

As soon as I can, I will talk to my mom.

MOM DOESN'T COME DOWN FOR DINNER.

Her absence casts a pall over us all. After, Dad suggests we go into town for a movie. The kids agree and spend fifteen minutes in good-natured arguing over what to see— a Pixar animated flick or a new action-adventure featuring the Justice League. The superheroes win out. Since it's an American movie, language won't be a problem. The film will have French subtitles.

The kids disperse to get their jackets, Dad goes upstairs to tell Mom, Frey and I are alone at the table.

"You're not coming, are you?" Frey asks.

I shake my head.

"You're staying to talk to your mother."

Not a question so I feel no need to reply.

Frey sighs. But then he stands up and pulls me to my feet, too. "I love you," he says. "I stand behind your choice. But please, Anna, be careful. I don't want to see you hurt any more than you are."

I put my hands around his neck and pull his face down so I can reach his lips with my own. The kiss is full of longing, gratitude. "I love you, too," I whisper, pulling back. "I think I always have."

Then the kids are racing back down the stairs with Dad right behind them. Frey herds them to the door. No one has to ask why I'm not accompanying them. It seems to be understood. I will stay with Mom.

It's not without a certain irony—this choice of movie. My family has a real-life justice fighter in their midst and they don't know it.

Well, they don't *all* know it.

I start up the stairs to Mom's room.

And after tonight, there will be one more sharing the secret.

CHAPTER 18

MOM IS SITTING UP IN BED WATCHING A FRENCH news program when I peek around the door.

She smiles when she sees me and reaches for the remote. "You didn't go to the movie."

I step into the room. "Would you like some company?"

She pats the bed. "I'd love some." She clicks off the television and looks hard at me. "You look so tired, Anna. This should be such a happy time for you and I'm spoiling it."

Her words bring a rush of anger, and the ever-present urge to scream that it's not her, it's the fucking cancer, and that if there were any justice at all in this fucking world, this wouldn't be happening.

But in my head I see Frey's gently frowning face and a shaking finger. Not the language to use with your mother, he's reminding me, in a voice so real, I think he might be standing right behind me.

He's right. I take my mother's hand and squeeze it. "You haven't spoiled anything. In fact, you made me realize how silly it is for Frey and me to wait to get married. And you know me." I wink at her. "If you hadn't made the suggestion, Frey and I would have dragged our feet, finding one excuse after the other to hang on to the status quo. I'm such a procrastinator. It would have had Dad climbing the walls."

She laughs at that. "I can't believe how silly he acted this morning. You'd think you were a child."

"To him, I am. But I am sorry to have embarrassed him. I didn't know—"

"That he was going to intrude on you so early in the morning? Don't be silly. I told him to leave you alone. That you'd get up when you were ready, but he insisted. He should never have been at that bedroom door to begin with."

We're both laughing now, at the memory of Dad's embarrassed reaction to having heard Frey and me behind that closed door. Still, though, I give myself a mental thump on the head. We are not at home and it could have been John-John or Trish dispatched to fetch us. Frey may be right about forgoing sex until after the service.

Realistically? How likely is that?

Our laughter fades. The silence stretches. Mom turns to me.

"What is it, Anna? What do you want to say to me?"

Her eyes search my face. My heart beats so furiously I'm sure she must hear. I turn away, suddenly afraid, suddenly unsure. What do I want to say?

"Anna?" Her soft voice with just one word pulls me

back, insistent, demanding as the magnetic pull on a compass needle.

I meet her eyes.

"You know you can tell me anything."

"Can I?"

Mom looks shocked. "Why would you ask that?" Her tone is hurt, reproachful.

I'm immediately swamped by guilt. I swallow hard, clench my hands in my lap. "Stupid thing to say. I'm sorry."

She watches my hand wringing. Her expression morphs to alarm. "What is it, Anna? You're scaring me."

Great start. "I don't mean to scare you. But I'm afraid I'm going to. It's why this is so hard."

"Go on."

"I have a story to tell you. It's not going to be easy for you to accept. All I ask is that you let me explain in my own way and wait until you've heard it all before you react."

Mom's eyes lock on mine, she nods. "Go on."

The words pour out— The beginning. How I was attacked and raped. How my attacker turned out to be a vampire. How he turned me into one, too. What it means—to need human blood to survive. *How* I survive, where I go to feed, how the human hosts are protected and that it's not painful for them. That I am the Chosen One, a leader who makes decisions that affect the entire vampire community— and as a result, the human community, too.

I edit as I go—some things I don't want to share. I don't tell her that their living in France was my doing, arranged for their protection. Or that Trish is not really my brother's child. When Mom is gone, I want my father and Trish to find solace in each other. I tell her that Frey knows my true nature and accepts it. I don't tell her that he and John-John are otherworldly, too. I speak quickly, afraid if I pause, I'll stop altogether.

Then I explain what I can do for her. That I can make her whole again and immortal. That she can have many more years with Dad and Trish and that it will be tricky, but—I think of Chael's offer—there are vampires in Europe who could show her how to feed safely. She wouldn't be a monster. She would be like me.

When I run out of words, the silence is ponderous, pressing in on my heart until I want to cry out with the pain.

When at last my mother speaks, it is so quietly I have to bend near to catch the words.

"I don't understand." Her tone is stammering, uncertain. "A vampire? They're not real. How can you imagine yourself such a creature?"

"I don't *imagine* it, Mom. Think. When was the last time you saw me eat food? Touch my skin. It's cold." I look around, spy what I'm searching for on the dressing table. I hold the mirror up so she can see only her face is reflected there. "I cast no reflection. I don't know why these things are, but it's the way it is. For vampires."

My mother's shoulders slump, her face crumbles. She begins to cry, rasping sobs that wrack her body. I start to reach out but hold back.

Maybe the tears are because she's repulsed. Maybe she would pull away from me in disgust. I couldn't bear that. I stand up, step away from her bed, tears of my own cascading down my cheeks and spilling onto my hands.

"I'm so sorry, Mom. I shouldn't have said anything. If you want Frey and John-John and me to leave, we will. We can be gone by morning. I'll tell Dad something's come up. That we—"

And in the next instant, Mom has pushed herself off the bed and is hugging me so tightly my words are choked off. "How long has it been like this for you?" she whispers.

"Almost two years."

"Oh, Anna." Her words are muffled against my shoulder. "How can you ever forgive me?"

I have to step back, too stunned by her words to do more than hold her at arm's length to study her face in disbelief. What is she saying? "You're not afraid of me? You don't hate me?"

She takes a step back, too, and sits on the bedside, pulling me down to sit beside her. She cradles my face in her hands. "I'm not crying because I hate you, I'm crying because of what I've done to you. You've had to face so much alone. When you needed me most, I made you afraid to come to me. Even before, when you left teaching, I was judgmental and cruel, trying to mold you into what I wanted instead of letting you find your own way."

I raise my hands to stop her words, but she grabs them and continues on.

"And you were *attacked* . . . My god . . . One of the worst things that can happen to a woman and you couldn't come to me. I made you afraid to come to me. What kind of mother does that to her daughter?"

I'm crying again now, too, and grasping her hands like a lifeline.

Mom's voice softens. "Instead of applauding the strong woman you are, I forced you away." She draws a sharp breath. "I've heard such awful things about vampires. The blood.

The killing. I never believed they existed, of course, I thought it was all fiction. But I only have to look at you to know that there is nothing inherently evil in what you've become."

I put my hands over hers. She doesn't wince at the contact. "I could make you well," I say simply. "It would be painless. There's a period of adjustment, but I would take care of you. We could tell the family we're going to a clinic—to try a new treatment. When you come back, you will be strong again. The cancer will be gone. You'll have your life back. Yes, it will be different, but I'll stay with you as long as you need me to."

Mom is quiet for a long moment, her eyes straying to a picture on her dresser. It's a family portrait, taken when I was a child. My mother, father, brother and I, all in our Easter best, posing with broad smiles and happy faces.

"Thank you for offering," she says at last. "But I can't accept." Her hands tighten on mine. "My faith is strong and I believe in an afterlife. I know it will be hard on Dad and Trish when I'm gone, but they have you and Daniel and each other. I think it was God's plan to bring Trish into our lives, knowing I had not long to live."

She pats my hand. "We will be together again one day. You and your brother and the daughter he never met. All of us, when it is time. For now, it seems you have a destiny to fulfill. An important destiny. And you will soon have a husband and a wonderful little boy to raise. Make the most of your time with them, Anna. Don't let it slip away."

Then we're hugging again, holding each other tightly. Mom's voice at my ear. "I am so proud of you, Anna. So proud of the woman you've become. You are so much stronger than I have ever been."

After a long moment, she breaks away. She's frowning. "I suppose this isn't something we should share with your father." Her expression is serious, but her words carry a hint of humor.

"Probably not," I agree. "At least for now. He has enough to deal with, I think, without the knowledge that his daughter is not exactly normal anymore."

"Then it will be our secret." Mom pats my cheek. "Don't you worry about it. I'll tell him when I think he's ready."

A shudder wracks her body. She leans back against her pillows, her face drained of color. "I think I'd better rest now. We have another big day tomorrow."

I bend over her, tucking the blankets around her, trying to keep the alarm from my face. "We will take care of everything," I reply. "If you want to spend the day in bed, you just do it."

She smiles—a real, genuine smile full of love and acceptance and it warms me. Suddenly, I feel better, lighter in spirit, than I have in days. I sit at her bedside until she drifts off.

It's only as I tiptoe out of the room that sadness descends once again.

I glance back at my sleeping mother. In some ways, telling her about me, offering her the chance to overcome the illness strafing her body was a victory.

In other ways, though, it was a bitter defeat, because for all my talk of immortality, I can do nothing now to save her.

FREY FINDS ME LYING IN THE DARK—CURLED ON OUR bed, knees drawn to chest. He shuts the door quietly and slips into bed beside me, letting me burrow back against him.

"I guess I don't have to ask how it went," he says.

My voice is a soft monotone when I recount the conversation. When I finish, he strokes my hair.

"Your mother's faith in her own kind of eternal life is strong," he says. "She does not fear death. It isn't surprising that she wouldn't agree to be turned."

"But she's not thinking of anyone else," I snap. "She's being selfish. She's not thinking of what her death means to Trish or Dad or me. We need her."

I'm crying again, angry tears that burn hot and seem to sizzle on my skin. Frey's arms tighten around my waist but he doesn't say what I know he must be thinking. He simply waits for me to say what he knows I will.

"That was stupid, wasn't it?" I struggle into a seated position, wiping my face with the sleeve of my shirt and shifting so I'm facing Frey. "I just called my dying mother selfish. She accepted what I told her. Made me feel accepted and loved. Even apologized for criticizing my life choices when I left teaching. And I just called *her* selfish."

Frey is smiling, one arm resting behind his head on the pillow. "You didn't mean it. I understand."

I snuggle back down beside him. "How do you put up with me?"

"It's a constant struggle."

I push myself back up. "One thing I didn't tell her," I say, half turning so I can look at him. "Is the part sex plays in the vampire dynamic."

"Probably a good thing," he says, slipping his free arm around my waist. "That might have been a little too much information."

Then I'm smiling, too. To a vampire, sex and feeding

warm the blood. They are the two things that make our bodies feel alive, feel *human*. The two things that make what would be an intolerable existence endurable. I read the fire in Frey's eyes, know what he's thinking, feeling. He understands. He always has.

"So do you really think we should practice abstinence for the next couple of days?" I ask, pulling my sweater over my head.

Frey sits up straighter. "Probably. We don't want to cause your dad any more embarrassment."

Leaning down, I gather Frey's T-shirt at the waist and strip it off, dropping it on the floor.

"Or we could be very, very quiet." I've got his jeans unzipped about the same time he's managed to lower mine and we kick out of them together.

He pins me beneath him. He's hard and ready and I raise my hips. When he slides inside, he moans, a deep, guttural cry of joyful abandon.

"Yikes." I push a finger against his lips. "We have to be quiet, remember?"

Even in the dark, I see the color spread up his face. He drops his head momentarily, then with a wicked gleam, begins to move. He drives my passion ahead of his own with each thrust and at the moment of climax, when I forget myself, he smothers my own joyful cry with his lips.

After, when we're lying together, spent, sated, I hear his soft laughter. "See?" he says, tracing a finger along my backbone. "Being with you is a constant struggle."

CHAPTER 19

MOM IS DOWN EARLY FOR BREAKFAST THE NEXT morning. She looks so much better, rested, relaxed. I'm determined to see she stays that way. We share a conspiratorial smile and a quick hug before taking our places at the table. Trish and John-John are deep in a good-natured discussion about who would win in a duel to the death—Iron Man or The Hulk. Even with the age difference, John-John seems to be holding his own.

Frey and Dad discuss the wine business; Mom and I go over the wedding list one last time. There really is nothing to do today but fill out that questionnaire from the wedding planner and wait to hear back about when we'll meet. The real action takes place tomorrow when David and Tracey get in and the grounds are turned into an open-air wedding chapel.

I insist Mom spend the day relaxing. The next two days are going to be more than a challenge. She gives in reluctantly, but does give in. She rises from the table to go up to her room when the front doorbell rings.

"I'll get it," she says, switching directions to head for the door.

Conversation between the rest of us—me, Frey, Dad and the kids—swirls around how to spend our Saturday.

But as soon as I pick up on what's happening at the front door, I'm on my feet. Frey raises an eyebrow, but I wave him off and make my way to join my mother.

She smiles when she sees me. "Look who's here, Anna. Your friend Monsieur Chael." She switches her smile to Chael. "Have you come for the wedding?"

Smooth as only the best charmers can be, Chael has taken my mother's hand and raised it to his lips. "Of course, Madame Strong. I wouldn't miss it."

My eyes widen. *You speak English?*

I've been practicing.

Mom shepherds Chael to the dining room, looking back over her shoulder to mouth at me, "Is he—?"

I bob my head in quick affirmation. Her eyes widen and she opens her mouth again in a silent "Oh my." But she doesn't miss a beat; she makes the introductions and at Chael's acknowledgment of each person in English, Frey's eyebrows shoot up, too.

Chael turns down an offer of coffee and turns to me. "I apologize for disturbing your breakfast. But I have a message for you from another old friend."

Dad motions to the kids. "Nice to meet you, Mr. Chael. If you'll excuse us, we'll let you speak in private."

I wait until they disappear through the kitchen door, Mom following, and turn to Chael.

"You speak English?"

"I told you I've been practicing."

"So why didn't you tell us?"

"You didn't ask."

I ball my fists to keep from smacking him. "You have a message for me?"

Frey puts a finger to his lips and bobs his head in the direction of a cacophony of cheery voices coming from the kitchen. "Let's go outside."

Good idea. I motion Chael ahead and we step through the front door into the bright sunshine. But before Chael tells us what he came for, he puts a hand on my arm.

"I am sorry about your mother. She is very sick. I am glad you are here. It will make her last days easier."

My stomach lurches. "What do you know of her last days?"

He touches the tips of his fingers together. "I felt it when we touched. She doesn't have much time." He looks at me from beneath a furrowed brow. "If you wish it, I could arrange for her to be brought over. It would be painless. We could spirit her away to another land where she could learn to live as we do. In time, you could be reunited."

I see Chael in a different light. For the second time, he is offering me a gift—he's offering to *save* my mother. There is sincerity in his words just as there is sympathy in his thoughts. In his way, he is trying to be kind.

"I appreciate the gesture," I say, finding I mean it. "But my mother believes in a god that offers her a different kind of eternal life. She is at peace."

Frey takes my hand as he directs his words to Chael. "You said you could 'feel' that she hasn't much time. How is that possible?"

"In my mortal life, I was a healer," Chael replies. "I was born with the ability to diagnose through touch. The gift has become stronger with time."

We have been strolling toward the vineyards. I wonder why I wasn't given such a gift. My talents seem to lay in brute strength and physical prowess. Worthless talents. If I could have *felt* Mom's illness in December, maybe—

You are wrong. Chael is in my head. *You have the ability to lead. That is an extraordinary gift in itself and not to be thought of as worthless. As the Chosen One, you determine whether we live in peace with mortals or war against them. Given the choice, I'm sure your mother would prefer you as protectorate.*

I think back to her words last night. In a way, she would. She said I had a destiny to fulfill.

Frey stirs beside me. "I'm assuming the message you came to deliver is from Steffan?"

His words bring Chael and me back to the reason for his visit. For a moment, I'd almost forgotten.

Chael nods. "Yes. King Steffan is requesting the honor of your company at a small party tonight. If it is convenient, of course."

Frey and I look at each other.

"If it's convenient, huh?" Frey is grinning. "Well, Anna, it's up to you. This will be one of our last free nights before the wedding."

I release a noisy breath. "Okay. Tell Steffan we accept. Let's get this over with. Will you be taking us?"

"I will arrange transportation. Shall we meet at the café in the village at seven?"

Frey and I agree and walk Chael back to his car—a sleek new Jaguar sedan—brand-new. The dealer plates are still in place. Impulsively, I run a gentle finger over a door panel. "Nice car."

"I thought you would like it. It is yours to use while you are here if you wish."

The offer is tempting. But I decline. No way do I want to become further in Chael's debt even for a small thing like the loan of a car. If, as we suspect, he is responsible for getting the law off our backs in the deaths of Warren and Judith Williams, that bill will be high enough.

Chael has his hand on the door. "Oh, by the way. The dinner is a formal affair." He reaches in and produces a garment bag from the passenger seat. "For Anna. Steffan wasn't sure you would have anything appropriate to wear. Except your wedding dress, of course." He winks at Frey. "We all know the old adage about the groom seeing the bride before the wedding."

He thrusts the bag at Frey, whose expression is thunderous. He looks past Chael to the backseat. "What? Nothing for me?"

Chael smiles another of his most charming smiles and settles himself into the driver's seat.

I watch the Jag purr its way down the drive and sigh.

Then I take the garment bag from Frey's hands. He gives me the evil eye.

"What? I'm curious." I draw the zipper down and peek inside.

Wow. Steffan has very good taste.

* * *

WE PASS THE DAY IN FAMILIAL COMPANIONSHIP: DAD, Trish, Frey and I. A trip next door to meet the horses (and the neighbors, of course; they are almost as excited about the wedding as my family). A trip to town to the outdoor market for fresh vegetables and bread. A trip to the vineyards to supervise the cultivating of the fields.

Frey and I hold hands, the kids never stop chattering and Dad does his best to appear cheerful. Once, when he doesn't realize I'm watching, the mask falls. Sadness is stamped in dark bold relief on his face.

I leave Frey's side and link my arm through his. "You doing okay?"

He squeezes my arm. "I'm fine."

"No. You aren't. And it's all right if you aren't."

He smiles. "It's wonderful to have you here. And the kids. I worry how it will be with Trish when you leave. She puts on such a brave front."

"It's not just Trish putting up a brave front," I remind him. "You're doing a pretty good job of it yourself."

"Am I? Sometimes I wonder." He lets his voice drop.

"When the time comes," I say, not able to bring myself to say the obvious, "why don't you and Trish plan to spend a few weeks in San Diego with me? Frey will have to go back to Monument Valley so John-John can finish up the school year. I have plenty of room."

He squeezes my arm once again. "I'll think about it. See what Trish wants to do. I thank God every day for that girl. You and she are the only things holding me together."

John-John comes skipping back to ask Dad a question

about the grapes and he lets himself be pulled ahead to where Trish is waiting. Frey steps up beside me. "Everything okay?"

"As okay as it can be." I put my arms around Frey's waist and give him a hug. "He's very glad we're here."

Frey's lips brush the top of my head. "Me, too."

WE PLAN TO LEAVE THE FAMILY AT DINNERTIME TO GO into Lorgues. We retreat upstairs late in the afternoon to shower and change. Frey has qualms about my wearing the dress Steffan provided.

Until he sees me in it.

It's a simple design, a shift of cream chiffon with strategically placed beads and sequins that seem to follow the silhouette of my body. It has a modest boat neckline and short sleeves and hits just above the knees with a scalloped fringe hem.

Not revealing. Not formfitting. It's beautiful without being ostentatious. Feminine without being overtly sexy. There is a pair of silver sandals in the bottom of the bag to complete the ensemble.

I slip them on and pirouette for Frey to get the full effect. "So. What do you think?"

"I think Steffan knows too damned much about you." But his eyes shine and he steps closer to trace a curving line of crystals from the top of the dress to a point just above my right breast. "I like it. Take it off."

I wave a finger in front of his face. "Later. Right now, we need to get on the road."

He groans and shrugs into his jacket. He's wearing a

blue Armani suit with a pale silk shirt and a conservative striped tie. I reach up and straighten the knot. "Just like an old married couple," I tell him.

The family is at the dining room table when we appear. We get a chorus of whistles and a round of applause, which makes Frey take me into his arms and dance us around the table.

Mom has come down to join the family for dinner, too, and her presence makes it hard to pull myself away. Once again, her skin glows, her eyes burn bright. We'd excused ourselves from the family dinner with the pretext of one final romantic dinner between Frey and me before we tie the knot.

"Good idea," Dad says with a grin. "After you're married those romantic evenings will be few and far between."

Mom swats his arm. "Don't listen to him. We've had plenty of romantic evenings. He's just too busy watching football to notice."

"Football, huh?" Frey says. "I'm a baseball man myself."

"You are?" I blink up at him. I can't believe I didn't know this about the man I'm about to marry.

He gives me an amused smile. "Well, when was the last time we discussed sports?"

He has a point. "Guess there are still a few things I don't know about you."

He puts an arm over my shoulder. "Honey, there are a lot of things you don't know about me."

Mom laughs. "Uh-oh, Anna. A man of secrets."

"It's good to have a little mystery in your life." This from Dad. "Keeps the marriage fresh."

I give Frey another good-natured slap on the arm. "As

long as none of these mysteries is named Susan or Elizabeth."

Frey points to the door. "I think it's time we were on our way."

"Evasive, isn't he?" Mom says.

I let Frey pull me toward the door, turning back to mouth, "I'll keep him on a short leash."

Dad has taken Mom in his arms. He leans down to whisper something in her ear. The sound of their laughter as they hold each other warms—and breaks—my heart.

CHAPTER 20

CHAEL IS WAITING FOR US IN FRONT OF THE CAFÉ. He's in the Jag, the engine running. The sound is like the quiet growl of a big cat waiting to spring. I tip my face to Frey. "Sound familiar?"

He rumbles a growl of his own and holds the door open for me to slip inside.

Chael puts the car in gear and gives it its head. He glances over his shoulder. "You look quite beautiful in the dress, Anna."

"What about me?" Frey says. "Don't I look beautiful, too?"

Chael grunts and turns his attention to the road. I noticed when we got in that he was in *very* formal dress—a black tux and pleated white shirt. He's concentrating on the driving, his manner relaxed.

"Tell me," I say after a moment. "Who will be at this party tonight?"

He shrugs. "I am not privy to the entire guest list. But I do expect one or two dignitaries from the EVL." He pauses, reading that I don't know what that is, before continuing. "European Vampire League. Counterpart to our Thirteen Tribes. Many are in town because they are curious about you." He glances over his shoulder once again. "This is your chance to make an impression on the oldest vampires in existence."

"Older than Steffan?"

"Oh yes." He chuckles. "I think you will be surprised."

"But Steffan is their leader."

"For the moment."

His nonchalance raises the hair on my arm. "What do you mean?"

"I did not want to say anything before but there are rumblings in the community. We may be witness to history in the making tonight."

Frey's grip on my hand tightens. "What kind of history?"

"You'll see. Shifter, you should feel honored to be included as consort to the Chosen One. Few such as yourself have been granted the privilege."

Frey grows restive beside me. I sense an end to his patience with Chael.

"You forget yourself, Chael." I bite off each word. "Frey is more than a match for any vampire. I suggest you don't give him the opportunity to prove it."

Chael takes the admonition calmly. He turns his thoughts inward and closes them off. Frey, meanwhile, is still fuming. I bring his hand to my lips. When his eyes snap to mine, I watch the transformation from anger to warmth as I rub his hand against my cheek. He nods that he is once more in control. Our hands remain clasped tightly together and we relax in our seats.

I let my eyes drift to the world outside our car. We are traveling the main road out of Lourges—to the west instead of the route traveled last night. Up into the gentle hills that surround the village. In the lingering twilight, we pass several side roads that end in huge houses perched like jewels on manicured lots.

Suddenly, an icy finger touches the back of my neck and I shiver.

Frey feels it. His eyes snap to mine. "What's wrong?"

But I brush his concern away with a hand wave. "Nothing. Really."

I turn my face away. Glad once again that he can't read my thoughts; carefully locking those thoughts away from Chael's prying mind.

Because it *is* something. This night reminds me of another night, almost two years ago. A ride up another hill in another part of the world that ended in a fight to the death against an old-soul vampire.

Avery.

Instinctively, my hand touches the hem of my dress. I was wearing Avery's gift that night. Just as I'm wearing Steffan's now.

I was driven to the house then, just as I'm being driven now.

My throat is dry. I have the terrible feeling I shouldn't have accepted Steffan's invitation. Worse, I shouldn't have brought Frey along. I may have read too much into Chael's show of goodwill, his compassion for my mother. Was it all just a trick to win my confidence?

Blood pounds through my veins, heat rising as the vampire seizes control.

Frey can feel it. My skin hot against his. He turns a puzzled frown my way. "Anna?"

Chael senses a change, too. He can't see me in the mirror, but he is acutely aware of the transformation taking place in the seat right behind him. It makes him nervous enough to pull the car over.

Once the car is stopped, I'm out of it, at the driver's door in a heartbeat. I fling the door open, grab Chael by the neck and pull him out, moving too fast to give him a chance to fight back. His vampire nature flashes, then retreats. He acts like a dog showing his stomach to an alpha, submissively waiting for whatever I choose to do.

I choose to shake him until his teeth rattle. *What game are you playing?*

None. I am doing as you asked. Taking you to King Steffan.

His mind is open, his thoughts as passive as his body.

I shake him again. *There must be more. All this talk of making history and of King Steffan's unseating. Do you expect me to fight him?*

At this, a smile, thin, unnerving. *No. Not you.*

Then who? I shove him away, stand ready to defend myself if he unleashes his beast.

He tugs at the hem of his jacket, straightens his tie, smoothes his hair back with both hands. *You are still too impulsive, Anna Strong,* he says through gritted teeth and tight jaw. *Has it ever occurred to you to ask first before you resort to violence?*

Not when it comes to you. Now answer the question. Who do you think is going to attack King Steffan tonight?

Chael shoves his hands into the pockets of his jacket, locks his eyes with mine. *Ever heard of a vampire named Vlad?*

CHAPTER 21

CHAEL'S WORDS SNAP THE HUMAN ANNA BACK IN a heartbeat.

I stare at Chael. "Vlad is a mythical creature." I speak the words aloud as if by doing so they will carry more conviction.

We are all mythical creatures, is Chael's heated but mocking reply. *Or have you forgotten?*

Frey is standing beside me. I was so caught up with Chael, I hadn't heard or seen him climb from the car. But he has obviously been there long enough to catch the gist of our conversation. His voice at my elbow makes me jump.

"Vlad the Impaler? Not possible."

"Oh, then, shifter," Chael says, his voice dripping sarcasm. "You must be sure to tell Vlad that he does not exist. Your opinion will be valuable to him."

Frey lunges at Chael, moving almost as fast as the panther, catching him off guard and connecting with a solid right to Chael's jaw. Chael lands on his butt, but when he jumps to his feet, the vampire has surfaced. I step between them then, knowing unless Frey shifts, he is no match for an enraged Chael. Much as I'd love to see the arrogant Chael brought down by the panther, this is neither the time nor place.

"Enough." The roar of my voice, of vampire's voice, brings both men to a halt. Their heads snap around.

Frey's blood is still running high, the panther lurks behind his eyes. The growl that erupts from his chest is more animal than human. Chael's eyes flash yellow slits, the vampire full-blown.

"Heel your pet," Chael snarls.

Frey lunges again. I step between them again, stop Frey with a look and an upturned hand.

A rumbling, hostile murmur of protest spews from his gut but he backs away.

I touch his cheek. "Not now."

Panther gradually retreats from his eyes. He shakes his head as if to clear it and takes another step back.

I whirl on Chael. *You should tread lightly. I stopped Frey this time, but I may not always be able to. Or want to.*

Chael has turned away, going through his grooming routine again, straightening his jacket, smoothing his black lacquered hair. His thoughts are shielded. A good thing. I imagine they are filled with images of Frey, torn and bleeding, his neck at Chael's mouth.

He has never seen panther in action. I glance at Frey. He is leaning back against the car but his eyes are locked on

Chael. Similar scenes are most likely playing in his head, too. But in his, it is Chael's throat torn and bleeding before he severs it completely with a snap of powerful jaws.

The showdown will come. I'm sure of it. Just not tonight.

I take Frey's hand. "We need to go."

Frey straightens, pushing himself from the car. "What about this Vlad nonsense? You should make Chael tell you what the hell is going on."

Chael glares at Frey. "You will soon know what is going on. You should pray Vlad doesn't take umbrage at your attitude and snap your neck like kindling."

Frey's back stiffens. Once more, I intervene. "Enough, Chael. Get back into the car."

Chael moves, slowly, grudgingly, taking his place in the driver's seat. Once Frey and I are seated, too, he steers the car onto the road.

The silence in the car is suffocating.

Great. This is going to be some party. I may end up acting as a referee between Frey and Chael the entire evening. I hope Steffan has lots of champagne.

I let my eyes drift to the road, to the soft spring greenery on either side. We are still climbing. To the top, I'm sure.

Where else would a king have his castle?

WHEN WE FINALLY REACH THE END OF THE PUBLIC road, we are faced with a guardhouse and tall, iron gates. A watchman, a vampire, comes to the car, glances inside, then presses a remote. The gates swing open.

Chael drives on, up and up, the driveway bordered by a

brilliant display of spring color. Lavender and Lavendula, almond trees in full bloom, roses. I roll the window down to breathe in the fragrance.

This may be the last peaceful moment I have tonight.

When the house comes into view it's a surprise, though not an entirely unexpected one. I've come to know that old-soul vampires do not stick with the stereotypes most often associated with them. Steffan's castle is not a stone fortress, but a modern one built of steel and glass.

The turnaround in front of the house is filled with cars—I'd guess close to fifty. Chael pulls up to a valet stand.

"I thought you said *one or two* of the old guard would be here," I mumble to him as he comes around to open my door.

He shrugs and waits for me to alight, turning away quickly when it's Frey's turn. I smile as a guttural sound like a dog's soft snarl rasps in Frey's throat.

A valet has already whisked the car away; a doorman stands on the porch. Both vampires. The double front door is gigantic, solid mahogany, at least twenty feet high and as wide across with opaque leaded-glass inserts. The glass displays a mosaic of a spider's web, intricate, ornate, done in gold leaf.

No spider.

How appropriate. A work of art that also delivers a warning. The spider is inside.

You are very perceptive. Steffan's amused voice from the top of the porch stairs has infiltrated my thoughts. *And very beautiful. Welcome to my home.*

He waits for us in the doorway, light spilling out from a

tiled entryway. He is resplendent in an artfully tailored black tuxedo, the cummerbund and tie exactly the same shade as a lilac rose boutonniere. Frey takes my arm and we move to the door, Chael following behind. When we are face-to-face, Steffan holds out a hand to Frey.

"Welcome. You are a very lucky man to have landed this woman," he says. "Also, a very special one if Anna has chosen you as consort above all others."

I sense Frey bristle a little at the title "consort"—one that keeps coming up among the vampires we meet. But Steffan's tone is not condescending and his greeting is warm. Quite a contrast from Chael and his constant, grating derision.

Frey responds by returning the handshake and a smiling "thank you." He gestures to the house. "And you are lucky to have such a beautiful home."

Steffan offers an arm to me and leads us into the interior of the house. Frey is at Steffan's left. Chael follows behind. I notice Steffan has not greeted him and I feel Chael's aggravation at the affront. It means I must be even more alert to Chael's conduct tonight.

There may be more than one drama played out on this elegant stage.

From the great room in front of us, the soft strains of an orchestra serve as backdrop to a hum of conversation. Some of it is vocal, some of it is telepathic, all of it swirls on the air like pollen in a gentle breeze. Steffan pauses to let us appreciate a sight that I'm sure has never failed to impress.

It is a large room, so large there are two huge chandeliers, one at each end, dripping four-foot ropes of crystal and pearl. Under the diffused light of a thousand candles, the gathering mills in relaxed comfort. There must be one hundred vampires here, along with two dozen or so mortals partnered with vampires, and a half dozen otherworldly guests.

Frey looks around, too. He nods toward a group of five men standing together near the orchestra. "Shifters."

Their eyes turn to us in the doorway as if sensing, too, another shifter in their presence and it is to Frey that they bend their heads in acknowledgment.

We continue to drink in the scene. Every female dressed in the finest couture, every male in a custom suit or tuxedo. The jewels glittering on earlobes and necks and fingers could bankroll a small country. There are liveried servants with trays of champagne-filled glasses or thick, crystal goblets of something dark and viscous. And red.

I raise my eyebrow at Steffan, who has been following my thoughts. "Volunteered blood only," he assures me.

Do I believe him? I think of Avery and his treachery and a shudder racks my soul.

Steffan reads it. He glances at Frey, acknowledging openly that he knows as a shifter Frey can pick up on his thoughts if he allows it. He does.

I knew Avery, he begins. *As you can see, he and I were neighbors. I was shocked to learn of his death. Angry. We who you call old-soul vampires, who have had hundreds of years, look on it as an affront when one of our own is snuffed out. Especially by one so new and ignorant of the way. But you killed him in defense of your own life. Something none of us could overlook. There was no vendetta waged, no call for your head.*

He pauses, catches the eye of a server and motions him

to come to us. He chooses blood from the tray, Frey and I champagne. We tip glasses and drink and he continues.

When your family showed up to claim Avery's estate, the question was raised again. Did you have the right to dispose of his property? He had never aligned himself with us, choosing an American affiliation, but his roots were here in Europe. We are rather a closed group, steeped in tradition. But just as we have our ways, we respect those of others. When you were declared the Chosen One, it was decided to forever forego any act of retribution on Avery's behalf.

Another pause, another long pull at his glass. He wipes his lips with a silk handkerchief. The handkerchief comes away with a faint red smudge.

I watch his eyes as he speaks. *What is your point, Steffan? Are you asking that I respect you and stay out of European politics?*

A shiver runs up my spine at the moment I finish speaking. I look around quickly, senses alert. It's as if someone reached out a hand to run an icy finger up my backbone. Cold, first, then hot as the path of that finger turns to fire. The feeling unnerves me, as real and visceral as a passionate kiss. It awakens something deep and primitive in the pit of my stomach. Not fear. Not anger.

Lust.

My eyes scan the crowd. If Steffan is speaking, I don't hear. I've closed the conduit between us and to any other prying mind. I'm open only to whoever is causing this stirring in my gut. It's like nothing I've ever felt.

And in an instant, it's gone.

No one looks up from the crowd to catch my eye. No one winks or nods or grins a "gotcha" grin.

I drain my champagne glass, motion to the server for another. When I can focus again, Frey and Steffan are both looking at me with puzzled frowns.

Frey speaks first. "Anna? Are you all right?"

"Yes." I put a hand on his arm. "I felt dizzy for a moment. But I'm fine now." Switching my gaze to Steffan, I add, "I'm sorry. What was I saying?"

Steffan laughs. *I think you were about to put me in my place.*

His laughter is contagious. My own face splits into a grin. *Nothing so overt. Perhaps I merely wanted to remind you that there is more to the world than Europe. And if you act precipitously, we are all affected.*

Well said, Anna Strong.

My shoulders jump.

The unexpected voice comes from right behind me but I neither heard nor sensed an approach. The same gut tingling sensation as before spreads through my body, ice and fire. I know without looking that whoever just spoke is dark and dangerous.

And a threat.

CHAPTER 22

M Y FINGERS CLOSE AROUND THE CHAMPAGNE glass and with a crack, the fragile crystal shatters. Champagne sprays, my palm convulses and a shard of glass slices into my skin. Blood mixes with the bubbles spilling onto the polished hardwood floor. Both Frey and Steffan leap to my aid.

But not quickly enough.

Someone steps between us, taking my hand gently in his own. He pulls the sliver of glass free and brings my palm to his lips. His face is half-hidden by a veil of long, dark hair but instinctively, I know he's the stranger whose voice I heard before. Where his lips touch my palm, a tingling begins. It travels up my arm, warms my face and neck, makes my nipples harden. I close my eyes, wanting to moan with pleasure.

Another's hand is pushing the stranger away. When I open my eyes, Frey's face is red with fury. He puts an arm around my shoulders and leads me to a bench along the wall. I let him. Not looking back. Not wanting to see who it is that has such power over me.

Frey examines my hand. "It's healed."

There's nothing remarkable or magical in that. Vampires have the ability to heal. But it's the way Frey is looking at me, as if he knew I was feeling more than the healing process. I remember wanting to moan in pleasure—sexual pleasure.

Could I have actually done it? Moaned out loud at a stranger's touch?

Anger shakes me back to reality. "What the fuck?" I look into Frey's eyes.

Relief softens his face. "There you are. What the hell happened?"

I look past him to Steffan. He is talking with the stranger who has his back to me but Steffan's body is rigid, his face a mask of surprise and anger. All I see of the stranger is a long black duster that stands out in stark contrast to the formal dress of everyone else in the room. The coat brushes the tops of leather riding boots much as his long dark hair brushes the upturned collar of his coat. Even with my ability to penetrate most vampires' thoughts, this one is completely closed to me.

"Who is that with Steffan?" Not the question I really want to ask. But asking if this powerful vampire could be Vlad Dracul sounds like something out of a bad Goth novel even if it is what is going through my head.

Frey glances over his shoulder. "I don't know. Listen, maybe we should get out of here. This place gives me the creeps."

Frey stands up and extends a hand. I take it and get to

my feet. "I'm ready but where's Chael? We should tell him we're leaving."

Frey looks over the crowd. "I'll find him." Then his eyes focus on my face. "Are you sure you're all right?"

"Yes. Go."

"Okay. I won't be long."

I turn my back on Steffan and his mysterious guest and watch Frey work his way through the crowd. In a moment he's lost from view. I try to pick up Chael through mind links, but there are so many conversations going on, it's like trying to distinguish a single drop in a bucket of water. When I do focus on an exchange, all I get are snippets. Local gossip, some of it about me and my family; who's been turned recently; who's met with the second death. I pick up nothing about a take-over plan or a hint of dissension or unhappiness with Steffan.

Of course, we are in Steffan's house.

Anna?

Damn. Steffan is in my head. I don't want to turn around. I don't sense anyone with him but I didn't sense the creepy stranger before he grabbed my hand, either.

Creepy stranger? Over the centuries I've been called a lot of things but I do believe that's a first.

My shoulders bunch. I know I had shielded my thoughts. How was he able to hear?

Reluctantly, I force myself to turn. Slowly. And find myself staring up into a face that could have been sculpted from granite. Sharp angles at the jaw and chin, high cheekbones, a thin Roman nose that seems a physical trait of every European royal family. Only his eyes are soft. Deep brown with flecks of gold. They give character and compassion to an otherwise stern visage. There is too much steel in his bearing to call him handsome. His hair is too unruly to be stylish; his clothes under the coat not fashionable or couture.

But there is something. He has *presence*. What the old ones might call *gravitas*.

Even so, I find myself wondering if this could possibly have been the man who affected me so dramatically a moment or so ago. In spite of it all, standing before me so solemn and serious, he seems—*ordinary*.

Steffan pulls me back, frowning in concern. "Are you feeling better?"

Shit. It's the second time I've shown weakness and both times it was because of the vampire standing beside Steffan. I drag my eyes to Steffan's face at the same time the stranger says to him, *You may leave us.*

Steffan moves off without another word, crossing the floor into the great room and disappearing into the crowd. It's unnerving.

Then the stranger turns back to me, extends a hand. *Vlad Dracul, former prince of Wallachia. Ordinary? First creepy, then ordinary? I must be losing my touch.*

Embarrassed, I force myself to take his hand. The smile on his face sends blood rushing to mine. He knows everything I'm thinking—everything I'd been thinking since he approached. It overcomes my sense of astonishment that I am face-to-face with the legend.

As our hands touch, I steel myself for another thunderbolt of sexual heat, determined not to react this time.

Nothing happens. We shake briefly, then both step back. I want to laugh with relief. And he grins. Shit. He's done it again. Gritting my teeth, I snarl, *I'd appreciate it if you'd get out of my head.*

Sorry, he says. *Force of habit.*

You can read anyone?

Anyone, anytime.

Is there anyway to turn you off?

Only if I wish it.

Great. How do I get him to wish it?

I doubt you could.

This time my skin flushes with anger instead of embarrassment. I turn away to scan the crowd again for Frey. The sooner we get out of here the better.

He will return in a short while.

The simple pronouncement raises goose bumps on my skin.

Where is Frey? What have you done with him?

He holds up his hands. *Nothing. Please don't alarm yourself. He is with friends. Fellow shifters, in fact. They are having a very pleasant conversation.*

But he was coming right back. He is not the kind to be easily distracted.

He taps a finger against his forehead. *He has many admirable qualities, but he can be controlled. I'm sure you know that.*

The next instant, it's as if he's linked directly into my brain and is replaying a scene from the car ride on a screen that only he and I are privy to. It's the standoff between Frey and Chael.

My temper flares at the intrusion. *I don't control Frey. Chael is a nuisance not worthy of his wrath.*

I agree. But all the same, it is because of you he backed down.

No. It's because he was smart enough to realize the time wasn't right.

As you wish.

His smugness pushes me over the edge. *Is this what you do, Vlad? After hundreds of years on this earth the only way you can get off is playing little mind games? You're not much better than a common Peeping Tom.*

I expect to get some kind of knee-jerk reaction—most likely negative—from a six-hundred-year-old vampire who is obviously used to running the show. So I brace myself. And I play a little mind game of my own. I use his same technique, linking our minds to let him see how I vanquished Lance's sire—one who purported to be a direct "descendant" of Vlad—months ago here in France.

But there is little reaction.

Just a casual lifting of his shoulders. *I do not know this Julian Underwood. Through the centuries there have been many who claim I was their sire.* He smiles. *It is like your wonderful Woodstock festival—if everyone who says they attended actually did, the numbers would have been staggering.*

Then he sobers. *But you acted righteously in bringing an end to this vampire. Histories written about my own mortal life portray me as an indiscriminate butcher. Very seldom is it noted that I strengthened my country's economy, improved life for the peasants, built an army. Sometimes being a leader means doing what no one else is willing to.*

I find myself staring. Okay, so I didn't get the reaction I was expecting but what was the point of this trip down memory lane? What is he trying to tell me?

There is a rustle from the great room, anxious voices, a shuffling of feet. Vlad takes my shoulders and turns me so that I'm facing into the room.

Steffan is being pulled into the center of the floor by three Hulk-like figures. Chains, huge silver links that even Steffan as an old-soul vampire cannot break, bind him. His face is battered and bleeding. Behind him, six more vampires are led in, tied together with the same kind of chains. Their clothes are torn, blood seeping through the ripped fabric.

My breath catches in my throat. *What is happening?*

But Vlad is no longer by my side. Moving faster than the eye can follow, he has left me to reappear beside Steffan.

And in his hand he holds a sword. A curved blade with a jeweled scabbard. One side of the blade is smooth, the other jagged like the teeth of a shark.

From somewhere behind me, a hand touches my arm. A voice whispers in my ear, "It's me."

Frey. Without turning, I pull him close. I can't seem to draw my eyes away from the spectacle taking place in front of us.

Frey follows my gaze. "I guess Chael wasn't bullshitting us after all. The sword—it's a Turkish kilij. Reputed to have been Vlad Dracul's weapon of choice."

I don't have to ask how he knows this. As Keeper of the Secrets, he has studied the history of the supernatural down through the ages.

"Do you know what is happening?" I ask.

"Not everything. But from what I gather, Vlad is not happy with Steffan's power play."

"I thought Steffan was their leader." My voice sounds strained and incredulous.

"Evidently only serving at Vlad's pleasure. And Vlad

was not pleased at the idea of bringing about a revolution, no matter how carefully orchestrated."

Vlad has raised his arms, calling for quiet. It takes less than a heartbeat for it to be achieved. He lowers his arms and starts to speak, pacing as he does.

Some of you know why I am here tonight. He glances back at a cowering Steffan. *Certainly not because I was invited. I was made aware of a plot being spun, a plot involving Steffan and those you see behind him. It was a crafty plan. A plan to integrate vampires into every office in every country in Europe with the aim of asserting domination.*

It would take time, part of the plan's cleverness. When full assimilation occurred, this generation of mortals would be in the ground. There would be no bloodbath, just a gradual assumption of power. So gradual, mortals would not be aware of what was happening until it was too late.

Vlad pauses, as if appreciating how that must sound to a gathering of vampires. I listen transfixed, impressed by his intuitiveness. He *knows* what they're all thinking, just as I do: the many who are thankful that they have not been included with the hapless ones bound together inside the circle; those who are asking why the plan would not work and seeing no negative side to it; the wiser, older ones who know what would happen if the seemingly flawless plan was put into action.

Vlad finds my eyes. He nods and I know it is to the latter that he will address his remarks. He begins to speak again.

We are arrogant, we vampires. We think that because we are immortal, we should reign over all life on earth. But mortals are smarter than we give them credit for. It is to them that we owe much of the earthly delights we enjoy. A smart vampire once said that man has created the world we vampires merely inhabit. We lack the wisdom of mortals because we lack the urgency to create and innovate.

His last words give me a jolt. He is quoting my speech before the Council. How could he know about it?

Vlad looks at me and smiles and sends the answer right into my head. *Chael, of course.*

I smile back. Chael. Of course. I look around. Wonder where the sneaky little bugger is right now. For this at least, I owe him an apology.

Vlad continues to speak. *But the very worst thing that can happen will inevitably happen. At some point, we will expose ourselves to mortals. Then predator becomes prey. It's happened before. During the Crusades, the Inquisition. Those among you who lived it know.*

Throughout the room, heads bob, soft voices murmur an affirmation. Vlad recognizes them and continues.

There are billions of humans. Our numbers are small in comparison. How long do you think we will last when we have bounties on our heads? We have survived this long because we have been content to hide our true nature. We have assimilated in a way that allows us to walk among our symbiotic human partners unmolested. To pursue any type of lifestyle we wish. Why threaten a system that has brought us peace and prosperity? It is my contention that we should not.

A pause as those mesmerizing eyes sweep the crowd. I know it's not possible that he is connecting individually with everyone in the ballroom and yet, when he raises the sword again and shouts, "Who is with me?" another murmur starts at the fringes of the crowd and crescendos. Shouts of "Vlad" and "Dracul" echo off the walls. He holds both arms high in acknowledgment.

Good. It is settled. We continue to live in peace.

He faces Steffan and a hush once again descends—complete and immediate, like the throwing of a switch. It's as if Vlad is controlling the crowd with nothing but the power of suggestion.

Steffan, however, is feeling something quite different from the rest. Fear rolls off him in waves as visceral as smoke. He blanches and cringes back under Vlad's gaze.

Vlad once more begins to speak. *Steffan, I have long given you free reign to serve our community as you will. You have taken advantage of my generosity, even proclaiming yourself a king. That I could overlook. But now you have put the well-being of the entire European Vampire League at risk. That is an arrogance that cannot go unpunished. You must pay for such treachery. As the eldest of our tribe, I condemn you to the second death.*

Those closest to Steffan step back. Steffan sees the reaction and his eyes sweep the crowd. No one comes to Steffan's defense, not a word is raised in protest of Vlad's proclamation. The hush that descends on the crowd becomes even more intense but it is intermingled with a sense of relief—relief that it is only Steffan and the six who have been singled out for punishment.

Vlad reads the crowd, too, and I have the feeling he is taking stock of those who think they have escaped his notice.

Steffan's body stiffens at the realization of all he has lost and a new emotion radiates from him. Anger.

But there isn't time to reflect or react to what Steffan is feeling.

Faster than a heartbeat, Vlad swings his sword.

CHAPTER 23

A COLLECTIVE GASP GOES UP AS STEFFAN'S HEAD separates from his body. Blood geysers for the instant it takes the vampire's body to die. The blood turns to red ash and falls like a gentle rain over those standing nearest to Vlad and Steffan.

I've never seen a vampire die like this. Steffan's body bursts into flame, then crumbles into dust so quickly, there's soon nothing left but a few remnants of fabric not caught in the maelstrom. I find myself clutching Frey's arm, horrified but unable to look away.

But there's another reason I stand transfixed. At the moment the sword touched Steffan's flesh, there was a flash. A fleeting burst of energy. My skin crawls. Did anyone else . . . ? I grasp Frey's hand as the implication hits me.

"What's wrong?" he asks.

"Steffan." My voice is barely a whisper. "I don't think he's gone."

My eyes search the crowd. I don't know what I'm looking for but I'm guessing Steffan has made the leap, just as Avery had when I staked him. Just before *his* body dissolved to ash. Avery picked another species, a werewolf, to inhabit. I didn't know it then. But if Avery could do it, and if Steffan had a suspicion Vlad might show himself tonight . . .

A lot of ifs. Still, I search out the shifters standing transfixed to one side.

"Frey. Weren't there five shifters when we came in?"

He nods, his gaze following mine.

"There are only four now. We need to talk to Vlad."

I start for the staircase, Frey at my side.

Vlad has turned to the six coconspirators huddling like frightened rabbits between their captors. I have no idea who these vampires are or how long they have been on this earth, but it is clear from the fear on their faces that mortal or immortal, facing death in some brings out cowardice.

Except in my mother. Unbidden, the thought flashes through my mind. My mother is facing death heroically.

Vlad senses my approach. He turns to face me. *What is it? Steffan. I don't think he is gone.*

There is no hesitation on his part. *Transmutation? If that's what it's called.*

The conversation is between just the two of us. Around us, the crowd grows restive.

Vlad casts his eyes around the room. *I must finish this. The others must see. Then we can talk.*

He doesn't wait for my acknowledgment or concurrence.

He approaches the six. His bearing, authoritative, commanding, makes me remember the name he was given after his death, the name Frey called him . . . Vlad Ţepeş. Vlad the Impaler. I catch the fevered thoughts of his captors and they are thinking of the stories, too. It's hard to reconcile the man in the duster who talked so passionately about living in peace with the images of a bearded, steely-eyed tyrant who is reputed to have killed thousands.

Vlad stops and turns to look at me. *Would you free these six?*

I shouldn't have been startled that he had been reading my thoughts. He'd already demonstrated his prowess. Still, I take a moment to choose my words before replying.

Are they are a threat?

These six? They are Steffan's sycophants.

Then perhaps you can win the loyalty of those present by showing mercy.

He flashes a smile. *Would it win yours?*

My loyalty? I have others to whom I owe my loyalty. But it would demonstrate that we share a common bond: the willingness to protect our worlds—vampire and mortal—with . . .

Another smile as he finishes my thought. *Justice tempered with mercy?*

I nod.

Vlad gestures to the guards on either side to remove the chains. Still uncertain as to their fate, the vampires remain hunched together, heads bowed, shoulders slumped.

You are free to go, Vlad says simply, dismissively. *But you are banished from Europe. If you return, it is in peril of your lives. Do not go to your homes. Your belongings are forfeit. They will be sold and the money used to ferret out the mortals working in concert with Steffan.*

He walks slowly as he talks, pausing in front of each vampire as he makes his pronouncement. One by one, they look up at him, whether by their own volition or because he is mentally compelling them, I can't tell. There is no relief on their faces. Banishment is almost as dreadful in their minds as death. But they are all resigned to their fate. No one is willing to argue or plead.

Vlad motions to the guard. *Take them to the boat docks at Marseilles. Give them enough money to book passage on the first ship out to . . .* He glances back at me again, telegraphing his intention before giving voice to it. *Any ex-Soviet republic. I will alert Alexi to expect them. He knows how to deal with insurrectionists.*

I'm impressed with Vlad's knowledge of the world outside his own domain. Alexi is one of the heads of the Thirteen Vampire Tribes. I met him when I was declared the Chosen One and I remember his stern, unyielding posture and harsh, uncompromising demeanor. Vlad has picked his choice of "jailer" for the six well.

The six are shuffled off; Vlad is surrounded by sycophants of his own. Whether they agree with his decision or not, no one is letting anything but admiration and pledges of loyalty color their thoughts. Steffan's ashes are trampled underfoot as the orchestra resumes playing and glasses are refilled.

I stir restlessly. *Vlad, we must talk.*

His eyes meet mine. He nods, excuses himself and leads Frey and I off to the side of the hall.

"Tell me."

"I saw a burst of energy at the moment your sword touched his flesh."

"And you know of transmutation?"

"I didn't know what it was called then." I pass a hand over my face. "I'd never heard the term before but I know what it is. Transmutation is an ability possessed by only the oldest vampires to leave their bodies at the moment of the second death. I have first-hand knowledge. Avery."

He pauses, as if turning the idea over in his mind. "I hadn't heard. You were not hurt?"

"Not because he didn't try. He used a friend's body as host—a werewolf. Then tried to coerce her through pain to attack me."

"But you vanquished him."

I think back to that terrible scene in the basement of Avery's house. Avery had possessed the werewolf Sandra, tried to force her to attack me. She had the will and strength to resist and in doing so, drove Avery from her body to perish.

"No. The were vanquished him. I think Steffan used the same tactics. There were five shape-shifters when we arrived here. There are four now."

Vlad looks to Frey. "Do you know the shifters you were talking to?"

Frey shakes his head. "Met them for the first time tonight. But they seemed to know each other."

"Then we need to speak with them." Vlad waves a hand and a vampire steps to his side. "The shifters. Bring them to the library."

The guard leaves and another memory from that terrible time with Avery surfaces. "There must be a talisman. Something of the shifter's that Steffan now possesses. For the werewolf, it was the talisman she wore to effect the change. I don't know what it would be for this shifter. But I'd bet he took something that belonged to one of them. It's what makes the magic work."

"Magic." Vlad sniffs. "More like devilry."

VLAD LEADS US ACROSS THE BALLROOM AND through a door at the far wall. He is obviously familiar with Steffan's home and we find ourselves in a large square room lined on three walls with floor-to-ceiling bookcases and on a fourth with a fireplace and raised hearth. Next to the hearth is a paneled bar.

Vlad shuts the door behind us and goes to the bar. He pours some dark amber liquid into three heavy, squat glasses. He keeps one for himself and pushes the others toward Frey and me. Frey picks one up, hands me the other. The aroma is heady and smells of oak and vanilla.

Frey takes a sip, rolls it around in his mouth, swallows. "Whiskey. Good stuff."

"The best," Vlad agrees. "Fit for a king."

I lay the glass untouched on the bar. "I'm a beer gal," I say.

Vlad raises an eyebrow but says nothing.

In another moment, the door opens. Vlad's guard escorts the four shape-shifters into the room and bows an exit.

Vlad continues to sip, his eyes focusing like lasers on the faces of the four men.

They look to Frey and I wonder what thoughts are transmitting themselves between them. They don't appear nervous. Only curious and maybe a tiny bit uncertain. They are all dressed, as were the vampires in attendance, in formal

wear, tuxes, silk shirts, colorful cummerbunds and handker-
chiefs. They are clean-shaven, all dark haired, three look to
be in their late twenties. The fourth is older, forty maybe,
hair touched with gray at the temples. They are handsome
in a tough, old-style-gangster way, more Italian than French.

There is no indication that Vlad frightens them. They
are not vampire, after all, and it is improbable that they
would have played a part in Steffan's scheme. Steffan was
old school, relegating any species other than vampire to the
ranks of the subservient.

So why did Steffan invite them tonight?

Vlad's thoughts echo my own. *Why indeed?*

Once again, he is following my thoughts without my
being aware that he is doing so. I heave an irritated sigh and
turn to Frey.

"Do they speak English?"

Frey nods. To the men, he says, "This is Anna Strong
and Vlad Țepeș."

I glance at Frey. He has purposely used the name associated with the historically cruel figure instead of the more
benign "Dracul." And it gets a reaction from the shifters.
Worried glances exchanged one to the other. Finally, one
speaks.

"Why have we been called to speak with Vlad Țepeș?"
asks the one who looks to be the older of the four. He
speaks English with an accent I can't place. "We are only
invited guests. We have nothing to do with what transpired
with Steffan."

The three behind him stir and nod in quick agreement.

Vlad smiles. "We do not accuse you of being a part of
Steffan's intrigue."

His voice is as smooth as his oily smile. It makes my blood run cold and I am not on the receiving end of his attention. I see a bit of the legend now and wonder . . .

Vlad continues. "Why were you invited? What connection did you have to Steffan?"

The four look at each other. Once again, the one who appears older than the others speaks. "We are not sure why we were invited. The invitation came by way of messenger only yesterday. It said as leaders of the shifter bands we were to be in attendance at a grand convocation. An announcement was to made that would affect us all—vampire and shifter alike."

Vlad raises his eyebrows. "What connection is there between vampires and shifters? I know of no such alliance."

This time, a spark of concern flashes in the eyes of the shifter. "Recently, Steffan reached out to our community. We were not aware he was violating any accord in doing so."

"What did he ask of you?"

"Nothing." The shifter glances back and meets the eyes of the others. All nod in quick agreement. "We supposed he wanted to widen the circle of his sphere to include all supernaturals. We were not aware it was only shifters that he approached."

Vlad takes another slow drink from his glass. The silence hangs heavy, seems interminable.

What are you doing? I finally ask Vlad.

Waiting, is his curt reply.

The numbing quiet stretches on.

Frey shifts at my side. His patience is growing short.

So is mine.

If we wait too much longer, Steffan is going to get away, I remind Vlad.

It won't be much longer. Watch their eyes. They are communicating among themselves. Can Frey understand what they're saying?

Frey must have answered in the negative because Vlad is shaking his head.

Unfortunate that there is not communication among shifters as there is among vampires. Frey has no knowledge of the language they're speaking.

I sigh. Vampires think communication is like Esperanto . . . universal to all.

Vlad continues, *But Frey did say the timbre of the conversation is becoming heated. I don't think it will be long now.*

Vlad is right. The spokesmen for the group steps forward once again.

"We do not know what plan Steffan had for us. But one unusual thing transpired tonight that we will share with you as a token of our goodwill. One of our ranks, Louis Archambault, disappeared shortly after you . . ." He clears his throat, starts again. "After the unfortunate scene with Steffan."

"Disappeared?" Vlad's tone is sharp.

"We were all transfixed, as you might imagine, by what was taking place in front of us. When it was over, we noticed that Archambault was gone. None of us saw him leave nor did he tell us where he was going." He looks away, almost as if afraid to continue, but feels he must. "We thought he was overcome by the brutality. It may indeed be the case."

Vlad ignores the knife-sharp accusation, "Where does Archambault live?"

"Near Paris. Asnières-sur-Seine." He rattles off a street address.

"If he took a car," I say to Vlad, "we could beat him cross-country."

Vlad crosses to the door and, opening it, calls to his guard. He snaps something in French and the guard disappears, to return an eye blink later. His answer brings a smile to Vlad's lips.

"His car is gone."

Frey addresses himself to the shifters. "What form does Archambault take?"

"Bear," the spokesman answers.

Frey's expression is almost blissful as he looks at me. "A challenge. It's been a long time."

"No, Frey," I snap back at him. "It's too dangerous. You can't come."

But Frey has already retreated to a corner behind the bar. We hear rustling and I know he's stripping off his clothes in preparation for making the change.

I sigh. Unless I'm prepared to hog-tie him, arguing with Frey when he's made up his mind is useless.

Vlad is waving a hand to dismiss the shifters when I stop him. There is still one more piece of the puzzle to snap in place.

"Did something happen tonight between Archambault and Steffan?" I ask. "Did Steffan borrow something of Archambault's maybe or—?"

One of the younger of the shifters speaks up for the first time. He looks to his friends. "The tie?"

"Tie?" I say encouragingly. "What happened with the tie?"

His face reddens. "It seems Steffan liked Archambault's tie better than the one he was wearing. He asked if they might trade. At the time we all laughed, it seemed silly. But the two did trade. And Steffan put Archambault's tie on immediately."

I nod to Vlad. He waves the shifters off and they waste no time beating a hasty retreat back to the party.

"Well, at least we have more than suspicion. Even if Steffan's leap to Archambault was unsuccessful, he was planning on trying it if things didn't go his way."

I pause as another thought strikes me. "Which means Steffan must have suspected you might show up tonight."

Vlad shrugs. "Ours is a tight-knit community. There are those whose allegiance to me is strong. Word can and does pass both ways."

"And was it Chael who told you of Steffan's plan?" I speak the words without giving them conscious thought. Chael played a major role in getting me here. And his cryptic words in the car about history to be made all make sense now.

"Chael is a friend," Vlad replies.

He says nothing more.

The rustling in the corner stops. Frey emerges, a sleek black panther, and flashes us a green-eyed greeting—a growl emanating from deep within his chest.

He pushes against my legs until my hand lies on the top of his head.

Vlad watches, a smile touching the corner of his lips. "I may have been wrong about your panther," he says. "He is not so biddable as I thought."

Frey snaps in Vlad's direction and I swear, I see him smile.

Vlad looks down at himself, then over to me. *We are not so fortunate as your cat. We cannot shed our human forms, but we can shed these clothes. Steffan has a gymnasium in the house, which means he must have something we can use to make our travels more comfortable. Come.*

Once again Frey and I follow Vlad through another door and up a staircase to the second floor. Frey bounds up the stairs with feline grace. Every time I see him in this form I'm amazed at the powerful muscles that ripple under midnight black fur. He is beautiful. My heart races. And mortal. I will protect him at all costs tonight.

The "gymnasium," as Vlad called it, is in fact an exercise room: recumbent bike, free weights, a treadmill. Attached is a shower room and then another door that leads into what I guess is Steffan's bedroom.

Not what I would have imagined a "king's bedchamber" to be. It is spartan. A plain bed of rustic wood, a huge armoire with simple lines, a writing desk. And yet, a search of the closet and armoire yields Steffan's clothes, finely tailored suits, slacks, silk shirts of the palest hues. In a drawer, we finally find what we are looking for. Sweatpants and shirts, sports shoes.

Vlad hands me a sweatshirt and pants, a pair of socks and a pair of Steffan's shoes. *They may be too big,* he says, *although I have found American women to have surprisingly large feet.*

I would object but for the fact that Steffan's shoes look to be a pretty good fit. I head back for the shower room to change. As I shut the door, I see Frey take up position in front of the door and it brings a smile.

When I've changed, I lay the dress Steffan bought for me on the bed, reflecting that I never thanked him for the gift.

A moot point now.

CHAPTER 24

VLAD, FREY AND I LEAVE THROUGH A BACK EN-
trance. The house being perched on the top of the hill
makes the first part of our journey effortless. Downhill all
the way, we easily pace each other, panther and vampire.
Vlad is our guide. He knows the countryside, and once we
reach the main highway to Paris, he keeps us to underbrush
when we can find it or out-of-the-way back roads when we
can't. An auto trip of five hundred miles takes about eight
hours. We should make it in three.

Vlad and I exchange very little communication during
our race. He once comments that I have remarkable stamina for a new vampire. That gets a chortling snort from
Frey and no comment at all from me.

The countryside goes by in a blur. I can't distinguish
village from town from city. It's still dead of night and at

our speed, even farmland and gently rising hillock flow under our feet and paws like a smooth river. The star-dazzled clear sky above is a Milky-Way smudge. It's a most wonderful feeling—as close to flying as an earthbound, flesh-and-blood being is likely to get.

My worry that Frey would be unable to keep up with us is unfounded. He sometimes bounds ahead like a frisky puppy off the leash and I realize we, he and I, need to make sure we set ourselves free like this on a regular basis.

It's almost as satisfying as sex.

Then you must not be doing it right.

Vlad. Impertinent and insolent as ever.

Keep out of my head.

I can't help it. You American women think such delicious thoughts. Like children, whatever pops in your mind, you express.

My mind, Vlad. My mind. You don't find me violating your privacy.

He chuckles. *You should. Oh, the things I could teach you. Frey would thank me.*

Frey would chew you up.

So provincial. Wait until you've been around as long as I have. Morality becomes an archaic concept.

And love? Does that become an archaic concept as well?

No reply. Vlad turns his thoughts off like a curtain coming down. Good.

We're approaching the outskirts of Paris. Vlad stops and Frey and I gather near him.

"Archambault lives in a northwestern suburb of Paris. Rue de Château is a main street. We have beat him by many hours. We will go directly to the address. We can rest there and wait for him to show up."

Frey presses against my legs and I scratch the top of his head. An act that sets Vlad to laughing.

"A girl and her pet," he snorts.

Frey raises a paw and growls a retort.

ARCHAMBAULT'S HOME TURNS OUT TO BE A BIG VILLA on a street studded with them. It is approaching three in the morning yet there are lights on inside. We can only guess that he must have called ahead to let someone know he was returning—perhaps a servant. Or a wife. I realize we should have asked for more particulars about his household.

Too late now.

The house has a huge walled garden in the rear. Frey bounds over the fence easily. In a moment, he is back, taking my hand in his mouth to pull me toward the yard.

"I think it's clear," I tell Vlad.

Frey is gone again, clearing the six-foot-plus wall in one graceful leap. I follow, Vlad close behind. We alight in a garden, newly planted along one wall, centered by a stretch of green lawn, bordered on two other sides by flowers and what look like fruit trees. Nothing much in the way of shelter. But Frey has already found a place between the greenery of some big, flowering vines and a cherry tree. He lays down and looks up at me. I snuggle next to him, my head on his chest. He nuzzles the top of my head before letting his body relax. His breathing becomes deep and regular, his heartbeat slows. In a moment, he is asleep.

Vlad has picked a spot a few yards away to hunker

down, his back against the trunk of a willow tree. I feel him watching.

You should get some rest, too, I tell him.

I don't require that much sleep anymore, he responds. *One of the benefits of age. But you should close your eyes. I'll stand guard.*

There is a moment of silence and just as I'm drifting off, Vlad's voice is in my head once more.

How did you know it was Avery who possessed your friend? he asks.

She was not a friend, is my immediate reply. *Far from it. She was another victim of Avery's. But at first, I didn't believe it was possible—transmutation. Until Avery started to manifest himself in the were more and more, giving himself away with cruel words and acts. He tried to coerce a friend of his host's to kill me and when that didn't work, set the werewolf upon me himself. It was only because the host he chose was strong enough to thwart him that he was vanquished.*

Vlad is quiet. I let a moment go by before I ask, *How will we know for sure if Steffan is present in Archambault?*

Steffan is nothing if not egotistical, Vlad replies. *I think he will give himself away the moment he sees us. He will want us to know how clever he has been.*

I let another moment pass. *How will we kill him? With Avery, with the werewolf, he was defeated because he could not stop Sandra from changing. With a shifter, there is no imperative to change. He could remain in the shifter's body for as long as he wants.* Another thought strikes me. *I don't know if he could impart immortality to a host, do you? If he can, and he's smart, he will not give himself away to us.*

Vlad chuckles softly. At the sound, Frey stirs and opens his eyes. I stroke his head and the panther relaxes again, falling back into a deep sleep.

If only it were so easy for me.

Vlad is watching us again. *I think I was mistaken. You two may be well suited after all.*

I take that as a compliment.

You should. I haven't met too many mixed-species couples that have made it work. Your strengths balance each other's. You are strong, a leader. He is strong in his own way, but a follower.

I bristle. *Frey has his own mind. If anything, he gives me strength. He is clear-headed and loyal—*

Vlad raises a hand. *I was not disparaging your mate. To the contrary, I was complimenting him. You have chosen well and I hope you have many good years together.*

Not what I was expecting. I release a breath. Let my mind wander back to the problem at hand. *Why did you laugh when I asked if Steffan could impart immortality to a host?*

Vlad rests his chin in his hands. *Because I cannot answer you. It is unclear.*

Unclear? In all your years on this earth, you have never known a vampire who transmuted and continued in his host as an immortal?

No. Vlad's clipped answer is followed by a brief pause, during which he climbs from his crouched position and stretches his arms over his head. When he feels my mind probing for more, he continues.

Vampires who transmute do it because they are escaping—someone. In every case of which I am aware,

*the someone they are escaping eventually catches up to
them. It may seem a good choice at the time, but inevitably
it leads to permanent death.*

For the vampire, surely. But what about the host?

*I do not know the shifter Steffan chose as his host. If he
was a willing participant in the plan, he accepted the risk.*

And if he was not a willing participant?

In the dark, I see Vlad shrug. *It makes no difference,
does it? The only way we can be sure Steffan is gone is to
destroy the host and its parasite.*

CHAPTER 25

I FINALLY DRIFT OFF, UNEASY THOUGHTS OF WHAT lies ahead for us transforming themselves into uneasy dreams in which Avery and Steffan lie in wait. I had reason to want Avery dead. I can't even remember what Steffan's host looks like. I had only one brief glimpse of the five shifters standing together when we walked into Steffan's party. Their attention had been on Frey.

Frey.

I absently run my hand along his sleek neck. If Steffan's shifter goes after him, I will gladly end both their lives. We have a wedding—

I bolt upright. We've been gone almost eight hours. What are my parents going to think when they wake up and find us gone?

Shit. I look at my watch. It's close to five. If Steffan and

Archambault are traveling by car it will be another four hours at least before they get here. Frey and I have an appointment this afternoon with the officiates of our wedding ceremony.

Shit. Shit. Shit.

This is not supposed to be happening.

Frey and I are supposed to be at home with our families.

What was I thinking agreeing to come with Vlad?

As if speaking his name in my head is an invitation, here he is.

I'm sorry I have usurped time with your family. I promise we will end this thing as quickly as possible and I will get you and Frey back to your family.

In a few hours, they will miss us. We don't even know if Steffan is on his way here. I can't believe I let myself get dragged into this.

Did you have a choice? Vlad's tone is shock with a touch of annoyance. *Weren't you the one who first uttered the eloquent words I quoted today about protecting humanity?*

I close my eyes, breathe in and out. Yes. Damn it. And thanks to Chael, here I am.

Chael.

Do you have a cell phone with you? I ask Vlad.

He digs one out of a pocket.

I don't suppose you have Chael's number?

No. But I have the next best thing. He punches some numbers into his phone. There is just a moment's hesitation before he is speaking rapid-fire French to whoever answered on the other end. He holds the phone away from his ear. *Shall I have Chael tell your parents that you took a romantic last-minute road trip to Paris? We'll say you'll be home by early afternoon.*

Can we be home by early afternoon?

I will see to it.

Miserably, I nod.

Vlad finishes his call. *My assistant,* he explains. *He will take care of everything.*

I mumble a thank-you, but it's without heart. What if something happened to my mother last night? I'm miles away with no way to get back until we've taken care of—

Frey suddenly comes awake with a growl. At the same time, Vlad jumps to my side. An outside light has come on over the front door. We steal across the yard to get a better look.

A cab is pulling up to the curb in front of Archambault's house. The door opens and the shifter steps out.

Vlad shakes his head. *Of course. He must have flown to the party from Paris. The car was to take him back to the airport.*

A thrill of relief washes over me—small and maybe inconsequential. But at least our wait is over.

Vlad cuts my optimism short. Archambault pays the driver and is turning toward the house when he suddenly stops. He is still shrouded in shadow from the trees lining his street, but this is the first chance I've had to really look at him.

Bear is an appropriate totem for the huge hulk of a man dressed in a tux that had to have been customized to accommodate his six-foot-six, three-hundred-pound frame. His complexion is coarse, features blunted, lips drawn and thin. He is breathing through his mouth, teeth bared, as if his flat nose is merely a placeholder on his face and has no useful purpose. Suddenly, he raises that nose, sniffing the air, adding to the illusion that we are watching an animal.

Does he sense Frey, the panther, hiding in his garden?

I reach down to touch Frey, an unconscious gesture to reassure myself that he is here, beside me. The panther is crouched and growling so softly, no human ear would pick it up.

I look to Vlad. *What now?*

Maybe he'll make it easy for us, Vlad says. *Come through the back into the garden.*

But Archambault doesn't accommodate us. After a long moment, he continues up the front walk to his door. From our viewpoint, we hear but cannot see a female greeting him and the closing of the door as they go inside.

Shit.

Could you tell if it was Steffan? I ask Vlad.

He shakes his head.

What now? Impatience sharpens my tone. *Maybe I should walk right up to his door and see if he recognizes me. Steffan would. I doubt Archambault could. We were never introduced. At least we'd know for sure if we were on the right track.*

Frey suddenly tenses beside me. No longer growling softly, he rumbles a warning as the back door is flung open. I reach down to steady him, eyes on the rectangle of light spilling into the yard.

No longer wearing his tux jacket, Archambault steps into the garden. "Is that you, Anna Strong?" he asks in a voice instantly recognizable. "I should have known with your experience, you might suspect I'd have an escape plan."

I motion for Frey and Vlad to stay hidden and step forward to the center of the garden.

"You and Avery have a lot in common, Steffan." I smile. "How did you know I was here?"

He touches the tip of his nose. "Funny thing. As a vampire, I had many heightened sensibilities. I never appreciated that of smell. Seems it's one of the few I have left now in this form. Your perfume in the car the other day, and tonight, it is memorable."

He is holding a wineglass and he takes a sip. "Why have you come here? I have been effectively neutralized, have I not? I will spend eternity in the cumbersome body of this ignorant shifter." He gestures toward the house behind him. "Hardly the domicile of a king."

"Ah, but you have plans, don't you? Like Avery, you would never be content to remain an *ignorant shifter*."

"Perhaps." Another sip of wine, a slow smile. "But that is not your concern. You are here for a short while and then you will return to America. Don't let me interrupt those plans. It would not be in your, or your fiancé's, best interest."

He gestures toward the corner where Frey and Vlad wait. "You know, I could have taken your pet. That would have been interesting, would it not? And not without it's pleasurable aspects. But I have no desire to be consort to the Chosen One."

"A wise choice, Steffan. Though a shortsighted one. I have no reason now to delay ending your existence."

He smiles. "Think carefully before taking action, Anna. After all, one funeral in a family is hard enough. It would devastate your father should he lose a daughter as well as a wife."

I don't sense Frey approach until he attacks. Like a specter, he rushes by on silent paws and launches himself at Archambault, fangs bared. Archambault retreats back, Frey clawing his way up his torso to snap at his neck.

"Frey, no."

But my words are lost in the thunder of his growls. Frey has tasted blood and he continues to rake at Archambault.

Instinctively, the shifter under attack loses control. Clothes shred as bone and sinew transform themselves into fur and muscle. Archambault's face contorts, snout forming with teeth as sharp and fearsome as Frey's. His head on a stout neck transforms into the round-eared mask of a polar bear and when he shakes Frey off with a huge paw, the panther is flung to the far wall.

Terror clutches at my heart as Frey lies still among the newly turned earth of a flower bed. Behind me, the bear roars, but my eyes remain fixed to Frey's still form. At last, he stirs. And when he looks up at me, I know. It's time.

CHAPTER 26

THE VAMPIRE UNLEASHES HERSELF WITH A SNARL. Vlad is instantly beside me. *Take care of Frey,* I tell him.

He doesn't argue or question. He moves away. When he is at Frey's side, I turn to the bear.

There is enough of Anna's consciousness left to make vampire wonder if it is Steffan or Archambault in control. No matter.

Vampire circles the beast. He watches her, wary. He makes no move to attack as if uncertain what type of animal he faces. That is fine with me. I, vampire, will choose the attack before he can make up his mind.

I glance to Frey. The other vampire has opened a wrist and is holding it to the cat's mouth. His own eyes are slit, too, like the cat's, like mine. Good. His blood will heal the panther.

A low rumbling sound from behind me. Bear is sounding a warning.

I turn. He has pulled himself to his full height, towering over me. He is snarling, showing his teeth. He waves paws with claws half a foot long in my face.

A plan forms. I need bear on the ground if I am to get to what I need. I reach up, grab one of the paws and, stepping back, twist until I hear the shoulder pop and the paw go limp. Bear screams and rakes at me with his good paw, but he does not fall.

I circle behind him. He stays with me. His useless paw hangs limp at his side, but the good one continues to stretch toward me, thrashing the air with those razor-sharp claws. One swipe connects, a blaze of red-hot pain sears my chest. Blood begins to seep through the rip in my shirt.

Blood.

My blood.

It awakens the lust. With a roar, I rush forward, catching the bear around his middle and throwing him to the ground.

I jump back, out of his reach. He squirms on the ground, gathering himself to stand. Before he can get legs under him, I am behind him. I bury my face in the thick fur, shielding it from the paw raking at me. I work my arms around his neck until my forearm is under his snout. I squeeze.

Bear bucks and twists. He slams me against the ground. He rears and kicks. I hold on—exerting more and more pressure until his attempts to shake me off weaken. Then, when I know the time is right, I shift my weight, grab his head with both hands. And wrench.

A sound, like the popping of dry wood. One ragged breath.

Stillness.

I back away. The bloodlust is unsatisfied. I kneel to open a vein, curious what the blood of bear will taste like.

"Anna!"

Vlad's voice from the corner of the garden. I look up. A woman has come into the garden. She is holding a shotgun and its barrel is pointed at my chest.

I see her finger tighten on the trigger, feel a draft of air as something rushes past me.

Frey. He knocks her to the ground, the gun spinning from her grasp as it discharges into the yard.

I beat him to his prey before he can seize her throat with snapping jaws. Lock his eyes with my own.

"She is human. Wait."

He backs away, staying close, growling.

The human Anna surfaces enough to form coherent words. "Who are you to Archambault?"

Her eyes are huge, reflecting horror and fear. She sobs. "I am his wife. Why did you attack him?"

I turn back, close my eyes, allow vampire to withdraw so it is a completely human visage she faces now. "Do you know King Steffan?"

"The vampire who rules his kind?" Sorrow retreats as another emotion surfaces. "Did he send you here to kill my husband?" Her fists clench in anger.

"No. Steffan was sentenced to death tonight. He escaped—by using your husband's body. This you see on the ground is no longer Archambault, your husband, but Steffan."

Even as I say the words, I think of Sandra. She was still in her own body, but bit by bit, Avery was taking control. Archambault was not a were. Would he have had a chance to fight Steffan's control?

From the corner of the yard: *We could not risk it.* Vlad's words are hard as flint. He has read my thoughts, felt my conflict. *You know that.*

I draw in a breath, hold out a hand to the woman. "I am sorry for your loss."

She ignores my hand. In the darkness of the yard, I see her expression toughen. She is not a young woman, forty or so, but her face reflects a life well lived. In other circumstances I imagine those eyes might sparkle, those lips smile more than frown.

Now she fixes me a glare of undisguised fury. "His friends will want revenge against the vampires," she says. "Steffan has unleashed the fury."

For the first time, Vlad steps up to join us. My breath catches. When the shotgun discharged, it struck him squarely in the chest

His shirt is shredded, his chest pockmarked with dozens of seeping wounds.

The woman recoils when she sees him. A glint of recognition sparks, and her shoulders lose some of their rigidity. She knows who he is.

Vlad fixes her with a look of hardened steel. "You do not wish to make enemies of the vampires," he says. "History has proven that to be an unwise choice."

CHAPTER 27

FOR A MOMENT, NO ONE SPEAKS. ARCHAMBAULT'S widow wants to fight for her husband's right to vengeance. But it's clear she recognizes Vlad and it's not only the vampire's legend she's aware of but the man's as well.

Vlad makes the first move. "You have a right to be compensated for your loss. I will see to it. But as for revenge, it comes at a steep price. Know that Steffan, a vampire, has lost his life as well as your husband. Try to be content with the knowledge that the scales have been balanced."

Tears are rolling down the woman's face. She looks down at her husband's body. It has morphed back to its human form.

"Do you wish us to help prepare him for burial?" Vlad's voice now is soft, conciliatory.

She shakes her head but does not meet his eyes. "I will

take care of it. I need to go inside to call his friends. I would like you to be gone when I return."

She reaches down to touch Archambault's cheek, then disappears back into the house.

Frey turns then to look at me.

I touch his flanks. "I'm all right," I say.

He rubs his head against the open wound on my chest. It's already starting to mend and once he's satisfied I am telling the truth, he goes to Vlad's side.

I follow. Once the woman is out of sight, Vlad sinks to the ground and closes his eyes. I've had my own experience with gunshots and they hurt like hell.

I kneel beside him and tear the shirt away. As I watch, buckshot works its way to the surface of his skin, falls away, and each lesion mends until by the time Vlad's eyes have reopened, his chest is fully healed.

He sits up.

Frey purrs and head butts him, making Vlad send me an eyebrow-arched look of surprise.

"I think he's glad you're all right."

Vlad climbs to his feet. "I think we'd better get out of here. Someone is bound to have heard that shot."

I glance toward the house. "Do you think she's accepted what you said about the scales being balanced?"

Vlad shrugs. "I'll make sure she's well taken care of. We'll keep an eye on her. It's all we can do. We spared her life—*you* spared her life. Let's hope she appreciates that."

We leave the garden, gather on the sidewalk in front of the house. Anxiety over being gone so long rears its head. "How are we going to get back to Lorgue?" I ask.

Vlad fishes in the pocket of his sweatpants for his cell.

"Lucky for us, she aimed high," he says, pulling it free. He dials, has a brief conversation once more in French, disconnects.

"There is a small municipal airport not far from here," he says. "There will be a helicopter and pilot waiting to fly us to Ampus. From there it's just a twenty-minute drive to Lorgues."

I glance down at my torn and bloody shirt and then to Vlad's. "Hope your pilot doesn't ask too many questions," I mutter.

"He'll be too curious about the panther traveling with us to ask about our clothes." He peers skyward. "Come on. We can make it before daybreak if we hurry."

WE MAKE IT TO STEFFAN'S HOUSE AS VLAD PREDICTED, an hour or so before sunrise. It seems strange to be back in the place our adventure began, a house now cold, dark and deserted. I wonder how long the guests stayed after the demise of their host but from the number of glasses and empty wine bottles strewn about, it appears the guests stayed until the liquor ran out.

Vampires are nothing if not resilient.

Vlad and I tramp our way upstairs while Frey retreats to the spot behind the bar where he left his clothes. I take a quick shower, washing away flakes of dried blood. There is not a hint of the bear's claw mark, not even a bruise or reddened skin.

Vampires are nothing if not tough-skinned.

I leave my torn clothes in a pile on the bathroom floor and slip once more into the dress Steffan chose for me. I finger-comb my wet hair, knowing there is little else I can do. If my parents see me in this disheveled state, I can only hope they attribute it to a fast ride in a convertible.

Vlad is dressed in his evening wear when I return to the bedroom. And perched on the end of the bed Frey waits, too, once again in his handsome human form. He rises when I come in and we embrace.

"Quite a party, huh?" he breathes in my ear.

"You're sure you're all right?" I whisper back.

"Thanks to Vlad."

Who clears his throat. "My driver will take you home if you are ready."

Frey slips an arm around my shoulder. "Actually, if you can take us back to Le Course café, we'd appreciate it. We left our car there."

"Of course. Shall we go?"

IT'S QUIET ON THE RIDE BACK TO THE CAFÉ. VLAD'S driver has raised the privacy partition though he needn't have bothered. Fatigue seems to have seeped our energy.

I'm laying in the crook of Frey's arm, my feet curled up on the seat. From the rhythmic rise and fall of Frey's chest, I'm guessing he has fallen asleep.

Vlad faces us, his head resting against the window, his eyes closed.

Are you asleep? I inquire gently, not wanting to wake him if he's dozed off.

No. He smiles. *Are you?*

He rouses himself to a seating position. I study the man sitting across from me. I've had a lot of unbelievable things happen to me in the months since becoming vampire—not all of them good—but sitting in a car at six a.m. with the one who might just be the original, the first vampire, has to top the list.

What would you like to ask me? His dark, intense gaze is as penetrating as his ability to probe my thoughts.

At first, the question seems too complicated to tackle. Until I realize it's really very simple. *Are you the first vampire?*

No. He frowns. *Legend bestowed that title on me. And that hack Stoker perpetuated it.*

Then who—?

No one knows. The vampire has been a part of every culture stretching back as long as man's memory.

Why do we exist?

Vlad reaches for my hand. *That is like asking why there are a million species of birds or insects or why there are different races.*

No. I shake my head. *Not the same thing. Evolution, environment, climate. They dictate flora and fauna on this earth. We are not evolved. We are made. One from the other. But for what purpose? We are parasites, feeding on the blood of mortals.*

You think we have no purpose.

I haven't determined one yet. I know I have little experience in this existence, but what I have has led me to believe there are more like Steffan in our ranks than like me.

Perhaps you just answered your own question.

He is stroking my hand. I pull it free. *I hope not, if you're saying I have nothing to look forward to but evenings like tonight—an immortal lifetime of fighting vampires intent on world domination.*

But you succeeded, did you not? The world is safe for mankind once again. He chuckles, raising an imaginary glass. *To humanity. The vampire's greatest weakness.*

I don't see the humor. *But safe for how long? I want to live a simple life. I want to marry the man I love and raise his child.*

Frey will die. Vlad utters the words without emotion, a simple statement of fact.

My own answer is more heated. *I know that.* I lean toward him. *But at some point one has to decide what is important. If we have forty years together, thirty, twenty, they will be good years and worth the pain of loss when the end comes.* I suddenly remember a fact of history. *Wasn't your time with your mortal wife Jusztina worth it?*

Vlad looks surprised that I would know his wife's name. I smile ruefully. *There is very little about your life that has not been recorded. Including the way she met her death.*

He looks away, briefly, as if unsure how to respond. When he meets my eyes again, they are clouded with remorse. *I was away when that happened—when she threw herself from the parapet. I've wished every day of my life since that I would have turned her before I'd left on that godforsaken mission.*

Why didn't you?

Instead of answering, he searches my face. *Your mother is facing death, is she not?*

Yes. Bravely. She is the most heroic woman I know.

I assume you considered turning her?

I gave her the choice. She turned it down. She believes in the immortal life her god promises.

Then you understand how it was with Jusztina. Do you hold your mother's beliefs?

I did when I was young. No longer. I have seen too much. I let a beat go by. *Do you still think of Jusztina?*

After six hundred years? He smiles, softly, sweetly. *Every day.*

Would you have preferred she never existed? That you never loved so deeply?

No. My memories of our life together sustain me. Life is too grim otherwise.

Then you understand how it is with Frey.

I realize suddenly that he is asking more questions of me than I of him. This isn't going quite the way I expected.

Vlad laughs softly, feeling my discomfort, and answers the question swirling around my head. *You are intriguing. I wanted to know more about this Chosen One.*

Why?

I believe we have a lot in common, you and I.

And what have you learned?

That the rumors about you are true. I saw it myself tonight. Still, I'd like to learn more. Will you meet me tomorrow?

I shake my head. *I'm afraid that's not possible. Frey and I are getting married in two days. After that, well, how long we stay depends on*— I can't bring myself to finish the thought, the words stick in my throat.

Vlad nods sympathetically. *Your mother. I understand. But we will meet again. When one has all the time in the world, one develops patience.*

All the time in the world. I sigh. *What history you have lived.*

Vlad shrugs. *History is just the present in retrospect. Times change but people do not. After a while you come to realize stepping back from mortals is the only way to survive. Otherwise your soul becomes deadened by the evil humans perpetuate upon themselves.*

Yet were you not mortal when you received the name Vlad the Impaler? I ask quietly.

Vlad doesn't shrink from the question but meets my eyes squarely. *Yes. I was a fanatic willing to protect my country against all threats—whether Ottoman Turks or German merchants. As ruler I thought I could eliminate crime by being pitiless against transgressors. I held myself as arbiter of morality and punished anyone whose conduct I deemed morally wrong. I deserve to be called cruel but not capricious. Those in my kingdom knew what I stood for and if they committed a transgression, they understood the consequences.*

His words are straightforward but the emotion behind them is great sadness.

Do you think history has judged you too harshly? If so, why don't you try to set the record straight?

He chuckles. *You mean write a book?* The Real Untold Story of Vlad Dracul the Third? *Who would believe it? My enemies were thorough. The portrait left behind of me is one of a monster who lived only to torture and kill. But I no longer care what history chooses to remember. It very rarely reflects the truth.*

Obviously. History says you were killed by the Ottomans, your head put on a stake outside of Constantinople.

Vlad smiles, stretches his arms over his head. *Inventing your own death is something you will learn to deal with as time goes by. Though it was far easier to disappear with no Internet or newspapers or even photographs to leave a trail.*

Hmm. *When the time comes, I hope I don't have to resort to leaving some innocent person's head on a stake to make it happen.*

Who said he was innocent?

The driver knocks gently on the partition, signaling we are nearing the café. Before I rouse Frey, I reach a hand to Vlad. *It has been a pleasure meeting you, Vlad Dracul.*

He takes my hand, raising it to his lips. *And you, Anna Strong.*

CHAPTER 28

WHEN WE GET BACK TO THE VILLA, THE SUN IS already snaking through the windows. We tiptoe in without waking the house, stopping only to erase a telephone message from Vlad's assistant.

"Some romantic road trip, huh?" Frey whispers.

I take his hand and steer him toward the stairs. Suddenly, the events of the evening, how close I came to losing him, have me shaking.

When we're safe behind closed bedroom doors, I waste no time slipping out of Steffan's dress. We don't say another word to each other. There's no need. Frey reads the urgency in my eyes, in my hands as I help him strip off his clothes. Then we're on the bed, and he guides my lips to his neck.

"Drink."

His hands hold me tight, his pulse thunders just under that fragile layer of skin. His breath is hot and ragged against my cheek.

"Drink, Anna," he says again.

And I do.

I WATCH FREY SLEEP. HE'S LYING ON HIS SIDE, NAKED under the sheets. I spoon my body against his and loop an arm around his waist. We've only been in bed an hour. I expect any minute to hear my parents and the kids as they make their way downstairs to start the day. I know I should be tired, should try to grab at least a few minutes' sleep. But sleep is slow to come. My body still tingles from feeding, my nerves still on fire from the kill.

Frey knew I needed to feed. The vampire had been denied the blood of the bear and bloodlust still raged— leaving me ragged and unsatisfied. He understood as he understands so much about me.

I'm tempted to slip down between his legs. Take him into my mouth. Watch as he awakens, surprise and pleasure lighting up his face. Give him something back for all he's given me.

But he needs to sleep.

I kiss his cheek.

I'll return the favor, though. In delicious ways.

The promise sends heat rushing through my body.

MUCH LATER, I AWAKEN TO THE SUN BEAMING IN through a gap in drawn curtains. Frey is still asleep. When he, too, awakens, he rolls over and catches me looking at him. His arms go around me and he pulls me close. "How are you feeling?"

I snuggle close, one hand trailing down between his legs. "Ready to return the favor," I whisper.

He glances over my head to the clock on the nightstand. He stops my hand. "We'd better wait. We're already late for breakfast."

I groan and he attempts to sit up. He doesn't get very far. His head barely off the pillow, he slaps a hand to his fore-head and falls back. He groans again, for real this time.

I lean over him, "Are you all right?"

"Killer headache." He looks at me and smiles ruefully. "Did I get hit in the head last night? I don't remember much."

I place a gentle hand on his forehead. "That bear did a pretty good job on you. Knocked you into a wall."

He sits up abruptly, pushing himself all the way this time. "Vlad. I remember now."

"He saved you. Twice."

"No offense, but I hope we've seen the last of him."

"We have," I assure him with a teasing grin. "I told him we were going to be busy for the next few days, getting married and all. And then we'll be spending time with the family. I expect we've seen the last of Dracul."

I trace a finger along the curve of his jaw. "Now kiss me. But keep it sweet, not sexy. You're not in any shape to get excited. And we do have to get up. The wedding planners are coming at noon. And this afternoon we have to drive to Cannes to pick up David and Tracey."

"Not in shape, huh?" Frey pushes me down on the bed.

He leans close and teases me with his lips, bringing them close, then pulling back. I finally tangle my fingers in his hair and settle his mouth on mine. At the same time, he's teasing another part of my anatomy, fingers tormenting until I arch my back and thrust against his hand and he slips his fingers inside.

"I thought we had to get up," he says, but he continues to probe, slower, deeper.

"I thought you had a headache," I gasp back.

But I don't try to stop him.

I'm shuddering with excitement, lost in the sensations flooding over and through me. If he tried to stop now, I would scream in protest. I move with the rhythm of his thrusts. When the climax comes, it lifts my hips off the bed. He holds me close, driving every wave of passion until the swell breaks and I collapse against him.

"What was that you were saying?" he says, stroking my hair.

I lift myself on my elbows to look at him. "It was supposed to be your turn."

He grins. "Oh, you'll make it up to me. Just wait."

FREY AND I CREEP DOWNSTAIRS WONDERING WHAT type of reception we'll get from my dad for being late once again. For the same reason, too.

We needn't have worried. I'd forgotten it was Sunday. On the kitchen counter we find a note:

Gone to Mass. Took John-John with us. Catherine has the day off but there are fresh brioches in the cupboard.

Thought you kids would want to sleep in since you got in so late last night. Remember the wedding planners will be here at noon.

Love, Mom

Frey grins. "Want to go back upstairs? We have two hours. We can make all the noise we want."

I raise an eyebrow. "First one up the stairs gets to be on top."

It turns out to be a tie.

CHAPTER 29

TWO HOURS LATER, FREY AND I ARE FRESHLY showered and respectable and sitting at the dining room table across from a man and woman who represent the company that's officiating at our wedding ceremony—tomorrow. My head swims at the thought.

The man is well dressed, suit and tie, carefully slicked-back hair framing what I've come to think of as a "French" face—closely shaven, well-groomed, thin nose, dark eyes. He's wearing a citrusy cologne or aftershave, I can't tell which it is. But it's strong. His name is Pierre.

His partner, Lorraine, is beautiful. Tall, model thin, expertly and subtly made up. Her dark eyes have a slight upward tilt and she has a mouth that begs to be kissed, wide, full-lipped and eager. I have to give Frey a surreptitious elbow more than once to stop him from staring at those lips.

Pierre is reading us examples of vows that we might choose from. We decide on a simple recitation that combines the traditional with a modern spin. The entire ceremony will take no more than fifteen minutes.

We are finished with the technicalities in less than an hour.

Frey gives them a credit card. They process the payment. Then we usher them to the door. As they leave, a truck pulls into the driveway. The crew who is to transform the back of the house into a tented, flower- and ribbon-strewn wonderland has arrived. Mom made all the arrangements, only consulting me on things requiring my opinion, so that Frey and I would be surprised. We have strict orders to point the workmen to the site, but not to peek as the work progresses.

When we are back inside, I look at Frey. "Can you believe we're getting married day after tomorrow?"

He puts his arms around me. "Getting cold feet?"

"Vampire, remember?" I tease. "Cold feet, cold hands."

"Not always."

And then we're kissing and he proves how right he is. But before things take their natural progression with us, we hear my folks' car in the driveway.

John-John is the first through the door, holding a white paper bag up high. "Guess what they call doughnuts in French?" he asks, running to greet us. "Beignets!"

I catch Mom's eyes over his head. The circle of life. Memories of my brother and I heading home after church, in the backseat of my parents car, a bag of hot, fresh doughnuts between us. My eyes fill with tears. The more things change, the more they stay the same.

*   *   *

FREY IS AT THE WHEEL OF DAD'S CAR AND WE'RE ON our way to Cannes to pick up David and Tracey. The pilot called to let us know they would be in at three. I'm slumped back on the seat, window open to the warm spring day, thoughts cascading through my head in a stream of consciousness that is making me dizzy.

"Anna?" Frey's voice. "What are you thinking?"

I swivel on the seat to face him. "You really want to know?"

His eyebrows shoot up. "Uh-oh. Am I going to regret asking?"

I give his knee a squeeze. "No. It's nothing like that. I'm not going to call off the wedding."

"Well that's a relief. I don't think I'd get my twelve hundred bucks back from Pierre and Hot Lips."

I swat his arm.

Frey's expression sobers. "No, really, Anna. Are you upset about something?" He catches himself. "That was stupid. Of course you're upset about your mother. But I get the feeling it's more than that. You have a very serious look on your face. Are you thinking about last night? Because I am fine."

I reach over and touch his knee. "I know you are," I kid. "You proved it this morning, remember?" But even his smile doesn't chase away the uneasiness still clouding my thoughts. "I don't know what I'd do without you."

He picks up my hand and kisses it. "I don't intend you'll ever have to find out."

I lay my head back against the headrest and close my eyes. "Do you remember the first time we met?"

"No. When was it?"

The tone of his voice gives lie to his words. There's humor there and a hint of a tease. He chuckles, then says, "Let's see. You came to see me at school, convinced I might have had something to do with Trish's disappearance. You were ready to tear my head off."

"You won't ever forget that will you?"

"Well, it turned out all right. Considering you bit me and almost sucked me dry to get at the truth."

"And considering how we ended up, your neck wasn't the only thing I sucked."

Frey laughs. "First time we made love. You did it for the blood . . ."

His voice trails off.

"I wish I had been smart enough to realize then what I know now. It would have saved us both a lot of mistakes. Me with Max and Lance and Stephen. You with—what was her name?"

Frey looks at me with a raised eyebrow. "I don't remember."

"Good answer." I pause a moment, sorting the images flashing in my head. "Then there was Belinda Burke. I almost got you killed the night of the demon raising. I'll never forget how I felt seeing you lying at that bitch's feet."

More mental snapshots, flying by like frames in a Power-Point presentation. "You saved Culebra by letting yourself be put under a spell because I asked you to. You saved me by coming to Palm Springs when I'd been burned. You helped me prepare for the vampire convocation that very probably would have resulted in my death if it hadn't been for you. Then, you stood by me when I dragged you to Monument Valley, even when John-John's mother was killed—" The flow of words stops, choked off by a strong surge of emotion.

Frey shakes his head, tightening his grip on my hand resting on his knee. "Anna, that's all water under the bridge. Why are you thinking of those things now?"

Why am I?

I don't know.

I close my eyes.

I do know. I look at Frey. "Do you know how important you are to me? You've been the only real constant in my life since I became vampire. You've never judged me or tried to make me change. You've been by my side no matter how difficult the situation or what it ended up costing you. I don't know why you love me. You shouldn't, you know. I don't give back to you half of what you give to me." I close my eyes, feeling tears threaten. "I don't know why you love me," I repeat softly. "I'm just so glad that you do."

Frey is quiet a moment. The muscles in his jaw tremble, then clench. He swallows hard and draws a deep breath. Finally he says simply, "I love you because it's all I'm capable of doing."

My heart leaps. I lean over and kiss his cheek. "That's the nicest declaration of love I've ever heard," I whisper.

DAVID AND TRACEY ARE SUITABLY IMPRESSED BY THE jet, by Cannes, by the drive to my folks'. They grill Frey and me about the details of the wedding, how we've been spending our time since we arrived (that gets a raised eyebrow from Frey), how John-John likes France. The subject that doesn't come up is Mom. I can tell David is hesitant to ask about her condition. I bring it up myself before we get to the estate. I assure him she's determined to play the mother of the bride to the hilt and that he'll be surprised at how good she looks. I also tell them not to treat her any differently than they have before. David is skeptical that he can pull it off.

But he needn't have worried. As soon as we stop in the driveway, the family is out the door to greet us. While my folks have never been big fans of David (bounty hunting was not their job of choice for their only child), Mom's greeting is so warm and welcoming, her demeanor so relaxed, any qualms David had about how to act around her are quickly forgotten.

Mom shepherds everyone inside, to a feast waiting for us in the dining room. Frey, John-John and I sit on one side of the table, David, Tracey and Trish on the other, Mom and Dad at opposite ends. Everyone I love is here. Except one.

I bump Frey's arm and whisper, "We didn't invite Culebra." Guilt that I hadn't thought of inviting him before now floods my heart. He's been as constant in my life as Frey and I didn't think of him before right now.

David hears my comment and pauses, a forkful of coq au vin halfway to his lips. "Oh, I invited him," he says. "Figured you'd want him here since you spent so much time in Mexico. You know, with Max . . ." His voice falters. Mentioning Max reminds us both that he is gone—killed in Mexico by a drug lord we helped put away.

The wound is raw. Still, I skewer David with a look. "How'd you know where to reach Culebra?"

"Searched your phone records."

"What?"

"Hey, it's what we do, right?"

I give him a mocking evil eye. "So. What did Culebra say?"

"Congratulations. And he sends his apologies. His niece is in her first drama production at her school and he has to attend. He said you'd understand."

That makes me grin. His "niece" is a girl we rescued on that same trip. One of the few bright points in an otherwise nightmarish experience. She must be doing well. Couple that with Culebra's reluctance to leave the confines of his supernatural kingdom in Beso de la Muerte, it isn't surprising that he'd elect not to come. And perfectly understandable.

I sigh and give David a grudging smile. "Thanks for taking care of that for me. But stay out of my phone records from now on, okay?"

Tracey shakes her head at David. "I told you she wouldn't be happy with your snooping."

"Yeah, but look at her face now. She's glad I did, aren't you, Anna?"

"Don't press your luck, David."

It's what I say, but I have to admit it, I am glad.

With the crowd at the table it's easy to pretend I, too, am enjoying a meal that has every face beaming. Between John-John and Frey subtly helping themselves to nibbles from my plate and Mom spiriting away a napkin full of food to replace it with a clean one, neither David nor Tracey, my Dad nor Trish notices that I haven't eaten a morsel.

After dinner Frey and I offer to clean up so David and Tracey can visit with my folks. We make short work of clearing the table, storing away leftovers and loading the dishwasher. As the machine cycles on, I lean against it, pulling Frey close.

"Just a few more hours of freedom. How do you want to spend them?"

At that moment, David appears in the doorway, Dad by his side. "We've been discussing that," David says. "You need a bachelor party. Let's go."

"Go where?" Frey's tone is as surprised as his expression.

"I know just the place," Dad says. "In the village. Come on. It's your last night of freedom."

Frey glances at me. I lift my shoulders. "Sounds like the menfolk have it all thought out." I stand on tiptoe, peck his cheek, give David a hard look over Frey's shoulder. "No strippers." Then I whisper in Frey's ear, "And no shifters."

Dad and David take Frey by each arm before he can resist and hustle him toward the door. "No promises," David says.

"Don't wait up," Dad adds, winking at me.

"Good luck," I call to Frey as the door slams behind them.

MOM MUST BE TELLING TRACEY SOMETHING ABOUT tomorrow she wants to be a surprise because when I join them in the living room, conversation comes to a halt.

"Well. Should I leave and come back?"

Mom laughs and pats the seat beside her on the couch. "Course not. I was just giving Tracey a hint about what to expect tomorrow."

Tracey's eyes sparkle. "It's going to be beautiful, Anna. I'm so jealous."

Trish and John-John are sitting across from us, and John-John says, "Aren't you and David going to get married, too?"

Trish gives him an elbow nudge. "That's not a polite question."

He turns wide innocent eyes her way. "Why?"

Tracey interjects before Trish can reply. "No. It's an honest question and, John-John, I wish I could answer it. David and I care about each other very much, but I'm not sure David is ready for marriage."

She sounds wistful and a little frustrated. I can't help thinking one of the reasons David is reluctant to commit is a bombshell bitch named Gloria.

But it's not my place to offer an opinion.

Mom deftly steers the conversation to another topic. "I hope you can stay on after the ceremony. It's so beautiful in Provence this time of year."

"We can stay a day or two," Tracey replies. "But I'm afraid we have work waiting for us. And we don't want to take advantage of your hospitality."

And so the discussion turns to how best to make the most of a short trip, what to see, where to go. I watch Mom closely for any sign of fatigue, any indication that she's not feeling well. All I see are bright eyes and a luminous smile, an erect bearing radiating happiness.

Maybe the doctors are wrong. Maybe Chael doesn't know what he's talking about. This glowing woman cannot be dying.

It has to be a mistake.

CHAPTER 30

I SPEND THE NIGHT DOZING, WAKING, CHECKING THE clock, impatiently waiting for Frey.

After the night we had last night, he must be exhausted. Of course, no one else knows about that.

Finally, at three a.m., I get up. I go to my parents' room and listen at the door. I hear Dad snoring softly. At David's door, I hear him and Tracey doing something other than sleeping. Where the hell is Frey?

I tiptoe downstairs and look outside. The car is parked in front. I take a quick trip through the house and finally find him.

Stretched out on the couch. His clothes are in a pile on the floor, a quilt has been thrown over his hips.

I kneel down, bend over him and whisper, "What are you doing?"

Frey sits up with a jerk. "Jesus, Anna. You scared the shit out of me."

"When did you get back?"

He glances at the glowing dial on his watch. "About an hour ago. You didn't hear us?"

I shake my head. "Must have dozed off. What are you doing down here?"

He gives me a "do you really have to ask?" look.

"Ah. My dad."

Frey nods. "He thought it inappropriate for us to sleep together the night before the wedding." He smiles and lifts a corner of the quilt in invitation. "But if we're really quiet, we can have some fun and you can go back upstairs and he'll never be the wiser."

I open my robe and let it drop to the carpet. "I'm so happy you're not the superstitious type. And if I remember correctly, I owe you."

Then I go to work with hands and tongue and watch Frey become even happier.

AT SEVEN, MOM IS AT MY DOOR, KNOCKING SOFTLY. I'm back in bed, alone, and feeling smugly like a kid who has pulled one over on her folks. I slip on my robe, adjust the blankets and cheerily call, "Come in."

She enters with a breakfast tray of coffee and croissants. "Anna, I can't tell you how sorry I am at your father's ridiculous insistence that Frey sleep downstairs last night." She puts the tray on the nightstand, goes to the window and yanks open the curtains. "When I found Frey on the couch this morning, I couldn't believe it. But you know how important these things are to your father."

Now the "we fooled you" mind-set morphs into something that feels a lot like guilt. "Ah. Where is Frey?"

"He's in John-John's room showering."

"John-John's room?"

Mom shakes her head, frowning. "Another of your father's hardheaded ideas—that the bride and groom should not see each other before the ceremony the day of the wedding. Honestly, I don't know where he comes up with these things. You'd think it was the eighteenth century."

I start to get out of bed, but she waves me back.

"Stay in bed a little longer. You have a big day ahead." She pours me a cup of coffee. "Your father will take Frey down for breakfast and I'm supposed to move his clothes into John-John's room. Those three must have had quite a time last night if your father convinced Frey to go along with this nonsense, to say nothing of talking him into sleeping on the couch."

He may have talked him into sleeping on the couch, I think, as I sip away on my coffee to keep from grinning, but not to forego a pre-wedding conjugal visit. Should I feel bad about it?

The pleasant lingering glow of good sex makes me decide no.

Besides, in a few hours, we'll be legal.

I finish the coffee, throw back the covers and swing my legs off the bed. "So what's the agenda?"

Mom wags a finger. "For you? Nothing for now. The hairdresser is arriving at eight. She'll also do your makeup."

I get a little tingle of panic. "Hairdresser? Mom, you know about me and mirrors . . ."

Mom holds up a hand. "Not to worry. Your friend Chael recommended this stylist. She does both vampires and . . ." There's just a moment's hesitation as Mom chooses her words. "Regular women. She'll do you first in here, then Trish and me in my room."

But I'm still hung up on Chael recommending a stylist. "When did you speak with Chael?" I ask.

Mom's hand flutters. "Yesterday. I think. He said he was calling to ask if he could bring a guest to the wedding. Of course I told him the more the merrier. We've ordered more food and drink than we can possible consume. Especially"—she gives me a conspiratorial wink—"if some of the guests won't be consuming any at all."

She helps herself to a croissant. "But then he asked a strange question. He asked if you and Frey had gotten back all right from the party." She pauses. "When were you with Chael?"

My brain shoots into overdrive. "Funny thing," I say. "We ran into Chael in Lourges the other night. He invited us to a party and we went along with him. But it was too crowded and noisy. We left before he did and didn't have a chance to say good-bye."

Did that come out all right? Most of it is even the truth. Chael doesn't know anything about what transpired with Vlad, Frey and I. And Frey and I never did get the chance to talk to Chael before we set off after Archambault. I wonder how long he wandered around the party looking for us before he gave up and left?

I wait for Mom to react.

She just nods. "I told him you were both right as rain." She looks up at me. "You are all right, aren't you?"

"Yep. We just left before Chael and couldn't find him to say good night." I throw my arms around her, "Mom, I can't believe how great you're being about—well, you know."

She hugs me back. "Anna, when I think of all the time I wasted being critical of you, I could kick myself. I'm so happy that you're here, now, that you've agreed to share this day with us. That you've forgiven me for the way I treated you."

The last is said quietly and with great emotion. There is regret and sadness in her voice, and my heart catches because I sense what she is not putting into words. That she will not waste any of the time left to her being petty or judgmental. That, finally, I have her approval.

There could be no better wedding present.

She and I chat while I drink coffee and she polishes off the croissants. She catches my lingering gaze as she pops bits of the buttery pastry in her mouth. "Do you miss this?" she asks.

"Do I. Especially Italian food and chocolate."

She nods appreciatively. "One of the good things about being ill," she says, "is being able to eat anything I want. Modern medicine is wonderful."

My shoulders tense. Wonderful? Her tone is cheery, but it chills me to the bone. If modern medicine is so wonderful, why can't it do more than improve her appetite?

Mom sees my reaction. She leans toward me and takes my hand. "I'm sorry I said that. This is your day. No more talk of illness." She makes a motion across her lips, a key turning. "Promise."

After a long moment, we're off to other subjects, the

weather (perfect for a late-morning garden wedding), the caterers (already setting up in the kitchen), the last-minute prep to the garden (chairs positioned, the archway decorated with flowers, the carpet being laid down).

At eight exactly, there is a discreet knock on the door and Dad shows the hairdresser in. His eyes are wide as he steps aside to let her pass into the bedroom. "Lisette," he says simply.

I understand immediately why Dad looks slightly uncertain when he shows her in. Lisette is a woman in her thirties, pretty in the way a wildflower is pretty, bright, tenacious, unconventional. Her arms are covered in tattoos, elaborate designs of intertwined vines and roses that climb her neck and up one cheek. She's dressed in dark slacks and a bright peasant blouse, leather sandals on her feet.

I leave the three to chat while I shower, wash my hair, towel dry it and return to take a seat at the vanity.

Mom hands Dad Frey's clothes then, and they leave me with the stylist.

Lisette is friendly and obviously comfortable with working in front of a mirror that reflects only her own image. She blow-dries my hair, fluffing and smoothing it as if the heft of it will determine what style to choose. I tell her not to do anything fancy, that I want a simple, slightly more polished look. That's all.

She assures me she knows exactly what I want, brandishing her hairbrush with a flourish. In a minute, she's done. Next, she applies a little eye makeup and blush. I haven't had makeup on in so long, I start feeling nervous that Frey will like this version of me better than the original and it's a look I can never hope to duplicate. Since becoming vampire, I only tried once to apply mascara without a mirror. After poking myself in the eye twice, I gave up.

While she works, she chatters in broken but passable English about what a beautiful bride I will be. Then she asks, "Is your groom also de vampire?"

"No," I reply quickly. "And you can't mention vampires to anyone else, okay?"

"Not to worry. Chael explained all to me."

Curious, I ask, "How do you know Chael?"

She gets one of those love-struck smiles that answers the question more eloquently than words. "We have been friends for many years. He spends a lot of time in Paris. It's where I live."

"Paris is almost five hundred miles away." I know. I ran it. "You came all that way to help today?"

"Ah, if Chael asks, I cannot refuse." She sighs. "Besides, he sent a first-class airline ticket to Cannes and the limo to drive me back to the airport is waiting outside. Chael is a very generous man."

Whew. Chael to the rescue once again. My thank-you note to him is going to be pages long.

Lisette finishes up, pinning the one simple rosebud I chose as my hairpiece over my right ear. She stands back, nods and proclaims me done. I take her down the hall to Mom's room where I know she and Trish will be waiting. I have to duck quickly back to my room when John-John's door opens. After all Dad went through to keep at least one wedding tradition intact, I'm not taking any chances. He's got me half believing in the superstition now.

It's almost nine.

Nervousness nibbles away at my self-assurance. After battling almost every conceivable enemy both mortal and not, why would the idea of getting married make me nervous?

I touch my hair. Wonder what I look like? I run a gentle fingertip over mascara-thickened lashes. Is it too much?

A sound from downstairs draws me to the window. Dad is greeting the first guests, the family from next door. He looks so handsome in his suit, white hair brushed straight back from a smooth forehead, smile erasing some of the worry lines that have formed around his mouth since my mother's illness. Father of the bride. A title that probably surprises him as much as it does me!

At ten, a knock and Mom and Trish walk in.

Trish looks radiant. Lisette pulled her buttercream hair back from her face, fastened it at the crown with a garland of flowers and ribbon the same rose color as her dress. The rest falls to her shoulders in soft curls. I can only shake my head at how splendid she looks.

As does my mother. Her hair, thinned by illness and medicine, has been transformed through the magic of a hairpiece. Lisette matched Mom's hair perfectly, adding fullness at the top and back by expertly blending a short cascade of curls with her real hair. She did Mom's make-up, too.

"No one is going to be looking at me," I say, hugging first Mom and then Trish. "They'll be too busy looking at you two."

"Oh, I don't think so," Trish says. "Look at yourself."

She says it in the offhand, casual way one does, but

Mom and I know that's not something that's going to happen.

Unless—

"Mom. Do you have a digital camera?"

"I do." She turns to Trish. "It's downstairs on Grandpa's desk. Will you get it please?" When Trish is out the door, she raises an eyebrow at me. "You can be photographed?"

"Not on film. But digitally . . ."

"Then quick, let's get your dress on. When Trish comes back we'll take a couple of pictures."

I take off my robe and Mom helps me slip into the dress. She stands back, eyes shining, her expression saying more than words. Trish is back, camera in hand, and she, too, gives me the nod of approval.

Mom takes the camera, but before she can start snapping away, Trish yelps. "We almost forgot! The 'something old, something new, something borrowed, something blue' thing!" It comes out in a rush, one long hyphenated word.

"You're right." Mom lays the camera down and pulls three small packages from the pocket of her jacket. She hands two to Trish, the third to me. "Your beautiful dress is something new. This is something old."

My hands are suddenly trembling. I tear at the tissue to find a small jewelry box. When I open it, there is a pair of pearl earrings nestled against black velvet. "Oh, Mom." I touch the earrings. I recognize them. "These were your mother's."

"And now they're yours." She turns to Trish.

Trish is grinning. "Something borrowed."

"Uh-oh," I tease. "Something borrowed from a teenager? What is this? Your iPod?"

But when I open the package, it's a simple gold bracelet of dainty heart-shaped links. "Trish, this is beautiful."

"It's the only thing I have from my dad," she says wistfully. "Mom said he gave it to her when he found out she was pregnant."

God. I have to fight to keep my expression from betraying a sudden wave of anger. Another in her mother's web of lies. The bracelet couldn't be from my brother. He died before knowing Trish's mother was pregnant. With another man's child.

But I'm lying, too.

Every minute of every day. Because I've perpetuated the lie.

When I look at the strong, courageous young woman Trish has become because of that lie, though, I know I made the right choice.

I accept the bracelet with a smile and slip it on.

Trish holds out the last package. "Your fiancé picked this out," she says with a mischievous smile.

"He did, did he?" I tear off the paper. A blue garter. I hold it up. "Hmmmm. Now whatever is he going to do with this?"

Trish is laughing and Mom motions for me to put it on so I slip the garter over my knee. Then she waits until I've made the last adjustment, putting on the earrings, to stand back and give me the once-over.

"You are a beautiful bride, Anna."

"Take a picture, take a picture," Trish says excitedly. Then, "Wait, wait. We forgot the bouquet." And she's out the door running down the hall for Mom's bedroom. There's a gasp as we hear her say next, "No. Don't look in. Aunt Anna has her gown on. It's bad luck. Go on downstairs."

Mom and I smile at each other. Frey must have snuck upstairs for a peek. He grumbles something, but we hear his tread on the stairs so he's heeding Trish's heated admonition.

Trish is back with the bouquet. Roses. The same pale color as my dress. When I'm holding the bouquet, Mom starts snapping. After half a dozen shots, I'm too impatient to wait any longer. "Let me see," I say, almost dancing with excitement. I haven't seen what I look like in over a year . . . and that was a fuzzy newspaper photo.

Mom hands me the camera and stands back to watch, her arms around Trish's shoulders, her eyes shining.

My hands tremble as I work the display. I can't believe I'm looking at my own image. My hair is lighter than I remember, honey blonde, with even paler streaks highlighting a face I expected to look drastically different. It doesn't. My eyes are softer than I would have imagined, still human, even after all they've seen. Lisette did a great job with a simple, subtle application of makeup that gives my tanned skin a glow. The dress hugs the curves of my body, my legs look long and lean, my arms toned.

"I don't look half bad." I don't realize I've said that aloud until Trish snorts.

"Are you kidding? Didn't you look in the mirror? You're drop-dead gorgeous."

Mom winks at me over her head and goes to the window. "I hear the orchestra. I think everyone's here." She hustles Trish out the door. "Go see if it's time, will you?"

When Trish has left, Mom takes my hands and stands

back as if taking her own mental snapshot. We don't speak, don't move, either of us. She looks happy, content. I *feel* happy, content. It's so strange and wonderful. Unexpected. Magical.

If only it could last forever.

CHAPTER 31

I PEEK OUT THE WINDOW WHEN I HEAR THE STRING quartet begin to play what I've chosen as my procession: Bach's Prelude in C.

Mom looks at me, her eyebrows raised.

I grin at her. "This is my surprise for you. I remember you saying it's what you chose when you married Dad."

Her eyes fill with tears, but I shake a finger at her. "No crying, remember? Your crying will ruin my makeup."

Another glance out the window. Trish is walking down the aisle hand in hand with John-John. They take their places in front, John-John at Frey's side, Trish to the left. I look at Mom. It's our cue. She takes my hand and we go downstairs to where Dad is waiting at the gate to the garden.

Mom gives my hand one last squeeze before she places

it in Dad's. He leans over and pecks my cheek. "Your hands are cold as ice. Don't be nervous. You look beautiful."

Mom winks at me. "Here we go."

She precedes us down the red carpet that's been laid from the edge of the garden to a flower-strewn pergola. The officiate is waiting for us on the steps. It's Pierre. I wonder with a grin if Frey will be disappointed that it's not Hot Lips performing the ceremony.

This is the first time I've seen the garden since the workmen arrived yesterday. Three rows of chairs have been placed in a semicircle facing a raised dais. The chairs are filled with Mom and Dad's friends and neighbors and at the front, David and Tracey. Lots of flowers. Everywhere. I sense Chael, too, though at the moment I'm too excited, nervous, terrified to look around.

My eyes focus on Frey. He's waiting for me, John-John at his side. He steps forward to give Mom's cheek a kiss and when she's taken her place in the front row, his gaze turns to me.

In that moment, all our history, all our mistakes, all our past evaporates. It's as if I'm seeing him for the first time. He reaches out a hand and Dad places my palm in his. Then Dad kisses my cheek, too, and joins Mom.

I can't take my eyes off Frey. His wonderful familiar face suddenly looks different. It's not a reflection of his clothes. He's handsome in his tux, but he's handsome in jeans and an old sweatshirt. It's something new in his gaze when he looks at me.

It's devotion. In his eyes. Shining from his face. A promise that he will never let me down. I knew he loved me. I didn't know until this minute how much. Or realize how much I loved him. It's magical. Joyous. I'm one of the lucky ones. I've found my soul mate.

He bends his head and whispers in my ear, "You are even more beautiful than I imagined you'd be."

And in that instant, nervousness and fear disappear. I throw my arms around his neck and hold him—so tight I feel his breath catch. And then he's hugging me back and I've never felt so safe.

Suddenly, laughter erupts from the guests seated behind us, and the officiate pulls us gently apart. "That's at the end," he quips.

And so I disentangle myself from Frey and we're both grinning as the ceremony really begins.

The vows are simple, promises to be faithful, to love each other through dark days and light, to protect and defend each other. Uncomplicated concepts to mortals, but to us, vampire and shape-shifter, they take on a special meaning. We repeat them solemnly, together, eyes locked. We exchange rings, gold bands each engraved with one word: *forever*. Then Pierre proclaims us husband and wife.

"*Now* you may kiss the bride."

And so Frey does. A deep, lingering kiss that has my heart pounding until the sound of applause brings us up for air.

The recessional blasts from speakers hidden among the foliage. Frey watches my face as I recognize the song. Since I picked the processional, he insisted on choosing the appropriate recessional. "It's perfect," I say. "But who picked it out, you or Dad?"

Then there's another gale of laughter and applause when the audience, too, recognizes the familiar composition.

What could be more fitting than the "Hallelujah Chorus"?

I'M MARRIED. I HAVE TO KEEP REPEATING IT LIKE A mantra to believe it. Even with all the people offering congratulations and my folks beaming, it doesn't seem real.

Chael approaches with his guests. Plural. He not only has a very young, very human, very French model type on his arm, but he's brought someone else, too.

Vlad's eyes twinkle as he bends low to kiss my hand. "You make a lovely bride," he says.

You kept a low profile, I say with a smile. *I didn't know you were here.*

I wasn't sure you'd be pleased at my coming.

Frey and I are in your debt, I reply. *You are always welcome.*

Chael looks puzzled by the exchange but I don't give him time to ask about it. I address myself again to Vlad. *You'll have to fill Chael in on our adventure.*

Vlad nods and laughs. He looks very handsome in a tailored suit, his hair pulled away from his face and secured at the back of his neck. He, too, has a woman on his arm, but this one doesn't look happy to have been brought to such a commonplace event. As a human, she no doubt expected more excitement from her vampire date.

Your date looks bored.

He grimaces and shoots her a sideways frown. *I made a mistake bringing her. She's too young and inexperienced to appreciate the beauty of this occasion.*

Young, yes. Inexperienced, I doubt it.

That brings a chuckle from both Chael and Vlad and a stern look from the date, who probably guesses that we are having a conversation and she is more than likely the topic.

"Allons, cher, je veux un peu de champagne," she says through pouty lips, pulling on Vlad's arm.

He bows an apology and moves toward the buffet and bar set among the trees.

I look around for Frey. He's chatting with some of my parent's friends. He had thrown a questioning look Vlad's way when he spied him among the guests, but he remained with the little knot by the buffet table. I join him now, slipping my arm through his. He nibbles my earlobe, using the diversion to whisper, "Everything all right?"

His eyes are on Vlad and Chael, now chatting it up with Mom and Dad. Vlad's date still looks like she wants to be anywhere but here, but the sour expression is hidden behind a glass of champagne so I doubt my exuberant parents notice.

"Everything is more than all right." I tip my face toward his. "I've never been happier."

Trish is suddenly at our side, John-John beside her. She holds a silver cake knife. "Come on, you two. It's time to cut the cake!"

She takes my hand and John-John takes Frey's and we're pulled to the end of the buffet table where the magnificent wedding cake is on proud display. Someone clangs a fork against a glass and in a minute, we're surrounded.

Trish hands me the knife. Now this is going to be tricky. If I so much as get a mouthful of cake, there will be serious repercussions. I cut two small pieces and offer one to Frey.

Luckily, Frey knows the drill. I go first, stuffing a

forkful of cake in his mouth; well, mostly in his mouth. He grins and uses his fingers to scoop up the excess, wiping them on a napkin Trish holds out. Then he holds up *his* piece of cake, but instead of aiming for my mouth, he swivels suddenly, leans down and pushes it at John-John.

An excited, surprised squeal and John-John grabs his father's hand, and the two are soon covered mouth to chin in chocolate cake and whipped cream frosting. The guests howl in laughter. It's a perfect distraction and before anyone notices I haven't had a bite of cake, I'm wiping my lips and smacking in feigned appreciation.

Well done.

I spy Vlad at the edge of the crowd, clapping his hands along with everyone else. Then more champagne is poured, the cake served, and I turn my attention to helping Frey and his son clean frosting off their clothes.

I sense the tenseness in the air before seeing David and Tracey approach. They are not holding hands. She tries to smile at me, but it falls a hundred kilowatts short of her usual high-beam grin. David is tight-lipped, shoulders bunched.

"Uh-oh," I whisper to Frey. "Here comes trouble." I hand him the napkin I was using to help John-John clean up. "You take Tracey, I'll take David." And I'm off to grab David's arm, pulling him to the edge of the garden where we can have some privacy.

"What the fuck, Anna?" he snaps, rubbing his bicep.

I guess I grabbed him harder than I realized. But he's not going to sidetrack me. "Fine way to talk to a bride," I snap right back. "What did you do to Tracey?"

His face softens from aggravation to something that looks a lot like guilt. "I broke up with her."

Now I wish I'd grabbed him harder. "You *broke up* with her? At my wedding? What the fuck, David?"

"Fine way for a bride to talk," he growls right back. But now it's guilt plainly stamped on his face. "I just couldn't let her go on thinking we had a future. It wasn't fair."

"Jesus, David. Tell me it's not because of Gloria."

"It's not because of Gloria."

Too fast, and not at all convincing. "So all that bullshit you fed me about you and Gloria just being friends was just that? Bullshit?" I don't give him time to respond. "You had sex with Tracey last night."

His head jerks up. "How do you know that?"

"Because I heard you."

Color floods up his face. "God. You could hear us?"

He's embarrassed. Good. No sense letting him off the hook by telling him it was because of my super-acute sense of hearing. "Yes. So, you had sex with her last night and broke up with her this morning. Real classy, David."

His jaw tightens. "We're both adults. She wanted to have sex. So did I."

"Last night. So did you just wake up this morning and think, today Anna is getting married. Good time to break up with Tracey."

He looks down at his hands. "It wasn't like that. Exactly."

"I don't even want to know what it was like. Exactly. John-John is more mature than you are." But I soften my voice. "Can't you make things right with Tracey?"

"How am I supposed to do that?" For the first time in

our conversation, his eyes spark defensively. "Tracey knew all along I wasn't prepared to get serious. I told her so. I told *you* so, remember? But with all the wedding preparations and watching you and Frey so crazy in love, it suddenly hit me that I wasn't being fair to Tracey. She deserves someone who can give her what you have. It isn't me."

I take his arm and turn him to face Frey and Tracey still standing by the wedding cake. "Are you sure? Look at Tracey. She's beautiful, smart, strong, sexy, and *she cares about you*."

He looks at Tracey. The sadness tugging at her mouth and clouding her eyes makes my heart heavy. But the look quickly morphs into one of grim determination when she catches David's eyes on her. She squares her shoulders and deliberately turns her back on him.

Tracey is a tough chick. A truth suddenly dawns on me with such clarity, I can't believe I hadn't seen it before. One of those "aha" moments you read about in books but seldom experience in real life.

This one hits me with the force of a sledgehammer. Maybe it's because of my mother or what Frey and I just went through or maybe it's because of the conversation I had with Vlad. Only one thing matters in this life. And it's about time I stopped trying to force David into a relationship he doesn't want because it's a relationship *I* think he should.

I take a deep breath and plunge in. "I can't force you to make things right with Tracey. And I'm about to utter words you never in your wildest dreams imagined I'd ever say."

David's face darkens. "What now?"

Are the words going to get caught in my throat? Choke me? Shit. Let's get this over with. I look David square in the eyes. "If it's really Gloria you love, don't waste any more time. Go get her."

I couldn't have surprised David more if I'd declared my own undying love for him. His eyes widen, his mouth falls open.

I don't wait for him to regain composure. I'm afraid if I do, I'll take it all back. I rush on, "I think you're going to regret it. Big-time. And please, don't bring her around the office. I may lose control and shoot her. But I've learned something these last few weeks. Life is too short and love is too important to squander. I'm doing this for Tracey as much as I'm doing this for you. Tracey is all the things I mentioned and more and you are absolutely right. There is someone out there for her. If it isn't you, she shouldn't waste any more time finding him."

David's expression changes from astonishment to deeply suspicious in the blink of an eye. "How much champagne have you had today?"

"Not enough. And I'm going to have to drink a lot more to be able to forget this conversation."

"Well, I'm going to call Gloria before you do." He glances at Tracey. "Will you tell Tracey I'm leaving?"

"Oh no. It's up to you to tell her. Maybe she'll want to stay on for a few days. Maybe she'll want to leave with you. In any case, I can have the pilot ready to fly in a few hours."

David leans down to kiss my cheek. "Thanks, Anna."

"Don't thank me yet. In fact, don't thank me for this *ever*."

But David is already off, moving toward Frey and

Tracey. I watch as Tracey listens to David tell her he's going back to San Diego. But there are no histrionics on her part, no recriminations. She's put on her big-girl panties and it's in that moment I know she's going to be fine. She merely shrugs and then they both move toward the house.

I move to Frey's side. "Tracey tell you David broke up with her?"

He nods. "They're going back to San Diego as soon as possible." He tilts his head to look at me. "So you couldn't talk him into trying again, huh?"

"Actually, I did." I slip my arm in Frey's. "But not the way you think. I'll tell you about it later." I watch David and Tracey disappear into the house. "Do you have your cell phone on you? I've got to make a call."

LUCKILY THERE ARE NO MORE CRISES FOR THE REST OF the afternoon. By four, Frey and I have said thank you and good-bye to all the guests.

David and Tracey have gone to dinner in town. They'll be leaving tomorrow to go back to San Diego—something about weather patterns making it impossible to leave tonight. It will sadden me to see them go, the only consolation being the knowledge that in time, Gloria will certainly fuck things up with David. If he's lucky, when it happens Tracey won't have found her Prince Charming yet and David might get another chance with her. Maybe then he'll be wise enough to appreciate it.

God knows, it took me long enough with Frey.

I look around. Only family left.

Now we're gathered at the big oak table at the side of the

house, out of the way of the cleanup crew. John-John has his head down on the table, an afternoon of partying finally catching up with him. Frey lifts him up gently and takes him upstairs for a nap while Dad pops the cork on a bottle of wine. When Frey returns, Dad has filled glasses for all of us, Trish included, though hers is less than a quarter filled.

He raises his glass. "To a perfect day."

We all drink and Frey offers the next toast. "To family. Those united by blood, and those united by the heart."

I'm close to tears now—something I've managed to avoid all day. But I'm next in the circle around the table and I know just what I want to say. I take Frey's hand. "To love. And we who are lucky enough to have found it."

Mom and Trish are side by side, arms linked. They raise their glasses together and Mom says, "To memories. As long as we hold those we love in our hearts, they will always be with us."

Tears I've been holding back want to flow freely now.

And I let them.

CHAPTER 32

"H APPY?"
     Frey's voice at my ear.

We're in bed, naked under cool sheets, limbs entangled. My arm is thrown over Frey's waist, his are around my shoulders. I'm floating in the afterglow of sex and feeding. I raise my head, trace his chin with a finger.

"Never been happier. How about you?"

"After what just happened, you have to ask?"

Light is beginning to filter through the drapes of our bedroom. "It's almost dawn. Think we should try to get some sleep?"

He takes my hand, slides it down between his thighs. "We only have one honeymoon night. Or morning. I hear that once a couple gets married, they lose interest in sex. If that's true . . ."

But whatever crazy thing he was about to say is cut short by a gasp of pleasure.

It's not just my hand that's found its way between his thighs.

"*Azhé'é?* Anna? Are you up?"

John-John's voice and timid knocking on the bedroom door sends me hustling from beneath the sheets and both of us scampering for robes.

Frey lifts an eyebrow and whispers, "Well, I was just about to be."

I slap his arm and grin, mouthing, *Later*, as I swing open the door.

John-John scampers inside and jumps up on the bed. "I'm supposed to tell you that breakfast is ready!"

I glance at the clock. "It's only six. Who told you to come get us?"

A giggle. "David. He said you like to get up *real* early. And today especially."

I grab John-John and tickle his stomach until he squeals. "David said that, did he?" I look over his head to Frey. "We'll get even with him for this."

Frey grabs one of John-John's hands, I take the other, and we swing him off the bed. "Well, he'd better have coffee made." I pump a fist in the air. "Or I'm going to sock him one!"

John-John laughs. "I want to see that."

And with John-John between us, we head downstairs to start our first day as a family.

I expect to see everyone gathered around the table, David with a wicked grin to let us know he can guess what John-John interrupted.

But instead, it's just David and Tracey waiting for us in the kitchen. And their expressions are somber, serious.

I look around. "Where's Mom?"

David leans down to John-John. "Will you please go upstairs and see if Trish is awake?"

John-John's face mirrors confusion. It's obvious to even a young kid, David's mood changed in the minutes he was away. "What's wrong?" he asks.

"I'll tell you when you get back with Trish, all right?"

John-John casts a look at Frey. "Go ahead, *Shiye*," Frey says, turning him gently toward the stairs. He, too, catches the undertow in David's voice. "And get dressed while you're up there, okay?"

Frey watches his son disappear through the door. "What's going on, David?"

He asks the question sounding an alarm in my head and gut—the question I couldn't give voice to myself. Impulsively, I slip my hand into Frey's, seeking its warmth and comfort.

David's eyes are on me. "It's your mother, Anna. Your father has taken her to the hospital."

The next words he utters register somewhere in the back of my mind—something about not being able to wake her, that when he finally did, she was incoherent. That he called her doctor, bundled her into her robe and brought her right down. That he told David and Tracey what was happening and left driving instructions to the hospital and keys for the extra car in the garage.

"Why didn't you call for me?" My voice is surprisingly calm and quiet when what I want to do is scream and shake David because he didn't come and get me.

"There wasn't time," David replies. "Your father was gone before I could. But I wrote down the instructions. You and Frey should leave right away. We'll stay here with Trish and John-John."

"No. Trish should come along, too."

David's expression grows even more solemn. "Your dad asked that you two come alone. At least until the doctors determine what's happening. You can come back for Trish when you know."

Frey is nodding. "He's right. Maybe what happened was caused by exhaustion. Or overexcitement. Something easily treated and we'll be bringing her home with us."

"Or maybe it was caused by the wedding." The words barely clear my throat, it's so tight and dry. The other possibility I can't say aloud—but it's shrieking in my head until I think surely David and Tracey must hear.

Or because the truth of what I told her—what I am—suddenly dawned and she couldn't face it after all.

"Come on, Anna." Frey is reading my expression. I can tell he guesses what I am thinking as he steers me toward the stairs. "Don't jump to conclusions. Let's get dressed. The sooner we get to the hospital, the quicker we'll know."

There's nothing else to say. Frey and I run back to the bedroom, dress with otherworldly speed, pulling on jeans and tees and little else, aiming to be out the door before Trish and John-John reappear. We have to be. I couldn't face Trish and tell her she can't come with us.

David and Tracey are startled by our sudden reappearance, dressed and grabbing for the directions and keys. But they don't question us, letting us go with promises to take care of the kids.

We find the car in the garage, a little vintage MG. Frey slips on sunglasses, the ones that allow his feline color blindness to be adjusted to human sight, and jumps behind the wheel. I let him drive. I couldn't trust my shaking hands. He expertly puts the car in gear and we're screaming down the driveway, my heart pounding so hard, my vision is clouded bloodred.

The directions Dad left for the hospital are clear and easily followed. In ten minutes, we've arrived. Frey lets me off at the Emergency Room door and drives away to find a place to park.

The ER is empty, save for an attendant in scrubs behind the admission's desk. I tell her who I'm looking for. She consults a clipboard and directs me upstairs, the Oncology Critical Care Unit.

The name does not inspire confidence. Still, I make it to the elevator without giving in to the impulse to break down. I can't be weak now.

I see my father sitting in a chair outside one of the examining rooms. He jumps up when he sees me coming toward him, opens his arms and cradles me the same way he did right after my brother died, crushing me to his chest, holding on as if to a lifeline.

I hug him back, mindful of my strength. So much has changed since I was that seventeen-year-old mourning the loss of her brother. When I feel my father shaking, I question whether I should make it all stop. I have the power to bring Mom back to the family, healthy.

But changed.

Frey's footsteps echo in the empty hallway. Dad lets me go, steps back. He clears his throat, turning his back to brush at his eyes with the back of his hand.

Frey pretends not to see Dad's distress, instead bending toward me to kiss my cheek. "Any word?"

Dad's voice is steady again, composed when he answers for me. "No. Not yet."

"Dad, what happened?"

He sits back down, motioning us to join him. Frey takes the chair to the left, I, to the right. Dad rests his elbows on his knees and buries his face in his hands. "I couldn't wake her up this morning. She didn't respond to my voice. She didn't respond to my shaking her. Her breathing wasn't labored. She just wouldn't wake up. I panicked. Called her doctor. He said it would be quicker to drive her here myself than wait for an ambulance." His voice drops, his shoulders sag but he straightens up in the chair. "So I did." He glances toward the closed exam room door. "Dr. Gerard has been in with her since we arrived."

"Has this ever happened before?" Frey asks, voice leaden with concern.

Dad shakes his head.

I take his hand, fearful that he'll flinch at its coldness. Instead, he takes my hand in both of his. "You're freezing." He begins kneading my hand, pulling me to lean my head against his chest.

Another flashback to another cold room—only this one was a morgue and I was seated by myself outside a set of swinging doors waiting for my parents to come back.

I close my eyes, trying to push the memory away, my body shaking with the effort the same way my father's shook a few minutes ago.

Dad's arms close around me. "Don't," he says softly. "Don't think the worst. Not yet."

I open my eyes to find Frey looking at me, his very posture humming with the need to do something and his face filled with frustration because he knows there's nothing to be done. Feeling powerless is not an emotion either of us can abide. I hold out a hand to him and he grabs it.

The door to Mom's room opens. Dad and I stand, step apart, focusing all our attention on the man approaching. I try to catch a glimpse into the room before the door snaps closed, but I see only the end of the bed and a nurse writing on a clipboard.

The doctor speaks to my father in French, adding to my exasperation. He's young, thin, sober-faced, head covered with the kind of skullcap doctors wear in surgery, body cloaked in white scrub pants and a spotless lab coat. But my father's face clears, his shoulders relax a little more with each word. Frey is at my side, has taken my hand again; he is interpreting Dad's reactions the same way. The news can't be all bad.

Finally, the doctor shakes my father's hand, nods to Frey and I, and strides down the hall.

I barely wait until he's out of sight before rounding on my father. "What did he say?"

Dad puts a hand on my shoulder, smiles. "We can bring her home today. She was dehydrated. Overtired. But they're giving her IV fluids. We can go in."

I'm the first through the door.

Mom is propped up, still in her own nightgown and robe, one IV tube pumping clear fluid into her arm. She smiles apologetically. "I'm so sorry."

But I've already caught her up in a hug that muffles her words against my shoulder. "Don't be silly. The doctor said you were dehydrated. That's what you get from drinking all that champagne. And overtired. I was worried that might happen."

She's shaking her head. "And I wouldn't change a thing. The wedding was so beautiful. And what's a French wedding without champagne?"

Dad waggles a finger at her. "Well, you gave us quite a scare. From now on, less excitement and more rest." He turns to me. "Why don't you two go back and let the others know what's happened. They must be beside themselves with worry. Especially Trish. Tell them we'll be home for dinner."

I look at Mom. "You sure you don't want me to stay, too?"

Mom pulls me forward for a kiss. "No. You and Daniel should be with the children. Assure them I'm fine. Tell Catherine to prepare a nice dinner for us. We'll eat outside—all of us—the family."

I hesitate, looking hard at her. Her voice is strong, her eyes clear, her skin radiant. "Okay. We'll go. I'll bring Trish back, though, if she insists on coming."

Mom shakes her head again. "No. I don't want her to see me like this. Just assure her I'll be home soon."

She's adamant. Dad interjects, "Really, Anna. There's no need for Trish to come. Maybe she and John-John can go riding this afternoon. Tell her by the time they get back, Mom will be home."

I hold up my hands in surrender. "Okay. Okay." I lean over and give Mom another quick hug. "I don't remember you ever being so stubborn."

"Who do you think you got it from?" Dad asks with a chuckle.

Frey has leaned over to peck my mom's cheek, too. "I'm not going to question it ever again."

I feign shock. "You think I'm stubborn?"

"Obstinate. Inflexible. Willful—"

That last gets Frey a sock on the arm. I'm not feigning this time. "Willful? You make me sound like a brat."

Dad and Frey both shoot me looks that in spite of it all, make me smile. "Well. Nice to know what my new husband and father really think of me. We'd better get out of here before this conversation about my character degenerates any further."

Mom is laughing and Dad smilingly waves us out the door. When I glance back, he's perched on the side of the bed, Mom's right hand clasped firmly in both of his own.

CHAPTER 33

R ELIEF THAT MOM WILL BE HOME SOON IS MIN-
gled with the knowledge that the next time something
like this happens, she might not recover. That eventually,
she won't recover.

That eventually, every human I know and love will be
taken from me.

Mom, Dad, Trish, John-John.

Frey.

I close my eyes, flashing back to the wedding. Am I
fooling myself with Frey? How many times will I repeat the
ritual, marry someone I love with a promise of forever?
Someone mortal, someone doomed.

Frey is quiet on the ride back. He has taken one of my
hands and rested it, covered by his own, on his knee as he
drives. The contact is comforting and familiar. I told David

yesterday life is too short and love too important to squander. I bring Frey's hands to my lips. I'm going to appreciate every moment we have.

Frey squeezes my hand. I smile, constantly amazed how my heart can soar one minute, and be plunged into despair the next. This is the saddest and happiest time of my entire life.

Trish rushes out to meet us when we pull up. I put my arms around her shoulders and tell her what happened to Mom, why, and that she will be back with us by dinnertime.

"I should be at the hospital."

"Mom knew you'd say that. But really, there's nothing you could do there. That's why I'm back. She kicked me out, too."

Trish's watery smile is coupled with a sigh. "She can be so stubborn."

"Oh no." I stop her with a hug then gently propel her toward the door. "We're not having this conversation again. Let's go get some breakfast. I'm starved."

She looks confused and Frey says, "Don't ask."

Just then, John-John, David and Tracey are at the door, and we hustle ourselves inside.

CATHERINE IS DELIGHTED AT THE NEWS THAT MOM IS recovering well and promises to prepare a special dinner for us. We tell John-John and Trish that it was Mom's suggestion that they spend the afternoon riding and after a little persuasion, they leave for the neighbors. David and Tracey insist on staying another night, as anxious as any of us to see for themselves that Mom is okay. They take the MG and Catherine's grocery list to the village to shop.

Then it's just Frey and me.

We're sitting side by side at the dining room table, coffee mugs drained, some of the morning's tension finally dissipating.

I stretch my arms overhead and sigh. "What a way to start our first day as a married couple."

Frey stands up, holds out a hand. "Well, this is still the first day."

I put my hand in his and he pulls me up. "And we did get interrupted. Mom is going to be all right. We have the house to ourselves. Now remind me, what is it we were doing this morning?"

Frey pulls me close with a hand at the small of my back. "This refresh your memory?"

The feel of him hard against me sends a rush of heat to my skin.

It does.

"DO YOU THINK IN TWENTY YEARS WE'LL STILL BE spending afternoons like this?"

I'm lying on my stomach, stretched out beside Frey. We're both naked, both spent after an afternoon of energetic and imaginative sex. I didn't know there were so many ways to give and receive pleasure.

And I've been around.

Frey makes a grumbling sound that is half purr, half growl. "I hope so. Or I'll have to trade you in for a younger model."

"Is that so?" I prop myself up on my elbows. "Let's see. In twenty years I'll still be thirty, and in twenty years you'll be—"

"Okay." Frey covers my lips with a finger. "I get it. I guess I'll just have to keep coming up with ways to keep you interested."

"Well." I draw the word out, my turn to purr. I lift myself so that I am now lying on top of him, stomach to stomach, hip to hip, my legs resting between his. I grind against him, feel a familiar stirring. "You're off to a great start."

He pulls my head down for a kiss, tongue teasing, advancing, retreating, until I grip it gently with my teeth and draw it in. He puts his arms around me and I know he intends to roll me over. I don't let him. Instead I sit up, straddle him, take him fully and deeply inside. His breath catches and his head falls back. He lets me take the lead, lets me draw pleasure from him as I lift and lower, thighs clenched tight, muscles contracting around and against him. His breath comes faster, his body tenses. I'm not there yet, but it doesn't matter. I watch him, watch his face, watch as the muscles in his abdomen grow taut, watch as his back arches. His hands grasp my hips. He's so close. A tiny movement, a tightening, and a moan escapes his lips as he empties himself into me.

A moan escapes my lips, too. Intense pleasure as satisfying as any orgasm. Frey's face, shining, open, so bright with love it's like looking into the sun.

This is what love is.

I collapse against him. We hold each other. He strokes my hair, and I feel hot tears burn the back of my eyes.

I think of my conversation with Vlad.

Yes.

Love is worth pain. Love is all there is.

I bury my face against Frey's chest, breathing him in, wanting to imprint his very essence into my brain, secure in the knowledge that I will remember this moment.

As long as I live.

CHAPTER 34

THE TABLE IS LADEN WITH FOOD—A PLUMP roasted turkey, bowls of potatoes, steamed carrots shiny with butter, green beans in a casserole crusted with onion rings. In the center of the table, a simple salad in a broad wooden bowl—various greens and kale and still-warm-from-the-garden tomatoes with a dressing made from freshly pressed olive oil and one of Dad's wines. The aroma from the breadbasket tempts even me. Thick slabs of a hearty, crusty baguette begging to be slathered with home-churned butter. Makes a vampire's mouth water.

Could be a typical American Thanksgiving feast.

Except that we're not in America. And this isn't Thanksgiving. It's my mother's wish.

I look around the table, my heart full. Dad is at one end, brandishing the carving knife like a miniature *katana*, much to the delight of John-John, sitting at his right, and Trish, sitting to his left. The kid's faces are alight with the simple joy of family together. Next to John-John, Frey watches, too, his wonderful smile a reflection of his son's. He has one of my hands clutched tightly in his own. Across from us, David and Tracey. Even they are smiling.

I sit, wishing the unbridled contagion of happiness would infect me.

But it won't.

It can't.

Mom leans toward me. She's next to me, opposite Dad, at a table in a storybook setting under big, broad-leafed trees in the backyard of their villa. She reaches for my hand.

I don't pull back. There's no longer any need. The coldness of my hand in the warmth of hers no longer requires fumbling excuses about poor circulation.

"Please, Anna," she says softly. "Don't be sad."

I meet her eyes, so warm and full of life. My heart beats with dull, irritating regularity in my chest. "This is so unfair."

She sits back, smiling. "How can you say that? Here we are together. You've found a wonderful man in Daniel and a child that will bring you as much pleasure as Trish has brought us. You have much to give the world. I am so proud of you."

I close my eyes, tears spilling over my cheeks, filled with so much sadness, my guts twist with it.

Mom reaches over again, touches the tears with the tips of her fingers. "No tears. This is a time of joy. A time to be together with no regrets. A time to make memories."

I take her hand in both of my own. "I love you."

"I love you, too, Anna."

Laughter from the other end of the table makes us look up. Dad has carved off a huge turkey leg and placed it on John-John's plate. John-John doesn't hesitate a moment, but scoops it up with both hands and takes a bite.

This time, a smile touches my lips, too. Mom is right. No tears today. They'll be plenty of time for tears later. When she's gone.

I'm both sad and elated.

I'm looking at my future. Here surrounded by those I love. These are the memories I'll cleave to in my lifetime.

More than a lifetime.

These are the memories I'll keep for an eternity.

EPILOGUE

NO ONE REALLY EVER GETS A HAPPILY EVER AFTER. I don't expect my story will be any different. There will always be conflict in the world—between mortal and immortal, between immortal and those who would challenge the way of things. I suppose that's why I am. It is my burden to keep the balance. Having Frey in my life, and John-John, lightens the burden. Having a family and friends, humans I care about, lightens the burden. I didn't choose this life, but I take comfort in the choices I do have. The choices I've made.

My name is Anna Strong.

I am vampire.

CURSED

by S. J. Harper

Coming from Roc in October 2013

**Meet FBI agents Emma Monroe and Zack
Armstrong. She's cursed. He's damned. Together, they make one hell of a team.**

Emma Monroe is a Siren, cursed by the gods and bound to
earth to atone for an ancient failure. She's had many names
and many lives, but only one mission: redemption. Now that
she works missing-persons cases for the FBI, it could be just
a rescue away. Unless her new partner leads her astray.

Special Agent Zack Armstrong just transferred into the
San Diego field office. He's a werewolf, doing his best to
beat back the demons from his dark and dangerous past. As
a former black ops sniper, he's taken enough lives. Now
he's doing penance by saving them.

Emma and Zack's very first case draws them deep into
the realm of the paranormal and forces them to use their
own supernatural abilities. But that leaves each of them
vulnerable, and there are lines partners should not cross.
As secrets are revealed and more women go missing, one
thing becomes clear: As they race to save the victims,
Emma and Zack risk losing themselves.

Siren (*noun*)

1. One of three sisters ejected from Mount Olympus by Zeus and cursed by Demeter for failing to prevent Hades from kidnapping Persephone.

2. An immortal goddess bound to earth who, in search of her own salvation, saves others from peril.

3. A beautiful and powerful seductress capable of infiltrating the minds of others in order to extract truth or exert influence.

*Y*OU'VE SEEN ONE DARK, RUGGED WEREWOLF, *you've seen them all.*

That's what I told myself the first time I laid eyes on Zack Armstrong. I was wrong. Dead wrong. And now it's come back to bite me in the ass.

I interrupt my best friend, Liz, in the middle of—something. I realize I lost the thread of our phone conversation the minute I spied Zack weaving his way through the maze of indistinct gray cubicles that make up the bull pen of the San Diego FBI field office. Save the hair and nine a.m. four-o'clock shadow, the man is all spit and polish. Tailored dark blue suit, starched white shirt, blue and gold silk tie and gleaming black shoes. The hair gives him a distinct edge—dark brown, slightly longer than regulation, no part. It's swept straight back, accentuating the lines of his square jaw.

S. J. HARPER

I resist the urge to crawl under my desk. "I'll call you back later. New partner's here. I've got to go."

"Not until I hear the details. What's he look like?"

Liz is forever trying to play matchmaker. Ironically, I rely on her spellcasting to make sure a match will never happen.

I turn around and lower my voice a notch. "Remember the guy from South Carolina I told you about? The one I was partnered with on that missing-person case in Charleston last year?"

"Really?" New interest sparks in her voice. "He looks like him?"

"It *is* him," I say. "Which you'd think Johnson would have mentioned."

"So what's the problem? I'll tell you now what I told you then. You shouldn't write off the possibility of a good romp with a guy just because he goes furry a few days every month. Weres have amazing stamina. Hey, did I ever tell you about Walter?"

You name it, Liz has dated it. Being a witch with serious magical talent puts her in contact with a wide variety of supernaturals. A strong advocate for equal-opportunity love, she's currently dating a vampire.

But Walter the werewolf was decidedly *not* one of her success stories.

"Yeah, Liz. A few dozen times. The problem isn't Zack's nature."

"The FBI has rules about fraternization?"

"No." I wish they did. I wish it could be that easy. Not that getting involved with a partner is encouraged.

"What, then?"

My eyes squeeze shut. I shouldn't have given Zack Armstrong a second thought in the last thirteen months, seventeen days. But I have. I've thought of him often. Too often.

Gooseflesh appears on my arms; the hair on the back of my neck rises. A sense of dread washes over me. That's why he's here. This isn't a coincidence. It's a test the Olympians have their hands in. Or, more specifically, one particular Olympian. Demeter. I'm a Siren—one of three. We were banished by Zeus and cursed by Demeter thousands of years ago for failing to protect her daughter Persephone, for failing to rescue her before she was dragged by Hades to the Underworld. It's for this I atone. For this I pay.

And pay. And pay.

I'm tempted to make something up, but this is Liz. She deserves the truth. "I liked him. *More* than liked him."

Her tone turns serious. "You never mentioned that. This could be bad."

The understatement of the year. Guys I get into meaningful relationships with tend to end up dead, courtesy of my favorite vindictive goddess. Partnering with Zack Armstrong could prove exceedingly dangerous. Even lethal.

For him.

"I've got to go."

I click off, the sound of Liz's protests ringing in my ear, and concentrate on the familiar six-foot-plus werewolf coming toward me. Deputy Director Jimmy Johnson emerges from his office. "Here's the memo I promised you about your new partner. Better late than never."

He may be chronically behind with paperwork, but otherwise Johnson's tenacious about his job, a real pit bull. And, despite being only five foot six, he's one of the toughest guys I've ever met.

I snatch the sheet from his hand and drop it on my desk. "Why didn't you tell me it was Armstrong?"

"I thought I did." His look is quizzical, but it doesn't stay that way for long. "Zack! Good to see you again."

The two men greet each other with a hearty handshake.

"Good to see you again, Deputy Director." The Southern accent is smooth; the cadence of his voice is, as I remember, low and lilting. It was the first of many things that got to me about Zack Armstrong.

Johnson dives in without preamble. "Emma Monroe's your new partner. I don't have to waste time with introductions. What's it been, a year since you worked on that case together?"

"Just over," Zack answers, flashing a sideways glance in my direction.

What Johnson couldn't possibly know is that we share more than a past case. We both have secrets—supernatural powers we've managed to keep hidden from the bureau, the world and, as far as Zack is concerned, each other. Unbeknownst to him, I sensed what he is the instant we met. We never discussed it. He's never revealed it. But of course he wouldn't, not to an outsider.

And then there is the other secret we share. Zack and I slept together.

Once.

It was during our last night in Charleston. We'd celebrated wrapping up the case, indulging in a good meal and too much wine. The attraction had been building for weeks, the sexual tension as thick as the South Carolina air. I wish I could say that one thing led to another. That I was impulsively swept away. But I'm not impetuous when it comes to sex. I can't afford to be. The potential consequences are too high.

We agreed that we'd go our separate ways after. There would be no telephone calls. No texts. No emails. No contact. Period. With twenty-four hundred miles between us, it seemed safe.

Johnson startles me with a slap on the back. "Show him the ropes. He's all yours."

I offer my hand. "Good to see you again."

Zack takes it.

A woman can tell a lot about a man from his handshake. Zack's hasn't changed. It's confident, firm and friendly. It's the handshake of a man who has nothing to apologize for and no regrets.

Johnson is already on his way back to his office. Zack doesn't seem to notice. His eyes are on me.

"I'm pleased to be working with you again, Agent Monroe."

Is he? The handshake. The demeanor. Both seem genuine. But despite the old-world charm, I can't shake the feeling that something is off.

Maybe coming here isn't something he wanted at all. Maybe it's strictly a bureau-initiated transfer. Maybe he's merely worried about how I'm going to react. My curiosity has gone into overdrive. The possibilities ricochet through my mind like bullets in a steel barrel. I want to know how he feels. To taste the truth, whatever that may be. And I could. All it would take is lowering the dampening spell that keeps my powers in check. But giving in to temptation like this would be uncharacteristic. Using my gift comes at a price.

"I thought we'd moved past you calling me Agent Monroe," I say finally. "Emma or Monroe will do fine."

Zack releases my hand, then subtly breathes in my scent before stepping back to continue his appraisal. His gaze, now cool and calculating, sweeps the length of my body. He's searching for a reaction, sizing me up. He sees what I want him to see, what he saw when we worked together before: a no-nonsense professional who is dedicated, capable, all about the mission. Denying my powers and disguising my beauty have become second nature to me.

Over the centuries I've become an expert at concealment, at blending in. My dark hair may be long, but it's never loose. I use a simple band to pull it back; some days I wind it into a tight bun. I wear sunscreen. No mascara. No lipstick. No makeup. Period. Today's suit, like all of my suits, is black and tailored. The white cotton twill blouse is classic, conservative. I don't accessorize. I don't wear jewelry. I don't wear silk where a man can see it.

Zack's eyes, an intense dark brown ringed with gold, linger a fraction of a second too long on my collarbone. I can't help myself. For one fleeting moment, I remember the feel of his mouth there. Suddenly, I'm conscious of the rise and fall of my chest. My throat is dry. I push the memory aside. The last thing I need to be doing right now is dwelling on what happened in Charleston. I know I should say something. I just have no idea what. Zack breaks the ice.

"It's been a while," he says.

"Yeah. So, how are you?" Before he has a chance to answer, I add, "I should introduce you to the others."

Zack lifts his hand in the air and shouts out, "Zack Armstrong, new guy."

There's a collective "Hey, Zack."

He turns back to face me square on. "I'm itching to get started. What have you got for me?"

I take a step closer and lower my voice. "That's it? You have nothing else to say to me?"

He matches my tone. "I was hoping to postpone the awkward 'What are you doing here?' conversation for as long as possible. At least until lunch?"

Since I'm not anxious to go down that road, either, I gesture to the desk facing mine. "Have a seat. This one's yours."

When he sits, I check my reflection in the window behind him. The glamour I rely on is firmly in place. The lock on my powers under control. He shouldn't be able to see through the wholesome, plain-Jane façade to discover what's underneath, what's real. Thanks to Liz, no one should.

"You heard what the man said." He leans back in his chair and spreads his arms wide, giving me a glimpse of what I know to be a well-muscled chest under the fabric of his shirt. "I'm all yours." His look is serious, expectant. "What can I do?"

A thousand possibilities rush through my mind. Not one of them has anything to do with the case.

Focus, Emma.

I pull a sheet from the file and give Zack the rundown. "Amy Patterson has been missing for two weeks. She's thirty years old, an artist. She lives alone. We got the case this morning."

Zack pulls a pen and a small notebook from his inside coat pocket. "What kind of an artist?"

I quickly scan the report. "Painter, Expressionist, mixed media mostly."

"Kidnapping gone bad?" he speculates.

"Could be. She's successful. But there's no known family and, according to her manager, no request for ransom."

Zack sets the pen and notebook down, centering them deliberately on the empty desk. "Who reported her missing?"

"The manager, Bernadette Haskell. She's known Amy for years. Haskell owns the gallery in La Jolla where Amy's art is exclusively exhibited, and handles Amy's gallery bookings and commissions worldwide. I spoke to her earlier this morning. She said Amy rarely leaves her apartment. She both lives and works there. Plus, she has a huge show coming up in New York. And before you ask, yes, she called there to see if Amy might have gone ahead to check the space out." I shake my head. "She's not in New York, either."

His brow furrows. "Why is the FBI involved in a straightforward missing-person case? Shouldn't the local police be handling this?"

I nod. "They should. They are. But Haskell has a friend in the district attorney's office, and he's calling in a favor. The relationship between Haskell and Patterson was more than purely business. Over the years, Patterson became like a daughter to this woman. SDPD hasn't made much progress. Officially, we're just reviewing the casework."

"Unofficially?"

"The fact that she's missing hit the papers yesterday. The story is getting a fair amount of press. The DA wants us to close the case. It's an election year and he's out to win the hearts and minds of the voters. Something with this amount of visibility, if handled right, could cinch what is sure to be a close election."

"Politics as usual. Where do you want to start?"

"SDPD already covered the usual stuff. They checked the psych wards, hospitals and morgues. There haven't been any recent credit card charges or bank withdrawals."

"What about log-in access for things like email, social networks and other accounts?"

"Nothing for a couple weeks."

"I almost hate to ask, but could this be a publicity stunt of some kind?"

I remember the sense of urgency and concern in Haskell's voice when we spoke. "My gut says no, but I don't think we should rule anything out."

Zack nods.

"According to Haskell, it's not unusual for Amy to go incommunicado when she's finishing a project. But it's highly unusual that she'd up and leave town without telling her. And Patterson's car is still in the building's parking garage."

"I assume they checked local taxi and car services?"

"Yup. That turned up zip, too."

"No signs of a struggle in her apartment?"

I push back from my desk. "Not according to the police report. I haven't personally searched the place yet. It hasn't been declared a crime scene. No sign of foul play. Haskell said she couldn't get away from the gallery this morning. She's the only one there. But she'll give us the keys so we can check the place out on our own. She's expecting us."

He rises. "Want me to drive?"

"Sure. The Haskell Gallery is on Prospect Street. I can give you directions."

Zack follows me toward the elevator. "I know where Prospect is." He punches the call button. The doors slide

S. J. HARPER

open instantly. He holds them and waits, allowing me to enter first.

He did most of the driving in Charleston, which made sense. We were in his territory. San Diego is mine.

"You aren't one of those guys who pretends they know where they're going because they're too stubborn to take directions from a woman, are you?"

We face forward. The doors close.

"Do I *look* like one of those guys?"

The elevator makes its descent. Our reflections stare back at us in the polished steel of the panel doors. Zack's expression remains neutral.

"Looks can be deceiving. Sometimes you think you know a person, then you realize you don't really know them at all."

He nods. "I suppose that's true." There's a hint of sadness in his tone. Zack's shoulders tense—a reaction so brief I doubt he's even aware he reacted at all. "Everyone has secrets."

He makes his way toward the exit, and I wonder again what really brought him to San Diego. I wonder why he left his pack behind in South Carolina. I wonder if he's joined one here. Mostly I wonder if he's been wondering about me.

We walk through the foyer of the FBI building into the light of day. I pause, close my eyes and tilt my face up toward the sun. How many more days will pass? How many more women will I have to save? I silently recite the same words I do every time I go out on a new case. *Redemption could be one rescue away.*

"You coming, partner?"

Zack has passed me and is waiting next to one of the

292

bureau's many black Chevy Suburbans parked near the entrance.

Before I can answer, a silver BMW convertible pulls into the lot. It whizzes by, making a sharp right turn and pulling up to the row of SUVs directly in front of Zack. The car's curves are sleek, its paint job gleaming. A woman steps out of the driver's side. Zack's eyes are glued to her. I can't blame him. Her long legs emerge first, toned and sporting a pair of expensive red heels that boldly accentuate her black-and-white dress. As she approaches Zack, she removes her dark designer sunglasses and the silk scarf covering her head. She's pretty, even-featured. Her makeup is meticulous. Long blonde hair spills out and hangs loose in waves that brush her shoulders.

The tension in Zack's body tells me the woman is more than a stranger stopping to ask for directions. He knows who she is and he's not happy to see her. His shoulders bunch; his mouth turns down. I can't quite make out what she says to him as she approaches, but his response is clear. He shakes his head and motions her away. The gesture is understated, discreet, but it carries with it a sense of finality. He looks past the woman, at me.

Her head turns, following his line of sight. Her eyes connect with mine briefly before she dons the glasses once again. The fraction of a second is all she needs to convey a warning. All I need to determine that she, too, is Were. One intent on marking her territory? I resist the urge to let my hand slide to my hip, where my gun rests securely in its holster. I choose instead to annoy her further by smiling and waving.

"You waiting for an invitation, Monroe?" Zack calls out

before climbing into the Suburban and closing the door, effectively dismissing Miss Fancy Pants.

As I approach she turns on her heel. A confident toss of her head in Zack's direction says she's gotten her message across. Now that she's seen me, now that she's convinced I'm not a threat, she doesn't bother to spare me a second glance. By the time I reach the Suburban, she's returned to her car, climbed inside and fired up the engine. With a squeal of tires, she's gone.

But not before I notice the license plate. South Carolina. It's reflex to store the number away in the back of my mind.

I open the car door. "I get the feeling she doesn't like me."

Zack is waiting behind the wheel, hands at the ten- and two-o'clock positions, knuckles white. He avoids looking me in the eye. "She doesn't like the fact we slept together."

He says it casually.

"You told her we slept together?" I ask, sliding into the passenger seat.

His gaze meets me head-on. "Would you have preferred I lied?"

"She your girlfriend?"

He throws the car into reverse and steps on the gas. "Ex."

I wonder if the status came before or after the revelation. It doesn't matter. In the month we worked together I came to know Zack's moods well enough to interpret this one. With one single syllable, he's effectively closing the door on that subject.

It's okay.

Zack can have his secrets.

I certainly have mine.

Photo by Kelly Weaver Photography

Jeanne C. Stein
now lives in Colorado, but
San Diego will always be home.
She is currently at work on a
new series. Visit her website
at www.jeannestein.com.

ISBN 978-0-425-25887-3

25887

72742 00799   9

"There are more books about young female vampires...but it's safe to say Anna Strong is contending for leader of the pack."
—*The Denver Post*

As a vampire, Anna Strong has an immortal life...but now she's running out of time.

Anna's relationship with shapeshifter Daniel Frey has given her hope for a future with him and his son—especially when Frey proposes...

But just when Anna starts to think her life couldn't be better, she must fly to France to be at the side of her dying mother. There she learns that not every vampire accepts her Chosen One status. And one such vamp is about to go rogue—by leading his followers in a fight to usurp humanity...

Praise for the Anna Strong, Vampire novels

"Packed with action that is sure to chill readers to the bone."—Examiner.com

"A kick-ass heroine readers will delight in."
—*Fresh Fiction*

www.jeannestein.com
www.penguin.com

$7.99 U.S.
$8.99 CAN